T0279145

A
MISFORTUNE
OF
LAKE
MONSTERS

A
MISFORTUNE
OF
LAKE
MONSTERS

NICOLE M. WOLVERTON

CamCat
Books

CamCat Publishing, LLC
Fort Collins, Colorado 80524
camcatpublishing.com

Hardcover ISBN 9780744309584
Paperback ISBN 9780744309607
Large-Print Paperback ISBN 9780744309645
eBook ISBN 9780744309621
Audiobook ISBN 9780744309669

Library of Congress Control Number: 2023950717

Book and cover design by Maryann Appel
Interior artwork by Alenaohneva, David Goh, Ninochka, Marek Trawczynski

5   3   1   2   4

"Monsters cannot be announced. One cannot say: 'Here are our monsters,' without immediately turning the monsters into pets."

—Jacques Derrida, *Some Statements and Truisms about Neologisms, Newisms, Postisms, Parasitisms, and other small Seismisms*, The States of Theory.

1

L E M O N

I F IT WEREN'T FOR THE dry suit strangling me from toes to tonsils, hypothermia would have set in thirty minutes ago—and graduating from high school with all my digits intact is a record I want to hold on to. Inside the Old Lucy costume, my toes and fingers scrunch. The good news is that I can feel them. Being the gooey human center of a neoprene and latex lake monster burrito isn't my favorite way to spend a Monday night. And here's more good news: things are about to wrap up—a cluster of shadowy figures is suddenly flitting like moths around the hazy lights on the dock about two hundred meters away.

That *this* is what's passing for good news is full-on crap, but whatever—it's go-time. A sudden flash of heat in my veins chases away the April-cold Lake Lokakoma water, and I clear my throat. It's sandpapered near raw from the oxygen I've been sucking from the tank strapped to my back. "Now, Lemon, it hain't no different than takin' a breath on land," is what Pappap's told me on more than one occasion. He keeps saying I'll get used to it—like the longer I'm the supersecret Old Lucy impersonator, it'll all magically feel normal one day.

Nothing about faking a lake monster is normal and ever will be. Not swimming around in a monster costume on a dreary night. Not hiding behind the boulders at Peter's Island to keep watch for people on the dock. Not constantly lying to my best friends. And definitely not being trapped in Devil's Elbow for the rest of my natural life.

The crisp air fills my lungs, even though it feels like it has to claw over broken glass to do so. Best get used to it now instead of wallowing in my misery. Hey, I *want* to wallow, but I can wallow when I'm dead . . . or at least after this impersonation is done. I check the silver dive watch strapped over the iridescent scales on my wrist and calculate how much time is left on my oxygen tank. Every thought in my head pares down until all I can do is visualize the Old Lucy impersonation routine, exactly as Pappap taught me. Nothing too showy. Just give them a taste, just a glimpse. And let them hear Old Lucy roar.

Light drizzle pings off the surface of the water and smacks my chin. I duck back behind the boulder, clear my throat again, and rip out the high-pitched ululation of an Old Lucy cry, complete with a long, eerie note that hangs over the lake as heavy as mist.

No wonder the oxygen doesn't hurt Pappap's throat—he probably doesn't have any pain receptors in there anymore after a lifetime of ululating.

A girl's voice is the first thing that comes sliding across the water. "Did you hear that?"

And then a guy's whoop. "Old Lucy's out there! Can you see her? Get some video."

"My phone's not picking up anything—it's dark as shit tonight."

I fit the regulator back into my mouth, swallow around the stale air from the tank, and adjust my goggles before clicking the face mask back into place. The new moon makes for a sky that might as well be a black hole, sucking all of Devil's Elbow and the towns surrounding it into nothingness. Low clouds obscure the stars, and there's a thick gloom hanging just above the water—all the better for that extra bit of mystery. It's the perfect night to stage an Old Lucy appearance, whether I like it or not.

The urge to think *and I don't* is hard to resist.

The words swim through my brain in big flaming black letters. Even the sweet almond perfume of forsythias blooming on Peter's Island temporarily masking the stink of sweat-embedded monster suit latex isn't enough to cheer me out of this funk.

The cold water closes over me as I sink into the lake. I've practiced the sighting route so many times that even my seemingly perma-depressed mood isn't a distraction. I've dreamed this route, woken up gliding through my blankets like a water bug. Ten yards clear of the island, five yards toward the dock for the tail flick. My body corkscrews up through the water like a drill, and I jackknife to thrust my legs and hips and the latex tail upward.

For a brief moment, the absence of water resistance is glorious, and I'm something close to triumphant.

Then it's off to the bottom of the lake, to the submerged wreck of a car that's been there for as long as I can remember. The rough texture of the old rope that Pappap installed as a guide is evident even through my monster mitts. Hand over hand, I pull myself along the line and shoot up to the surface again, just out of sight of the dock. There are a few spots like that between here and our boathouse—places where I can splash around, make some noise, and hope the people on the dock can hear it, even if they can't see me.

The satisfied feeling is fading now, though I've successfully just pulled off my first solo Old Lucy impersonation. The neoprene strangles tighter. Being trapped inside a generations-old, disgustingly smelly, fake monster costume is just the perfect metaphor for the dumpster fire of my new life.

The bridge of my nose prickles. I dive toward the bed of the lake and practice fake smiling around the regulator for the benefit of my grandparents while swimming for home. *I am a grateful granddaughter. I am a grateful granddaughter. I am a grateful . . .*

2

L E M O N

AIN BREAKS OVERNIGHT, LEAVING THE sky bright and clear, with a blue so blue it hurts my eyes. The sun bullies its way into the cafeteria of *Devil's! Elbow! High!*—that's the way it sounds when the cheerleaders scream it at pep rallies—and shines up the scuffed linoleum floor. A beam of light gleams across the cheery banner hung against one wall that reads "Home of the Lake Monsters" with a cute purple Old Lucy illustration smiling from one edge.

Tuesday's mystery meat glistens on Pepto-pink lunch trays around the room. The banana Troy left in my locker this morning looks safer by comparison, but the combination of blue, pink, and yellow is too cheerful for my mood. I set the banana on the fake wood table, close my eyes, and brood. I'm getting really great at it.

Pappap would tell me I'm being a baby, to soak up all the Old Lucy buzz and count it as a job well done. The talk in homeroom and the hallways this morning was *Did you hear* and *Well, he said.* That *is* a good thing. Danetta Harvey's about ten feet away right now, recounting last night's Old Lucy sighting for a rapt soccer team audience, which isn't doing much for my sulking capabilities—but maybe it means I won't have to do another impersonation too soon.

"I never really believed in Old Lucy until now." Her voice is high-pitched, melodramatic. "But Billy shined a flashlight out on the water and . . ."

She's even wearing a glittery Old Lucy T-shirt from one of the tourist shops on Front Street. She probably ran out this morning before school and bought it for this very occasion; it looks new. Maybe I *should* be proud of my contributions to Devil's Elbow—Danetta's family owns a pizza shop downtown called Monster Pepperoni that bakes up a special Old Lucy–shaped pie during the summer for tourists, and I can name at least two or three dozen more kids in this cafeteria whose parents make their living on summer visitors drawn to town for monster hunts at the lake. The monster *I* now impersonate. It's not like there's any *other* reason to visit this town. I know deep down that I'm doing a good thing, but I'd give anything for my biggest worry to be something more mundane and boring than keeping the economy of an entire town afloat. I mean, I'm seventeen, not forty-seven.

The table jolts, and I jolt with it. Skeet Jenkins slouches on the bench next to me, sitting backward, one elbow propped perilously close to my water. His eyes are aimed at what little cleavage I have in my V-neck. My stomach crawls like a wriggling pile of slimy worms have been let loose, squirming and poking.

Someone nearby stage whispers, "Oh my god—look."

"So, Ziegler." Skeet leers at me, all dimples and crooked teeth, topped with a lewd wink. It seems like my annual encounter with Skeet has arrived—he makes it a point to harass everyone with boobs at least once each school year. What I am *not* expecting are his next words: "Prom's coming up."

My guts go on turbo-spin. It's exacerbated by a strategic rip in his jeans at the thigh that shows off an overabundance of black curly leg hair. I have nothing against body hair, but showing it off so carefully seems so . . . intentionally icky. Everything about him feels like it's designed to cause a reaction. The sleazy way he feels entitled to hit on everyone regularly, the clear outline of a condom that's always visible in the back pocket of his too-tight jeans, the rifle rack on his truck, the retch-inducing smell of too much musky body spray. I'm reacting, all right: it's called nausea. He's the small-town cliché in every television show . . . on hairy legs.

This is *not* what I had in mind when wishing for more mundane worries.

"Prom, right. How could I forget." It's becoming painfully obvious that half the people in the cafeteria have abandoned their Old Lucy talk and are now watching the impending train wreck that's playing out at my lunch table. Why couldn't he just stick to making some disgusting comment about my body and then running off, like he usually does? The weight of all those eyes on me—including Skeet's—is almost as strangling as the Old Lucy costume.

"What do you think?" He licks his thin, chapped lips. "Me and you at the prom? I'm getting my pickup detailed and everything. I'll get one of my cousins to buy us a few cases of beer. We can party in the woods after. It'll be a good time." He runs the tip of his finger up my arm. "I'll even pack a tent for us to camp overnight."

The worms move from stomach to skin, leaving gross goo trails where Skeet touches me. A polite if tense smile is spreading over my face, and I hope like anything he doesn't mistake it for interest of any sort. He studies me, smutty-eyed and calculating.

Danetta whispers to her admirers and smirks in my direction.

I adjust my shirt over my chest and flinch away, trying not to be too obvious about it. "Uh, Skeet, wow. I . . . don't . . . I mean, thank you for asking. That's so sweet of you." My brain trips over itself. Anything I say is going to make him mad—and convincing people to forget I exist is my only goal in life these days. Confrontation gives me a raging headache. "It's just that . . . I'm already going with someone else. But really, I'm so flattered."

The lie hangs between us like a balloon blown too full of air. The urge to cram the silence with awkward chatter is loud in my head, and so is my silent, horrified screaming. Even though I've just said no, he has *Expectation* face.

Maybe he thinks I'll bail on my hypothetical date and go with him —or maybe he knows I've made zero plans for prom and will admit it if he smolders at me long enough. The pained smile feels perma-affixed to my face.

Skeet's mouth tugs into a scowl, and a small measure of fear hisses over my skin when I think again of his gun rack and that time I saw him punch someone in the lunchroom for stepping on his cowboy boots.

"Bitch. I don't want to go with you anyway." He jerks toward me, threatening, then stalks away, heels banging on the linoleum sharp as gunshots.

I slam my head into my hands as soon as my muscles loosen enough to move. I've had my fill of drama today. The thought of giving up, ditching school, and trying again tomorrow is attractive—if I was the kind of girl who did that kind of thing. I'm too afraid of Grammy and Pappap finding out. I suppose I should be grateful to Skeet on some level—Old Lucy has been out-of-mind for the entire four minutes of our delightful encounter.

Maybe if I concentrate hard enough I really will just—*poof*—dissolve into a hazy cloud of discontented smoke.

"Taking a nap, Lem?" Darrin Flanagan climbs onto the bench across the long, rectangle-shaped table ten minutes later and grins when I look up. "Or were you knocked unconscious by the glory of the cafeteria?" He tosses his brown bag down, and it spins like a top.

My anxiety calms to a dull twitch.

"Both, simultaneously," I say, just before Troy Ramirez slides into the spot beside Darrin and plunks down his own pink tray of shiny meat. His shoulders are suddenly taking up a lot more space than they used to. Sitting next to him, Darrin looks like a mouse next to a moose. To be fair, Darrin is the opposite in almost every way, with a light brown mop of unruly curls and a soft, round face that makes him look like a sixth grader.

I reach over and squeeze both their wrists for a few seconds. It's a relief to have company that doesn't actively make me uncomfortable for having skin.

Troy smiles at me, brown eyes sweet and untroubled as usual. "Hey, didn't see you this morning. Everything okay? I left you a ban—"

"Yeah, thanks." The banana still sits exactly where I left it. "You saved me from having to eat"—I gesture to his own tray of mystery meat—"whatever *that* is."

Troy laughs and gently nudges my arm. "Here to serve. I know you're opposed to Turkey Loaf Tuesday. Hey, heard about the Old Lucy sighting last night? Classic."

The polite, frozen expression crawls back onto my face.

"Oh, fuck Old Lucy," Darrin says. "Can't you see our Lemon is bored of that noise? She wants to discuss the mysteries of the universe beyond the limits of Devil's Elbow. She's all about the unending enigma of spontaneous combustion. False flag conspiracies and crisis actors." He cocks his head and looks across the cafeteria—everyone has gone back to minding their own business—before glancing back at me. The corner of his mouth quivers. "Or maybe she wants to talk about Skeet Jenkins."

Troy frowns at Darrin for a split second.

"Okay, someone has had one too many coffees today." I point my banana at Darrin for emphasis, hoping he won't see that my hand is shaking a little. *Drop it*, I think in his direction. *Drop it*. "That'll stunt your growth, you know."

"Not all of us can be giants."

Troy's mouth loosens. He rubs a hand over his short dark hair. "Heard Billy Voorhees was out at the lake last night. Said Old Lucy came right up to him and ate one of those fruit leather snacks out of his hand."

Before I can attempt another subject change, Darrin lets out a cackling laugh and bangs the table once with his hand. "Was he drunk? Because it sounds like he was drunk. More to the point, are *you* drunk? You believe him?"

It's apparently too much to ask to exist in a space where Skeet and Old Lucy don't exist, even for fifteen minutes. My sigh is barely audible next to the cafeteria din.

"Sure, I believe him. Why not?" Troy bites into his apple, chews, and swallows. "Look—not saying I believe there's a lake monster for real, but I don't *not* believe, either. Never seen it with my own eyes is all. Maybe it's a law enforcement thing—only believe what you can see and touch, but never rule out the possible. My dad says it all the time. Says it's something he learned from your grandfather when my dad worked under him in the police station, Lemon."

"That sounds like Pappap," I say, though inside my head is filled with sour laughter. Pappap puts on a good show in public, but he flatly refuses to accept there are things beyond his knowledge—and he's certain he knows everything. If people thought that way, Ziegler's Ferry Tours would go out of business.

No one would believe that Old Lucy could exist, so why bother looking for her on a ferry tour of the lake? For one brief moment, I fantasize about jumping up from the table and shrieking, *It's all fake! Old Lucy is a hoax! This whole town is a lie!*

See and touch *that.*

Darrin smirks. "So, Troy—you're telling me that you're agnostic about the existence of lake monsters because your dad absorbed the wisdom of sheriffing and receptiveness from Ike Ziegler?" He throws a napkin at Troy. "Something doesn't seem right there. Ike is a bit too authoritarian to be open to the existence of cryptids." He turns to me. "Come on—tell me the truth—does Ike come home and make fun of people for believing in our sainted lake monster?"

My brain repeats back one of Pappap's rules for the job: promote the hype—all day, every day. I hope I don't look like I want to throw up all over the place when I say, "We live with Old Lucy, plus with the ferry tour company, he knows she's out there in the water, and I guess . . . I guess I do, too."

Troy and Darrin both gape.

"Screw Billy Voorhees—are *you* drunk?" Darrin says. "In the entire time I've known you, you've been *sure* Old Lucy is fake."

"Not true," I say, fighting the bitter edge surfacing in my voice. "I've just never cared one way or another."

"And now you do?" Troy says. "You have a sighting we don't know about?"

I shrug. Grammy likes to say, *Encourage the talk, say you believe, but never admit to seeing Old Lucy yourself. It gets you noticed, and that's the last thing you want.*

And that don't do you no good, Pappap always chimes in. *You just blend into the woodwork, easy as you please.*

Here I am . . . blending like a champ.

"Ever heard the theory that the Loch Ness monster is really an elephant?" Darrin says. "You know I'm not an Old Lucy believer," he says. "I like conspiracy theories—I just don't believe them. So, maybe it's an elephant."

The struggle to keep my face neutral is real. Darrin doesn't buy into the conspiracy theories he's always going on about? Since when? "That is so random," I say. "Are you suggesting one of my neighbors has a pet elephant that regularly bathes in the lake?"

Darrin steals my banana and peels the first strip. "Elephants can live to be sixty years old or some shit."

"Yeah, but Old Lucy sightings go way back further than the mid-1900s," Troy says. "And elephants? That might be weirder than your conspiracy theory about the Denver airport."

"You believe in Old Lucy but not that American Nazi pukes could be using an airport as their base of operations?" Darrin finishes peeling the banana and eats it in two bites. "And hey, it's *a* conspiracy theory, not *my* personal belief. Nazis and anyone Nazi-adjacent suck, no matter where they operate."

"Fair enough. I'll give you that one because Nazis do, indeed, suck," I say. "If the elephant thing is true, though, it would make me the most unobservant person on the planet."

Darrin grins. "Don't sell yourself short—you've got that hot girl thing going for you."

"Hey!" I kick him under the table, but he's not Skeet: he doesn't say it like he's picturing me naked.

Troy taps Darrin in the arm with his fist. "Don't talk about Lemon like that."

Darrin rubs the spot. "Fine. Lem, you're the smartest goddamn girl I know, a feminist icon for the ages. And you just happen to be a blond Amazon."

I kick him again for good measure, but my heart isn't in it. Prom and graduation are only a monthish away, and Darrin and Troy will leave me behind not long after that. I'll miss Troy's directness and the way he's always looking out for me. Darrin's jokes. Troy's willingness to just be a nice guy.

Even Darrin's casual manly crap and constant trucker mouth and his wild theories about secret societies, although I'll never let on that I find that stuff endearing—at least on him.

"Just because I'm taller than you is no reason to be sarcastic," I say, poker-faced.

"*Everyone* is taller than me," Darrin says. "But I make up for it with my incredible charm and sex appeal."

"That has to do with elephants and lake monsters *how?*" Troy says, attempting a menacing growl that just comes off as too funny to be scary.

"Quit encouraging him." I smile to mask the fact that I want to bottle the two of them up to have their friendship with me always. There's no way to bright-side this because there's nothing good about losing my best friends while simultaneously having my future ripped away. I know I should be thinking about it like I've had a future handed to me on a silver platter instead, but it's hard to be excited when it's not the one I want.

"It doesn't have anything to do with anything." Darrin shrugs. "I'm just trying to make you forget I referred to Lemon as a hot girl. It's true, of course, but you get so testy about it. It's a good thing you ruled out following in your dad's and Ike's footsteps as a career move—you clearly do not have the temperament for being a cop. Or maybe you do. I've seen all those police brutality cell phone videos all over the place."

Troy rabbit-punches Darrin's arm again. We're all being a little loose with the violence today. I know why I'm all salty and tense, but what's Troy's excuse?

He opens his mouth to say something more, but the overhead lights flicker—once, twice, a pause, then another blink. The cafeteria is dead silent for a millisecond before it explodes into a din of nervous tittering and jokes.

Darrin says, "Well, shit, Lemon—you didn't have to go—" He breaks off and winces, clapping his hands over his ears. "What's up with the air pressure?"

A vibration like the buzzing of bees zings through the bottom of my feet.

Troy's face goes confused. "Whoa, feel that?"

"What *is* that?" As the last word leaves my mouth, the floor lurches. A grinding scrape tears the air. My head jerks toward the commotion, but then it's everywhere. The overhead lights swing. A voice—a boy—

screams, and the cafeteria turns into a tinderbox of noise, louder than before. The table shudders, and Darrin's brown bag goes flying.

Troy is on his feet. He clamps onto my arm and hauls me up. My feet hit the rolling ground. It's total chaos. Everyone running. Shoving. Bumping into me. My legs are too liquidy to work properly.

Darrin clamors over the table like he's in a movie, sliding over the hood of a car. Troy's tray upends and claps some first-year girl in the chest. She doesn't seem to notice as she bulldozes her way past, meat juice dripping off her. There's a sound louder than the yelling, something that rumbles and cracks. The lights still swing. Troy wraps his arms around me and lifts me, backing us both out of the crowd.

"What are you doing?" We are nose-to-nose, and it occurs to me to worry about my breath.

"Earthquake." *His* breath smells like apple. The fire alarm suddenly blares.

Earthquake?

Something cold and solid presses into my back, and Troy smooshes against me from the front. The sound of my ribs creak in my ears. I suck in my first real breath. My feet dangle. Troy has me pinned to a doorframe. I yell out to Darrin, but the rumbling and the alarm and the screaming drown out everything but what's happening inside my head.

The pressure against me lessens. I slide down the doorframe. My legs are still like jelly, but the ground is solid enough now. Troy hovers over me. Where once everything was on fast-forward, now it's all slow motion. People running by. Danetta puking into a garbage can. Nothing seems real at all.

Darrin appears at my shoulder. His voice shakes when he says, "You okay?"

"I think Troy tried to suffocate me." I touch an achy spot on my ribs.

"Sorry, Lemon." Troy shrugs, but his face doesn't look anywhere near casual. He has *High Alert* face. "You were frozen, so I moved you. The doorway seemed like the best place."

Darrin sags, hands on knees. "Wow. That was . . ."

"We should go," Troy says. "Aftershocks, y'know?"

In that moment, everything sharpens. "We just had an earthquake."

Darrin laughs once, incredulous. "Welcome to the party, Lem. Where the hell you been?" He jerks his head toward the corridor. "Let's get moving, hey?"

Troy herds me down the crowded hall like a sheep dog, rushing after Darrin. "Seriously—you're fine?" Troy says in my ear. He's close enough that the apples on his breath are still evident. His body heat clings to me, even as the cold of the doorframe lingers in my bones.

The worms are back in my stomach, but for a much different reason. "Yeah. That was unexpected." I glance around—it's all still intact: the Old Lucy mural, the lockers painted purple to match. "The whole building should be coming down, but it looks like nothing happened. Weird."

The doors ahead of us are open, but there's a bottleneck of bodies. No one seems to have any sense of urgency about getting anywhere. I clutch the back of Darrin's T-shirt and say to Troy, "How did you know what to do? To get in the doorway? It's not like we have earthquake drills."

"When would we have time?" Darrin calls over his shoulder. "Between active shooter drills and standardized tests, the school year is chock full of excitement to keep us from learning to think for ourselves."

The top of Principal Showalter's bald head is visible through the door. He shouts, "Everybody out. Come on, get moving."

Even with the principal partially blocking the exit, it's not too long until we pop through the front door of the school. The color of the sky has intensified, and it's oddly alarming—still a little too surreal for my liking. I eye the ground in case a sinkhole decides to open beneath our feet. Between officially taking over as the Old Lucy impersonator last night, Skeet asking me to prom, and now this, anything feels possible in the very worst way.

Darrin leads us across the lot until we reach Troy's massive puke-green Buick.

Troy leans against the car and plays with this phone. "What are we supposed to do? Assure my mom the school's still standing—and what then?"

Darrin says, "Watch the teachers lose their shit, I guess. I get it—earthquakes aren't exactly an everyday thing in Pennsylvania."

"That's not entirely true." I will myself to relax—that is, until the glowing neon from the Lucy-licious Fluff and Fold across the street blasts into my sight line. There's just no getting away from my destiny in this town. "Grammy told me once that there are usually one or two earthquakes each month around here, but they're tiny. There were even a few really small ones that registered on the seismograph at the lake the other day."

"There's a seismograph at the lake?" Darrin says.

"It's part of the equipment the police department keeps to monitor the water quality and rainfall amounts and stuff like that," I say. "Pappap keeps a few instruments out there, too—he says it helps him understand lake conditions."

Troy nods. "Dad was just talking about those little earthquakes. Some guy at the station said it could be fracking related. Started happening a dozen years back—the fracking quakes, that is. That's why Dad was rambling about earthquake drills. It's why I knew what to do when it hit today. Anyway, bunch of fracking operations are set up maybe thirty minutes from here."

"Figures." Darrin's nose wrinkles. "Old people, right? How much sense does it make to destroy the planet just so they can make more money? I'd like *not* to die before I graduate from college."

I catch sight of Skeet's pickup truck parked a few rows away. He's behind the wheel, glaring in my direction. My phone buzzes in my pocket, and part of me wants to ignore it in case it's a text from him. The last thing I need is a continuation of his *you're a bitch* crap.

"Should text my dad, I guess," Troy says.

Right. And I should check on Grammy and Pappap. I fish my phone out, about to speed-dial one of them, but the text that buzzed is from Grammy: *Are you okay, sweetie? Where are you?*

Me: *I'm good, in parking lot at school. You and Pappap okay?*

We're fine, cleaning the boats today. No real damage from the quake.

"Grandparents?" Troy says.

I nod, and Darrin laughs. "Speaking of old people . . ."

"It's Grammy, making sure I'm not dead. They're over at the ferry office."

Because *of course* they are. Tourist season is coming, and they've got to be ready to reap the benefits of my impersonations.

Everything to do with Old Lucy is turning me into someone I don't like—I can barely even give my own grandmother the benefit of the doubt. I know she loves me, but from here on out I'll never be sure if she's actually worried about me, or if she's just concerned I'll die and Pappap will have to go back to impersonating the lake monster and ruin their retirement plans. It's not like my Uncle Bobby, Aunt Nan, or my cousin are going to vote themselves to be the new heirs to the questionable Ziegler fortune, and Grammy knows it. They don't live in Devil's Elbow. They don't care about what happens here or about the family legacy. I don't care much about it, either—but saying no to my grandfather is impossible. My mouth tightens.

"Did you get a text from Ike?" Darrin says.

"Oh, please," I say. "Pappap barely knows how to use a cell phone beyond making a simple phone call. It's like magic to him." Right on cue, my phone rings.

"Hey, Pappap." I make a face at Darrin. He nudges Troy away.

"Well, hain't that a kick in the pants." Pappap's voice is rough as the ever-present stubble on his wrinkly cheeks. "All that shaking, and now it's like it ain't never happened. The lake's as calm as a baby and smooth as glass. Earthquakes are funny things."

"I told Grammy I'm fine."

"I know—she's standing right here. But you can't find no fault in me checking." He chuckles. "Are them kids at your school talking about Old Lucy?"

I suppress yet another sigh. Of course he doesn't care about how *I'm* doing—he only cares about how the family legacy is holding up. "Yeah, I heard some things this morning."

"Good. The earthquake hain't going to help none, though, I tell you what. We might have to schedule another sighting a few weeks from now."

My heart instantly fills with sand. "Do we *have* to?"

"There won't be no need if the earthquake talk dies down pretty quick. We'll see. If there hain't been a fresh Old Lucy sighting to get people talking, folks might go to one of them water parks in the Poconos instead of coming here. Best see if you can't get Old Lucy back atop everyone's minds."

"Sure, Pappap. Okay."

I say bye, hoping my voice doesn't sound too miserable. Maybe I can start a new rumor about an Old Lucy sighting. Maybe that'll be enough. *Anything* to avoid strapping on the Old Lucy latex and neoprene so soon. At least Skeet's truck is gone when I turn around. I'll take good news anywhere I can find it.

3

TROY

"**W**HAT'S UP WITH YOU, TROY?" That's Darrin, soon as we're away from Lemon. "Thinking big thoughts or something? You look all . . . I don't know . . . tense. If you're going to beef, let me know—I'll give you some privacy."

"Leave my sphincter out of it." I sneak a glance at Lemon, make sure she's not within earshot. The wind blows her hair around like a kite tail. She glances over at me and waggles her fingers, absent smile on her face.

"Let me guess what's running through your head." He coos, "Oh, Lemon, Lemon. I love you, Lemon. I want to have your sweet yellow-haired babies, Lemon. Why don't you love me, Lemon? Won't you thank me for saving you like the big, strong he-man that I am?"

"Shut up," I say. "It's not like that."

Except it is . . . kind of.

"What, it's not like that *today*?" Darrin says. "You're lucky Lemon is totally blind to it."

"Leave it alone. She's our best friend. *My* best friend." One of the only people who doesn't constantly hound me about what I want to do with my life.

"So? I hope you're not saying you have a thing for me, too, but that you're sparing me because we're tight." Darrin pounds my shoulder. "I love you like a brother and all, and under certain circumstances I'd consider—"

"Be serious. Me and Lemon, we're platonic. That's it. Besides, there's Skeet." Comes out casual—but I'm dying inside. It was only a matter of time, someone asking her to prom.

But *that* guy?

"Oh, right. Like Lemon's going to say yes to his promposal? Or like Ike is going to be okay if she does? Hasn't he arrested pretty much everyone in Skeet's family? He would lock Lemon in her room first before he let her out with Skeet." He eyeballs me. "Y'know, you could go to prom together instead—like I know you want to and have been stewing about for months. I can arrange it."

Lemon shoves her phone away in her pocket, walks toward us.

My teeth clench. "Leave it alone."

"More conspiracies that you claim not to believe in? What is it this time?" Lemon's ponytail bounces. "Let me guess—New World Order? Corporations paying politicians to say climate change is a Chinese hoax?"

I try to keep the murderous look off my face. Darrin's going to screw me. I can see it.

He plays innocent, of course. *Jackass.* "Funny you should ask," he says. "I'm planning to ask Cara Alexander to the prom."

"That doesn't sound like a bad thing," Lemon says.

"It's *not* bad," Darrin says. "She's going to say yes. Who wouldn't, right? Like I said, incredible charm and sex appeal. And here's the

thing—I know you told Skeet you're already going to prom with someone else, if the rumors flying around are true."

I shoot him a warning glance.

Lemon's ears pink up. She gets that look on her face—the one
where she's embarrassed but doesn't want anyone to know.

"Look, I get why you said no to Skeet," he says. "I'm pretty sure the
night would end with him puking all over you, a little cow tipping, a lot
of unwanted groping, maybe a little gas station robbery. Not exactly a
precious memory that you want to have forever and ever."

"Shut it down." I cross my arms over my chest. Darrin's dickish,
yeah. He doesn't mean it, though. That mouth races ahead of him.
Never should've told him how I feel about Lemon in the first place—
should've been enough just to keep it to myself.

"What I'm getting at," Darrin says, ignoring me, "is that your bestie
Troy here is planning on sitting out the prom because the girl he wants
to go with is, shall we say, unaware of his affections. That makes him
available. Since I know perfectly well that you do not, in fact, have a
date, and Skeet would be all up in his feelings that you lied to avoid
going with him, you should go to prom with Troy. Plus, then you two
can double with me and Cara. Problem solved for you. Problem solved
for Troy. Problem solved for me—because I get to spend the night with
an awesome girl and you two freaking turds."

"Gee, you make it sound so enticing," she says. "I'm a creepy looking
turd—and a clearly desperate and dateless one."

For crissakes. Now he's got her feeling bad about herself. He's a
dead man.

"I say that out of love, of course," Darrin says. "You're both my beloved turds. Turds of my heart, if you will. And you're never anyone's
second choice. Just so we're clear."

Lemon half smiles at me, but intense. Like being pelted with stones.
"Who's the girl? You never—I mean, I didn't think you were all that
interested in going to prom at all."

"I'm not. Darrin's being dramatic."

Darrin snorts. I manage not to punch him, much as the urge grips me.

"It's not a terrible idea," she says. "Or we can say we're going and then just not go. Maybe have a movie marathon. We haven't done that in a while. It'll be fun."

"Look, go to prom," Darrin says, still kind of laughing. "*That* will be fun. And who knows what could happen? I feel completely secure in my manhood to say that Troy is a delicious slice of hotness and will probably look like James Bond in a tuxedo." He jabs his finger at Lemon. "It could be the best night of your life."

"And I could hit you with a shovel," I mutter.

Darrin grins. "And again, there's the Skeet factor and his *hell hath no fury like a man scorned* schtick. No one would question that you and Troy going to prom together hasn't been the plan all along. It will help ease the rage of Skeet's fragile masculinity."

"Fine, I'll go." Lemon rolls her eyes. I can see it in her face that she hates the idea. "Any news on prom theme for this year?"

"That's the best part." Darrin's grin is massive. "Old Lucy is the theme. We're having a prom *de* lake monster."

"Jesus on a freaking cracker," she says quietly.

All our phones ping at once. Darrin gets to his first, smiles even wider. "We've been sprung for the rest of the day on account of the earthquake. Shall we go wreak havoc elsewhere? The day is young."

Lemon laughs, but it's humorless. Like I could feel any worse about how morose she is about getting railroaded. I've gotta give her an out for prom.

I tap her shoulder. "Want a ride home?"

Darrin's eyes cut toward me. "You want to celebrate our freedom by going home? I've got to loosen you up before we graduate." When neither of us answers, he groans. "Fine, drive me home, turd of my heart."

At least I can think about what to say to Lemon on the drive.

I unlock the doors to my old-ass Buick. The inside of the car reeks of pine, oil, and duct tape. Lemon's in the passenger seat, so close I can smell her, too. Warm, like vanilla. It's her hair—she always smells like that. Even during the earthquake. Yeah, my first reaction was to get us to a safe spot. My second was to bury my nose in her hair.

We rip out of the parking lot, past the Old Lucy statue in front of the school. Darrin's cracking jokes. Lemon's laughing. This is the way it should be. I don't know what the hell I'm going to do after we graduate. I wish nothing would have to change at all.

A time clock in my head's always counting down the rest of the school year, but the state of Front Street is a reminder that summer's almost here, too. Fall, winter, early spring—it's pretty dead. Now, though, people are out, painting store fronts, cleaning windows, getting ready. The guy from Lakebed Candies is shining up the clown face entrance to his place. Already a sign in the window advertising Old Lucy Poop, some weird fudge concoction. Dad says tourists love that kind of thing. I don't know how Lemon deals with working her grandparents' ferry business.

I take the next corner, listen to Darrin and Lemon chatter. I throw in a "yeah" and an "uh-huh" now and then. Finally, we pull up to Darrin's gray two-story. He slaps me lightly in the back of the head when he climbs out. I flip him off. He laughs and waves, jogs up his front steps to the porch. I'm almost sorry to see him go—the drive hasn't helped me come up with anything to say to Lemon.

"Hey," she says when I pull back onto the road. "You want to get ice cream first? Magic Monster is testing out new summer flavors today."

The shop on the next block stands out—it's got a new coat of pink glitter paint, almost the same color as the signs on Ziegler's Ferry Tours. "That's . . . uh . . . bright." I almost hit the curb.

Lemon shrugs, half grimacing. Maybe this is the part where she lets me down gently about the prom. Ply me with sugar, drop bad news, like I'm a kid.

Inside the shop, it's light blue walls, painted up like water. Old Lucy heads pop out of the waves here and there. Mrs. Day, the owner, flits out of the back room in her bright orange Magic Monster shirt, phone pressed to her ear. She wears a big smile 'til she sees it's just us. She nods, goes back to what she was doing. I hear her say, "If Charlie turns up, you tell him I'm pissed he didn't show up for work today. What does he expect me to do? I don't care if he went fishing."

"Beastly Bing," Lemon reads from the front of the ice cream case. "Bing cherries and chocolate. That sounds good."

"Who thinks of these names?" I say. "Cryptid Cookie Crumb? I Scream For Lu-Seaweed and Salt?"

"Come on—you wouldn't want to eat Lake Bottom Lychee?" She points. "Oh, look—there's one that's pineapple with ginger. You love pineapple." She peers over the case. "Hey, Mrs. Day, we're ready."

Lemon orders the pineapple ice cream for me and the Cryptid Cookie Crumb for her when Mrs. Day comes back, this time without her phone. I reach into my pocket for my wallet. Lemon puts her hand on mine. "This is on me. I owe you for the earthquake."

If this is what makes her feel better for dumping me, okay. She hands me a cone. We head out to the picnic table next to the shop. Mrs. Day hasn't made it out here yet with the paint. It's faded from last summer. Salmon-colored instead of Day-Glo. A perfect, sad-sack spot to get jilted.

"So, prom." Lemon sits next to me, hip against mine.

"Yeah, I wanted to say—Darrin strong-armed you."

She startles, turns to face me. "What, no? He strong-armed *you*. If there's someone else you'd rather go with . . ."

"He was just making shit up. You know him." The pineapple ice cream tastes . . . more ginger, less pineapple. Still good.

She laughs, takes a bite of her cookie crumb. "It's not a terrible idea, the two of us going together. You know I love you, and I bet you *do* look great in a tux."

She loves me . . . just not like *that*. I *could* pretend it's different between us, just for one night. Lemon doesn't have to know. It's all playing out in my brain. Two of us, swaying to the music. My nose in her vanilla hair. Her hand on my shoulder. My arm wrapped around her. The feeling of her against me.

Suddenly, this is the best idea Darrin has ever had.

"Then yeah, let's go," I say. "We'll have a good time. Like when we went to the freshman dance."

She grins, takes another bite. "Technically, you and Darrin went to that one, and I went alone."

Right. Because Mr. Z said it wasn't right for us to all go together. Something about Lemon being too young to date. Or about her going out with two guys. Whatever.

"But I do remember you and me danced to . . . that song about summer," she continues. "And Darrin wore those ugly shoes."

"You looked pretty." It just pops out of my mouth. Lemon doesn't seem to mind, though. She leans against my shoulder, smiles at me.

"Purple dress, I think, right?" I say, like I'm not picturing her in it, thinking again about how my arm will be around her waist, her hands on my neck.

"Right," she says. "Grammy donated it last year when we were cleaning out the attic. It was lavender with that little ruffle thing. I think that was the first time I ever saw you in a tie."

That's when I notice Lemon's eyes are wet.

"You . . . you okay?" I say.

She turns away. "Yeah. It's just . . ." She hiccups. Tears steam down her face in a gush. She tosses the remains of her cone in the trash, frantically swipes at her face before falling into my chest. My arms automatically wrap around her.

The irony of that—after I was just thinking about it—isn't lost on me. Her shoulders shake. I rub her hair, her back, say stupid things into the side of her head.

This is new. Lemon's not one for crying. Maybe it's the earthquake. Some people have delayed reactions to that kind of thing. I keep doing what I'm doing until she hiccups again, pulls away. Lets out a long, hitching breath.

"Sorry," she says. "Thanks for just letting me cry. I really am fine. I swear it."

"You sure?"

She nods. "Yeah, weird day, I guess. At least it probably won't get any weirder."

An inward cringe hits me. I keep my face neutral, though. Lemon's not the fragile type, but tempting fate like that—it almost always guarantees there's worse coming.

4

L E M O N

M Y EYES STILL FEEL SWOLLEN from crying, even thirty minutes after Troy drops me at home. I can't imagine what he must be thinking—and it's not like it's even a remote possibility to tell him about the guilt weighing me down, the sadness about losing him and Darrin while I stand still here in Devil's Elbow, seething with jealousy as they leave. I can't tell them anything.

Butterbeans, my grandparents' elderly bulldog, nudges me toward the ramshackle wooden staircase that leads down to the boathouse behind our cabin. His crumpled face is so outraged that I could dare to be depressed on this blue-sky day that I can't help laughing. The sound bounces off the pine trees that line the edges of our property almost all the way to the water's edge.

The other two dogs—Bob, the orange and white Brittany spaniel, and Snowflake, Grammy's giant ball of white dandelion fluff—pull at the bungee leashes. I grasp at the wooden rail, bleached nearly white with decades of sun exposure, and follow it to the floating dock and attached boathouse at the bottom. It's one of the few places I have a real memory of my dad.

"Hey, look over there," I say to the dogs' wiggling butts. They ignore me in favor of sprinting across the dock and toward the trail that leads around to the west side of the lake. "That's where my dad used to pick me off the dock, hug me tight, and jump into the water." I point with the hand that's not tangled in the master leash. The sound of Dad's shouts are still almost as real to me as my own voice.

Bob, half on point at the mouth of the trail, at least has the decency to smile up at me, tongue lolling out of the side of his mouth. "I know. I miss him." I pat the heart-shaped orange spot on top of his head, still hearing my dad in my head.

For the dozenth time, I check to make sure all the dog leads are tightly attached to the master leash. Butterbeans might have short, arthritic legs, but he still has the occasional sprint in him. Snowflake slaps Bob, still half on point, with her tail when she zooms ahead down the trail, pulling me with her.

Pappap thinks Snowflake might be part West Highland terrier. She's small and hairy enough, but she has the undereye bags and jowls of a shar-pei. Snowflake is even older than Butterbeans—she's been Grammy's dog since I was a kid, even before my parents died. She's the only one of the dogs who would know my dad if he ran up to us right now.

I jog after Snowflake and scoop her up, kiss her right between her rheumy brown eyes. "You'd remember him, right?" She squirms until I set her down.

Bob catches up with us and pants adoringly at me.

"Don't worry," I say. "I'm not mad at my dad for being dead."

Butterbeans gives me a look like he doesn't believe me, but it's true. Dad would have been voted in as the lake monster impersonator instead of me if he and Mom hadn't had a car accident. If I let myself get ticked off about what could have been—for them or for me—the wretchedness takes me. And I especially don't want to think about what I'm losing, at least for the next hour—because that time is for me and the dogs. I don't have control over much, but I can control what I'm thinking about for a short period of time, or at least try. So no thinking about my parents. No thinking about Troy and Darrin. No thinking about Old Lucy. Definitely no thinking about that scene in the cafeteria with Skeet.

Putting on a good face . . . my specialty. Most of the time anyway.

Butterbeans almost seems to be laughing at me. Bob and Snowflake are happy tapping—that's what Grammy calls it—at the ends of their leashes, so I put on a silly voice and ask, "What's it going to be?" All three are googly-eyed excited. "We have time for a decent walk. We can walk along the lake, or we can hike through the woods. Up to you."

Bob tilts his head up.

"Don't look at me that way, Bob."

Butterbeans howl-yawns and stamps his heavy feet on the dock boards.

I'd have a dozen more dogs if I could. There's nothing like a pack of squirmy, happy-to-see-you dogs as a distraction from, well, everything.

"Okay, fine. Lake trail it is." I'm glad we're alone out here—anyone watching me talk to the dogs would think I'd lost my mind. The gravel trail curves around the shoreline, the water just a few feet to the right of it. Here, the space between the trail and the lake is mucky, tall grass shooting up out of the water. The dogs are out in front before I can call to them, leashes crisscrossing as they zigzag toward a stand of pickerel-weed. Bob's deep, puffing inhales are nearly as loud as the wind rustling through trees up ahead.

The trail darkens, falling under the shade of enormous spruces that border the dry side of the path. It's like being pulled into a portal, through to a different, almost magical place. Up around the bend, the pickerelweed thickens and butts up against the curving trunks of several weeping willows. The dogs are on a tear, racing each other to the marshy strip beyond the trees, and the squelchy pebbled beach just wide enough for all three of the dogs to paw at the water and chase newts and birds and frogs off into the tall grass along the trail.

We're not quite a mile away from our floating dock, but I'm so far away from the problems that await me at home that it might as well be a hundred miles. This time of year, the air is all fuzzy with blowing yellow pollen. Bob lets out a joyous, high-pitched bark and pounces in the water, sending up small splashes.

It's the most relaxed I've been in at least two or three days.

There *has* to be a way to make the Old Lucy thing work for me. *Has to.* Maybe I can run a small pet rescue out of the house. I don't need to be a veterinarian for that. It won't interfere with my monster impersonation duties. Not really. I'll need the emotional boost and the company. And I can hire people to help with the ferry services. I'm going to have to anyway, eventually. Grammy keeps hinting around that New Mexico is a nice place to spend her and Pappap's "golden years," and I can't handle the business all by myself. I'm great at math, but the ledgers make me go cross-eyed. Maybe one day, but definitely not now.

I don't want to be so envious of Troy and Darrin, and I definitely don't want to be so weepy in front of either of them ever again. Troy doesn't really say much about what he wants to do for school, and I don't want to pry. Darrin decided last year to major in urban planning after years of telling anyone who would listen that he wanted to be a gynecologist like his mom. It's Dr. Flanagan's fault that he kept running around yelling, "I'm the other Dr. Flanagan, at your cervix!" Neither Darrin nor Troy has an unfettered path, and they're going to have to work hard to get what they want, maybe get lucky—but they have choices. They get to *choose.* They get to leave, and I don't.

I shake my head. Obsessing about all of this is breaking my pledge to just hang out with the dogs and pretend everything is okay. I push it all down until my mouth relaxes enough to smile . . . or at least not to grimace.

Butterbeans grunts, all googly-eyed, and licks my hand like the goof that he is. I don't want to laugh, but I do and give him a scratch between his brown ears. The edges of his mouth pull back toward his ears, giving him a gap-toothed jack-o'-lantern look.

"Yeah, I know." I grin back. "I'm not much fun today, am I?"

Bob flops down at my feet and rolls over onto his back, nearly twisting into the water. The orange spots on the underside of his chest are bright in the sun. His tongue flops out the side of his happy mouth, and his eyes squint.

My laugh floats over the water. It's almost a convincing sound.

Quick as a breath, Bob jerks to his feet. He plants himself between me and the water. He issues three sharp barks at the lake and growls low.

I pivot and pivot again, looking for what's caught his attention.

Butterbeans wriggles away from me and joins Bob, broad shoulders set. Snowflake stands farther away from them on the narrow beach. Her little body jolts with each high-pitched bark.

There's nothing there. Not even a ripple out of place on the water.

Snowflake barks again.

A low moan sounds over the lake, so quiet I'm not even sure it's real.

I shush the dogs. Wait for the noise. Everything goes silent—frogs, crickets. *Everything.* Goosebumps pop up on my arms. Even Bob, Butterbeans, and Snowflake freeze for a solid thirty seconds until Snowflake strains at the leash again. I reel her in closer, but her barking is relentless now.

Maybe there's a snake in the water, or the scent of geese in the air. Bob is a bird dog, after all. He'd be the first one to get all tense if he got a whiff of something different or interesting. Maybe he smells a hiker farther along the trail. He's a big old softie, but he at least likes to pretend he'd protect me from a potentially dangerous stranger.

"Who's there?" I yell, just in case. There's no answer.

Two steps away from the lake is all I manage before the water gey-sers up like someone's forcing it up through a hole in the silt.

There are suddenly teeth—long pointed things that seem to curve inward—and a rotten smell of death. The suggestion of mottled gray skin emerges through the water. A huge, anvil-shaped head with a dirty yellow crest and a long thick neck roars back into the lake a second later, taking with it a small, writhing spot of pure white.

Snowflake.

A shot of crimson splashes over the pebbles at my feet.

Another crash of water and a final yip, and everything goes silent once more, but only for a moment. Bob and Butterbeans strain toward the water, growling and barking, teeth bared. I scream, too, and stare at the spot where Snowflake was dragged into the lake.

What the hell just happened?

The dogs pull me closer to the water, straining to get at whatever is now below the surface. I yank at the leashes, tugging them away. The canvas lead bites into my hand. That thing in the lake has teeth. Giant, sharp teeth.

I haul Bob and Butterbeans back to the path, through the shadowed trail, staying as far from the water as possible. My throat hurts, but dif-ferent from the way it hurts from sucking air through a regulator—I'm still screaming. Like full-on horror film screaming. The noise of it is louder than anything else—the dogs, the water, the wind. My heart.

A million thoughts shout at me.

I should go back and look for Snowflake.

I need to get the dogs to safety.

I'm in danger.

There is something in the lake. With teeth.

Sweat burns my eyes.

My lungs hurt. My throat hurts.

Why is Butterbeans' fur red?

Is that thing chasing me?

My legs feel like lead.

Am I crying?

There is a *monster*.

Grammy and Pappap will be upset.

Who cares about Grammy and Pappap? *I'm* upset.

God, what will I tell them?

I sprint down the trail, back toward the floating dock and the boathouse. Bob and Butterbeans thump ahead, springing forward with ears pinned back. I've never seen Butterbeans move so fast—ever. The sound of his ragged, hoarse breathing is terrible. The weathered wooden dock dips with the weight of them, and in the resulting splash of wood against water comes the thought of that . . . *thing* . . . leaping out and taking another dog.

Or me.

Bob is a whipping streak of white and orange, but Butterbeans, despite his desperate speed, lags. Without breaking my stride, I scoop him up and tuck him into my chest before barreling up the steps to the top of the hill. The old staircase shakes and creaks. I don't look back. I don't stop running, even though I suddenly can't feel my legs. I'm sure if I pause, if I slow, the teeth will be on me. It will kill me. It will kill the dogs. And it'll keep coming.

What is that thing?

"Jesus, Lemon, what happened?"

I plow right into Troy at the top of the stairs and knock him back a few steps. He fumbles with Butterbeans. Bob is panting and whining, pawing at the grass.

"Is that blood? You okay?" Troy's eyes are huge and dark. "What's happening?"

"It . . . it ate . . . Snowflake." My voice sounds odd, too high and harsh, almost the chitter of cicadas. "It's coming."

I twist a fistful of Troy's denim jacket and jerk him around to face the lake. There's nothing but calm water and the dock and the boathouse and the sun and the wind in the trees. If not for Bob pacing back and forth, eyes alert, blood-streaked Butterbeans squirming in Troy's arms, and the rush of blood pounding in my eardrums, it could be any other day.

The sky is still entirely too blue.

Troy sets Butterbeans on the grass. The dog drops to his belly and lays chin on paws, making himself small. He whimpers. I understand completely. I want to disappear, to hide, to shrink down my tallness into something tiny and invisible and safe.

Troy's brows draw together on his *High Alert* face. "There's nothing coming. It's okay. You hurt? Where's Snowflake?"

"You have zero idea what you're talking about," I say. "I was walking the dogs, and a monster came out of the lake and ate her! It ate Snowflake!"

Monster.

There it is, that word on my tongue. It pushes at the corners of my brain. It can't be anything else—the irony of it sits in my mouth for a moment before my knees buckle. I feel like I'm falling in slow motion until my body heavily hammers onto the lawn. It's all very dramatic and swoony, and my ears burn with embarrassment until that word is back, and then I'm just terrified.

Monster.

Troy folds himself down next to me, his expression a mix of excitement and alarm. He bounces his fist on my knee. "Old Lucy? Ate Snowflake? You really saw it?" His face falls, and his fist stills. "Oh. Old Lucy *ate* Snowflake."

Bob climbs into my lap and shivers. He has *High Alert* face, too.

Troy's words repeat in my head, over and over. I peer at him like he's grown mermaid scales on his forehead. He's *serious*. Of course he is. Only believe what you can see and touch, but never rule out the possible—the blood all over the dog makes it more than possible that Old Lucy could be to blame. What else *could* it be to someone who doesn't know what I know?

An unexpected giggle bursts out of me and expands until I'm cackling for no reason. I can't stop. The feeling of it—and me trying to control myself—tickles. I absently reach over to stroke Bob's freckled nose as I laugh, and tears run down my face again. He whines and licks my hand.

Troy's rubbing my shoulder and whispering things to me, trying to calm me. "You going into shock?" he says. "Yeah. Yeah, of course you are."

I giggle harder. Such a strange sensation, like my entire stomach is lit on fire from the inside. I hiccup a few times.

"I can't believe you saw Old Lucy," he says.

And then I'm stone cold sober. I hug Bob and hiss at Troy, "Didn't you hear me? A monster—an actual, honest-to-god *monster*—a lake monster, no less—just *ate* Snowflake." I mimic the burst of water with my shaking hands. "It was there and gone before I could even breathe. There is a *monster* in the *lake*."

The lake I'd been *in* the night before. And a million times before that. How have generations of Zieglers managed not to get eaten out of sheer luck? This new job of mine suddenly sucks a zillion times more.

"What are you even doing here?" I say. Bob pulls away from me and starts circling us, jumping over Butterbeans.

"You forgot your cell phone in my car. You didn't answer the door when I knocked, figured you were maybe walking the—I should call my dad. Or should I call your grandparents?" He roots in the pocket of his jacket and pauses. "Wait, no. Let's get you inside. You're shaking." He jumps up and holds out his hand.

I snort but allow him to hoist me off the grass.

He holds up a finger and takes his phone from his pocket. A few seconds later: "Dad, Old Lucy killed one of the Ziegler dogs . . . no, I don't think so . . . Lemon was there. She's . . . no, she's not hurt, least I don't think so . . . yeah, okay."

"Who is your dad supposed to send out here for something like this?" I say when he ends the call. "Maybe have him alert the National Guard."

Troy's face goes comically blank. "Who responded the last time something like this happened with Old Lucy?"

"It *wasn't* Old Lucy."

Before I can stop myself, the words just slip out: "There *is* no Old Lucy." He says at the same time, "Okay, then what was it?"

My confession must have gotten lost in his question because he doesn't react other than to look around again, more nervous this time. Part of me is relieved. Part of me is disappointed.

He says, "A bear, maybe? Dad's had reports. Warm spring, y'know? Drives 'em out of hibernation early. Let's go inside, okay?"

My ears are burning again. "My dog is dead, Troy. Butterbeans is covered in blood."

Butterbeans whuffs.

"You're bloody, too." He wipes his thumb across my cheekbone, and it comes away streaked copper-red. He inhales through his nose. "Look, you're shook up," he says. "You should sit down."

"Just . . . grab Butterbeans, okay? Please?" I fume on my way to the back door of my house. I have no idea why I'm so mad. Okay, I do—I want Troy to zone in on my brain waves and understand what I'm saying without me having to tell him. I unlock the door with shaking hands, and Bob zooms inside, into the kitchen. He beelines to the living room. A few seconds later comes the sound of the front door pushing open.

"Lemon, honey, you here?" Grammy calls.

"That boy's car is out front," Pappap grumbles. "She knows I don't truck with that."

Great. One more thing I don't feel like dealing with right now— Pappap's old-fashioned notions of proper decorum for girls. My mouth tightens into an angry knot. And why hasn't he told me there's an actual monster in the lake? He's been doing the sightings for most of his life. He *has* to know.

"Kitchen," I call, trying to sound calm when I really want to crawl out of my skin at the very possibility of Pappap keeping that kind of secret.

"Who's a good boy," Grammy croons. "Bob's a good boy, yes he is."

I pull Troy all the way inside the kitchen and lock the door. One last peek out the window, and all is clear. No weird creatures, nothing horrible dashing up the staircase. Troy looks between me and the doorway of the kitchen, mouth soundlessly working, like he wants to say something but isn't sure what. I can empathize.

Butterbeans nudges my ankle with his head.

"And where's my Snowflake?" Grammy says.

I squeeze my eyes shut, but teeth snapping into poor Snowflake is what waits behind my lids. I don't want to have to relive it. My eyes pop open to see Troy walking through the door to the living room. A few seconds later, hushed voices, then Grammy's panicked, "Merciful heavens!"

Well.

"And she said it weren't Old Lucy?" There's a cautionary note in Pappap's voice, and I can hear the lecture already starting to form in his brain: when an animal goes missing, try to link it to Old Lucy. If a body goes missing or if some drunk falls into the lake and drowns, drop a hint that Old Lucy's been seen. "The myth of Old Lucy, it's as important as the sightings," he always says. "Your job ain't just swimmin' in the costume—it's planting clues. It's ginnin' up danger."

Yeah, there's danger, all right. It ate the dog.

"Troy," I hear Pappap say, "you should go. Lemon hain't going to want company right now. I'm sure she'll give you a holler later."

I'm so cold. I wrap my arms around myself and wait for the sound of the front door to shut. The sound of Troy's car turning over. Pappap's going to have things to say—and I should have things to say to him too, but I know better. Luckily, Grammy's the first one to the kitchen, a quilt from the couch in her hands. She clucks over me, wrapping me up.

Of course, Pappap comes stomping in and plants himself in front of me. "What on earth—"

Grammy frowns. "Ike, I'll thank you to tone it down some. Your granddaughter has been attacked by something."

"I appreciate that, Pearl—but look, ain't a scratch on you, is there, Lemon? If you was hurt, I'd be concerned." He glances over at Grammy. "But she hain't. She's fine. Troy's probably right about it being a bear."

"It wasn't a bear, Pappap. It was something else." I describe the monster, the whole time wanting to vomit—both at the memory and because asking him if he knows, has always known, is eating a hole in my stomach.

Grammy's eyes slide to Pappap. "Ike, that doesn't sound like anything we've seen around here. Don't you think—"

"Probably just a bear with mange." He pats my hand. "Probably trying to catch its lunch, and you and the dogs got too close. I'll set some bear traps."

What is he saying?

"Got some bear spray under the sink, too."

He really doesn't believe me. He's not going to do *anything*. Maybe he knows about the monster and maybe not—either way, he just doesn't *care*.

"Maybe keep Bob and Butterbeans up here in the yard to do their business for the next few weeks." Grammy's mouth trembles. "Poor Snowflake."

Pappap says, "Now when Gerry gets here, you just tell him straight what you seen, Lemon. Don't lie none, and don't say it weren't Old Lucy, either. Folk'll draw their own conclusions, and we'll do a bit of work to make sure them rumors spread. They'll be swarming the ferries to see if they can spot Old Lucy this summer!"

5

TROY

Mom's waiting for me when I get home. My hands shook the whole drive from Lemon's. My heart's *still* hammering. Mom doesn't say much. Takes one look, walks me into the house, and sits me down in the kitchen, right in front of the ugly centerpiece of dried orange flowers.

She kisses my cheek, gives me a hug. Leaves me be. She knows how to do that without it being weird. Must be all those years with Dad, letting him brood after a shitty case or a shitty shift.

I can't get Lemon's blood-spattered face out of my head. My fingers drum on the blue placemat at my seat at the table. It ends up in my hands. I roll it, bunch it up. Hands won't stay put.

I've never seen Lemon like this. Not by a mile. Darrin knocked over a wasp nest once when we were kids. That was bad. Lemon fell out of a tree at my house. Broke her wrist. That was worse. But today . . . blood on her, blood on the dog. That was something else. She's lucky I didn't bodily pick her up and drive her to the hospital. I wanted to. Like when I manhandled her into a doorframe during the earthquake.

I turned into a caveman—protect what you love, be a man. The kind of thing Dad's always spouting when he says he's trying to turn me into a grown-up. Surprised Lemon didn't kick me in the sack at school. Hell, it looked like she wanted to at her house when she said it wasn't Old Lucy that ate Snowflake. I still don't know what that was about. Shock, maybe.

I rub my forehead, sit for a minute more. Maybe Mr. Z's right that she'll call me when she's ready. I text her anyway: *You okay?* No answer, but hey, she's in the house. Her grandparents'll probably make sure nothing happens to her. I want to know she's okay, though. I want to know Mr. Z didn't haul her out to the lake to look for the bear or whatever it is that caught Snowflake.

Mom putters back into the kitchen, shakes her head when she sees the placemat all messed up. "Dad did tell me what happened before he left for the Zieglers."

"I figured." My leg starts bouncing like a jackhammer. Kitchen's too small and too big, all at once. Nothing to do with the white wraparound cabinets, the striped rug on the floor. None of that. I just . . . need to be somewhere else.

"I want you to be careful, okay?" she says. "Remember what your father said about earthquakes last week—about how wildlife gets spooked? Lemon got lucky today. That house is so isolated out there at the lake. I wish Ike and Pearl would take Lemon to stay in town until things calm down, but Ike's so stubborn about that house."

"Stubborn about everything," I mumble. She's not making me feel better.

Mom grins. "Noticed that, huh? I had a first-row seat when your dad was Ike's deputy all those years." She turns to the refrigerator, pulls out a bottle of water. "Regardless, just mind yourself. Your dad says the station's had lots of calls today. Cracked roads. Even a few missing people. I'm not saying that's related to the earthquake *or* wildlife, of course. What I'm trying to get at here is that I want you to be extra careful if you head out that way to see Lemon."

"You're not gonna tell me I *can't* go?"

She twists the top off the water and sets it near me on the table. "Oh, please. You're a little on the stubborn side yourself. Speaking of which, any luck making a decision about college yet? I heard one of the cashiers at Hitchcock Organics say she'd just mailed in her acceptance to some college in Philadelphia."

I groan. "I'd rather talk about dodging lake monsters or bears." My leg starts bouncing double-time, like my nerves are on fire.

Mom and Dad have let me handle college applications by myself, which I suppose I should be grateful for. Not like Darrin, whose parents practically filled them out for him, hovered while he wrote his essays. They had an actual cake when he got accepted to Cornell—guess his dad went to nursing school there.

My mom and dad . . . they've seen my response letters come in. They bug me about it, but they haven't demanded answers. Yet. I just . . . nothing feels right. How the hell am I supposed to know this second what I want to do with the rest of my life?

Is hanging out with Lemon and making sure she doesn't get eaten by bears an option? I'll go to school for that right now. Sign me up. Ready to jump up and drive back over to Lemon's anyway. Something *really* isn't right—even beyond the obvious.

"There's always the police academy," Mom says. "Your father can drop a word."

I shrug, jam my hands in the pockets of my jeans, feel my muscles bunching.

"You're graduating, Troy. The future's coming, whether you want it to or not. You have to make some decisions. Soon."

"Okay, Mom . . . but not now."

❧❧❧

DARRIN'S AT MY locker after homeroom the next morning. His eyes are bugging out of his head, like he got jabbed with a livewire. He's not the only one. Half the school's charged up, yapping about Old Lucy. Some sophomore asked me if I'd had to go identify Lemon's body—he heard it from half a dozen people that she was dead. Some kid whose parents own a motel out on Route 80 said his parents were on the phone all night, taking new room reservations.

Darrin pokes my chest with his finger. "Are you fucking kidding me? Lemon faces down Old Lucy, Snowflake gets killed, and no one calls me?"

At least *he* hasn't heard any of the wilder rumors.

I rub my chest. "I'm giving Lemon privacy. Try it."

"Oh, please. Privacy? In Devil's Elbow? There's a new girl in my homeroom today, and even *she* knows about Lemon." He points down the hall at a short girl. She's thin, red hair all wild, twisted up on top of her head. "That's her. She came up to me and was all, 'I'm real sorry about your friend's dog.' I didn't even know what to tell her."

"Tell who about what?" Lemon slicks past me, leans against the lockers. Her blue shirt's electric against the pink paint. Her messenger bag swings and hits, banging hard.

"And she rises from the goddamn dead," Darrin says.

Okay, maybe he *did* hear some of those rumors.

Lemon rolls her eyes, then turns to me, offers a sweet smile. "Sorry about yesterday. I was a little out of it." Something flickers on her face, quick and then gone. Something angry.

"What are you doing here?" I say.

"I didn't want to be at home, not with . . . besides, Pappap has determined there's nothing wrong with me," she says dryly. "Perfectly healthy girls go to school."

"You nearly got k—"

She flaps her hand. "But I didn't."

Darrin laughs. "The hearty Ziegler stock strikes again. I should have known. You scoff at danger. If I didn't know better, I'd swear you were part of a vast plot to make me feel like a wuss."

"Trust me. I scoffed. Troy will attest to that."

"Wait." His brows rise. "You were *there*, Troy?"

I shake my head. "I caught the aftermath."

"That adds a little something to the drama," Darrin says, eyeing me. I can see his brain whirring, looking for an opportunity to make this into something it isn't. Finally, he says, "Is Ike convinced Old Lucy's going to rise up and eat a boat of tourists?"

I open my mouth to mention the bear, but Lemon says, "He's pretty excited about the idea if it means more business."

Darrin barks a laugh, divebombs Lemon for a quick hug. "Well, hooray for capitalism. I'm awfully glad you managed not to die—but Snowflake . . . I liked that dog."

Her face crumbles before she can pull herself together. "Yeah, me too."

The bell rings. Darrin throws a wave, takes off down the hall.

She watches him go.

"You didn't tell him it was a bear," I say.

Her voice is flat when she says, "It wasn't a bear."

"Someone might want to tell my dad—he's got the rangers looking for a mangy bear. Wait . . . can bears swim?"

"Bears *can* swim," says a girl's voice.

I swing around. The new girl stands there, the redhead. She's all sharp angles and freckles, big brown eyes. That weird hair.

"They're fast, too," she continues. "Up to six miles per hour. Ever clock how fast *you* can swim? My guess is maybe two miles per hour, tops." Each word is like a hummingbird—fast, enthusiastic.

"Hey, where'd conspiracy boy go?" she says. "Er, Darrin, I guess, right? You're Troy?"

I nod. She turns to Lemon. "I already know who you are. You're like a celebrity."

Lemon makes a face. "Lucky me."

"I'm Amelia." She ducks into the classroom, darts toward the back row of desks. Slides into the seat next to mine. It's the last thing I need today, some new girl sticking to me like tape. I follow, sit down. Drop my backpack. Lemon takes the desk in front of me, as usual. People are whispering, pointing. There's a crudely drawn Old Lucy on the chalkboard. Lemon stares ahead, still as a statue. Even Mrs. Stempfel openly gawks at her.

I lean forward, tug on the end of Lemon's hair. She looks back at me.

"Seriously—if you need to bail for the day, say the word. The Buick's parked in the lot." I'm only half joking.

She grins. "You'll be the first to know." She digs into her messenger bag, emerges with the book we picked for our group project.

"*All Boys Aren't Blue*," Amelia says, a little too loud. "Hey, I read that. I love that book."

Mrs. Stempfel smiles. "Amelia, would you like to join Troy and Lemon for their group work? We've only just started our reading projects."

Amelia scoots her chair over to my desk. "Perfect. And I already feel like I know you from talking to Darrin and hearing all about Lemon from everyone else. Seriously—does everyone talk about you like this all the time, or have I just come on a special day?"

Lemon's shoulders sag. She stands, flips her chair around. A fake smile is pasted to her face. Gossip has a way of wearing people down at the best of times. Today's not Lemon's best anything.

"Was *All Boys Aren't Blue* really on your book list?" Amelia says.

"Nah," I say. "Wanted to pick something schools are banning. Show of solidarity with our fellow high school students and all that."

She laughs. "Nice. The last school I was at had a freaking fit because I was reading James Baldwin books in the cafeteria. As if I was capable of polluting their precious kids' minds with *Giovanni's Room* through proximity. Meanwhile, half the student body was stoned stupid every day. I ended up writing out an entire chapter of the book in black Sharpie on the inside of the bathroom stalls one night—just to give them something to read while they were smoking up."

"You must have been popular," Lemon says, deadpan.

"What else did I have to do while I was there? Might as well spread a bit of knowledge while waiting to leave. All these little towns in Pennsylvania are boring and weird. No weirder than here, though. Less book banning in Devil's Elbow, maybe, but more lake monsters. I've never been to a town with its own pet monster."

"Lucky you," Lemon says.

"You taking a tour of rural Pennsylvania?" I say.

"My dad's with the government." Amelia gives a half shrug. "As much as I wish we could stay in DC and miss touring the hinterlands of this godforsaken state, I go where he goes."

"What's he doing here?" I ask.

"Working, I guess." She swivels in her chair, glances over the class. "See that girl over there? The one with the curly brown hair?"

"Brylee," Lemon says.

"Brylee was planning to ask Troy to go to the prom. And that Skeet guy? Complete freak. From the way he tells it, you practically threw yourself at him to get him to ask you out, and then laughed in his face." Amelia snickers. "The laughing in his face part I totally buy. The rest is harder to believe. That guy is such a tool."

Lemon huffs out a quiet laugh. "How do you know all that? Isn't this your first day?"

"Yeah, but it's a small school. People tell me things. I listen." When neither of us responds, she says, "Like this lake monster thing. You wouldn't believe some of the stuff I've heard about your lake monster. It's pretty strange."

Lemon cocks her head. "You have no idea."

6

L E M O N

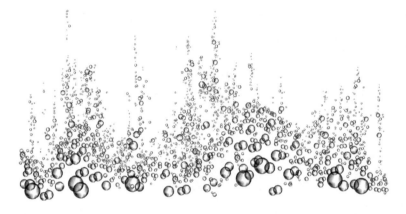

W HEN MY PARENTS DIED, GRAMMY talked a lot about the stages of grief. It's stuck with me. I've gone through denial, anger, and bargaining over being the family designee for the Old Lucy legacy. I'm probably midway between depression and acceptance, although I have doubts I'll ever feel good about doing the impersonations. Even still, having the evidence that Pappap and even Grammy, who's usually really great, value Old Lucy over my safety . . . well, I'm firmly stuck in the anger category and likely to live here.

The rest of the school day goes exactly the same as my morning: chaos, rumors, and rubbernecking. The general consensus in the hallways is that Old Lucy is irate because the earthquake shook up Lake Lokakoma, which is why she ate my dog. I suppose that goes in my favor: when the subject of Old Lucy and Snowflake comes up, I only have to look traumatized—which I am—and everyone automatically projects their thoughts onto me, assuming I'm just sad about Snowflake. I am, obviously, but it's way bigger than that.

"Hey," Darrin says to me in passing between classes, "I hear you're not all that pissed at Old Lucy because you're a loving and empathetic giver-goddess who is all forgiveness and light." He cackles and keeps walking.

The new girl turns up in several of my classes. At least she's a distraction. Each time I see her, I find something else new to notice about her—a tiny iridescent bat pin stuck into her hair, shiny black feathers edging the cuffs of her shirt. Even if she hadn't said she and her dad are from Washington, DC, it would have been obvious they're not from around here. No one dresses up for school except for maybe one girl whose mom owns a dress shop. Amelia's wardrobe may stand out, but her mouth fits right in—she's a never-ending stream of scandalous reporting. Every time I run into her, she vomits some bit of random gossip. I want to hate her, but she doesn't talk about lake monsters all the time, unlike everyone else. It's kind of a relief to hear that Aurora Hinkle might be pregnant or that Sam Karis wrecked his dad's car.

When I get home, Pappap is gone. That probably means he's at Marley's Diner—which also means hanging out with his old man friends, playing the part of the outraged grandfather, yowling dramatically about how lucky he is that his beloved granddaughter didn't meet the same fate as Snowflake at the hands of Old Lucy.

"He put out bear traps all through the woods," Grammy says while making me a cup of tea in our cheery yellow kitchen. It's pristine—Grammy's been on a trauma-induced cleaning jag this week. Even her bicycle got detailed; I saw it gleaming when I came home. The big white basket on the front is spotless. Butterbeans whuffs at Grammy when she steps too close to him, then curls up near her chair at the table.

While Grammy decided to deal with Snowflake's death by bleaching the whole house and everything in and around it, the dogs have reacted in their own ways. Butterbeans seems to have gotten it into his head that he has to protect Grammy at all costs. He's been following her around the house like a shadow.

Bob, after years of sleeping at night on the dog cushion in the living room, insists on sleeping in my room. It's nice to have company, but his long legs stretch out over nearly every inch of the mattress.

"Ike's so worried about you, Lemon." Grammy sets a cookie on the saucer next to the teacup. There aren't enough baked goods in the world to make me feel better, if that's what's going on here. I can't even force myself to get remotely near a window at the back of the house without needing to sit down and take a few deep breaths.

A moment later she adds, "He insisted the sheriff's office put out a general wildlife warning for the Lake Lokakoma vicinity, on water and off. Ike wants to make sure no one gets hurt, no matter what's out there."

"No matter *what*." I snort. "I told you what's out there."

Grammy pushes her long salt and pepper hair over shoulder and places the cup, saucer, and cookie in front of me. "How many times over the years would you imagine someone says they've been attacked by Old Lucy?"

"I'm not just *someone*, Grammy."

She sits across from me at the wooden table and smiles gently. "I know that, honey. Don't be angry with me when I say this, but you're not immune to memory bias. You *just* made your very first run as Old Lucy. It makes sense that anything around that lake would look like her to you."

I say through gritted teeth, "It didn't look like Old Lucy. At all."

She rubs my forearm. "Give it a few weeks, okay? If there really is something in the lake, we'll know. We're out there all the time. We know the lake as well as our own faces."

She's right about that, but it doesn't matter. A map of the lake forms in my head, unbidden. The lake is shaped like a kidney bean, with our boathouse and the cabin where we live at one end. At the other end of the bean are the ferry office and the boats for my grandparents' business.

The public dock and Peter's Island lie in the middle, sort of—at the outside edge of the bean bend. As much as they think they'd be able to see it if something new is living in it the lake, it's a big place. Grammy and Pappap can't be everywhere at once.

If I were a monster lurking below the water, looking for dogs to eat—or worse, a human—I wouldn't hang out near a lake ferry at the risk of being seen. I'd probably find a hidey-hole to hang out in and wait for a tender morsel to come to me . . . or cruise around in isolated parts of the lake where I could feed in secret. Maybe look for a snack where there aren't a lot of people, like what happened to Snowflake.

With luck, this thing in the lake has a brain the size of a peanut instead of, say, a brain the size of a dolphin's. I'd rather the monster be stupid as a box of rocks so it's easier to find, easier to see coming. Even if it is, though, Grammy and Pappap don't believe I saw what I saw, and I don't want them to die—or anyone else for that matter. And just like Grammy and Pappap can't be everywhere on the lake to find this thing, they can't stop everyone in Devil's Elbow from getting too close to the water, regardless of how smart the monster is or where and how it hunts for food.

Bob wanders into the room and nudges my hand, like he can tell sharp electrical pulses of agitation are zinging beneath my skin.

That night, with Bob's bad breath in my face and his feet jammed into my ribs, I dream about the family meeting where I was voted in as the Old Lucy impersonator. Pappap's just announced he wants to retire in the next five or ten years. Uncle Bobby is side-by-side with Aunt Nan on the gold couch in the living room. He leans forward, elbows on knees. "Lemon's the only logical choice."

Grammy's in her rocking chair, hair streaming over her shoulders. "She's only fifteen years old."

"My boy's too young, and we live a good hour away," he says. "It would never work for us. Nan and I both work—we can't up and leave our jobs."

"There's the ferry business," Pappap says. "And this house. You'd own them both, free and clear."

"Lemon knows the lake better than any of us," Nan says. "I know she'll do a great job."

She can't even look at me. Neither can my cousin Will. They know the life they're sentencing me to. They know how Pappap is about the legacy. I should say something in my defense, but there's nothing *to* say. No one cares that I want to be a veterinarian. No one cares what I want at all, because if I don't want to be Old Lucy, what then? No one else is going to do it—and I can't say no, not if I don't want to lose everything. I've got no other family, and even though Pappap's overbearing most of the time, he and Grammy have been good to me.

Pappap strokes his stubbly chin. "Let's put it a vote then."

I nearly start laughing. Even if I had the guts to protest, I'm too young to have a vote, and I'm screwed because of it . . . just like everything else in life.

In the next moment, my dream morphs. There it is—that low moan I'd recognize anywhere. It seeps into the house through every crevice. Snowflake, Butterbeans, and Bob come bursting past Grammy and almost knock her over. I smell the monster before I see it—the smell of rotting things. The monster bursts through the front window, all gray skin and long teeth and that thick, curving neck. It picks off my Aunt Nan first, spraying her blood all over the gold couch. Then Bobby and Will, Pappap and Grammy. The dogs. Then it comes for me, fangs dripping with gore.

I wake up gasping, Bob staring at me in the dark.

࿔࿔࿔

IT'S THURSDAY WHEN I throw open my pink locker door at school and shriek. A black rat as big as a toaster hangs in my locker, blood crusted on its snout. Troy comes careening down the hall, along with half the teachers. As the librarian is cutting it out of my locker, Skeet sneers at me from down the hall. My skin shrinks all around me until it's hard to breathe.

I let Troy turn me away from the spectacle in favor of our first period classroom. Right at the door, there's some kid from the school newspaper, his phone pointed right at me. "What's it like to come face to face with the town monster?" he asks, all breathless.

At first I think he's talking about Skeet, but then I remember that in this town no one thinks people are the monsters.

I can feel my face pinching. The only thing that comes out of mouth is, "Scary."

Troy accidentally-on-purpose bumps into the guy and knocks the phone out of his hand. The whole while, Amelia watches from her desk at the back of the room.

She's always watching. And just like yesterday, she's way too dressed for school. My uniform is jeans and a shirt, maybe a sweater. That's common at Devil's Elbow High School. Both days Amelia's been in head to toe black, and today she's wearing a wool cape that floats around her skinny knees. Maybe that's just how people dress in DC, but I'm now hyperaware of my wardrobe choices.

I come home and stare at my closet. Amelia stands out, but is it because that's the way people in the real world dress, and I really am some country bumpkin who will look like a hick outside Devil's Elbow? I have more important things to worry about, but I can't stop thinking about it, even when I go to bed.

That night I dream the monster from the lake eats Butterbeans and Bob, slowly and joyfully, sucking the flesh off each bone in their little bodies. When it's done with them, it comes for me, but Amelia is standing to the side of the boathouse, rating my outfit. She likes my shoes. The monster eats them first, then keeps going, crunching upward through ligaments and muscles, marrow and tendons. I bolt out of bed when it starts slicing through my hips with its razor teeth. Bob licks my hand. I don't sleep the rest of the night, and I still refuse to even so much as glance at the lake.

∽∽∽

PAPPAP GRUNTS *GOOD morning* to me as I walk out the door to catch the bus to school. It's the first word he's said to me since the attack. There's another dead rat, this time at the end of our driveway. Dread squeezes me. Living near a lake means the rat probably has nothing to do with Skeet, but still—I glance into the trees across the street, just in case he's there, glaring back. There's nothing there, but Bob barks from the front window. Not the most comforting thing ever.

Amelia sits with me, Troy, and Darrin at lunch at school. Today she's wearing black leather pants, and her red hair is braided around her head with tiny amethyst flowers tucked into the plaits. She volleys a constant barrage of questions about Devil's Elbow at us. How did the town get its name? What's with the watery circus clown atmosphere of Front Street, not to mention the actual store with the clown face entrance? How many people live on the perimeter of the lake? All of it's juxtaposed against her spilling dirt on half the student body.

When she takes a break to buy another orange juice, Troy says, "She's the nosiest girl I've ever met." His Pepto-pink cafeteria tray is home to a disgusting looking glop of bread and white gravy.

Darrin says, "You have to admit, she's entertaining."

"Don't you ever wonder what she's saying behind our backs?" I ask. "If she's willing to dish about them"—I gesture around the cafeteria—"to us, you know she's telling Danetta and Brylee and everyone else in the world *our* secrets."

Darrin grins. "What kind of secrets are you telling her, Lem?"

Nervous laughter bubbles up, but Amelia saves me. "You know what's odd?" She plops down on the bench and uncaps her juice. "Devil's Elbow doesn't have a bubble tea shop. Not one. You have a coffee shop that will shape the foam on your cappuccino into a lake monster and a shop that sells lake monster–shaped stress balls. But no bubble tea. Plus, do you know a couple of juniors went out to the lake last night to see if they could catch and kill Old Lucy?" Now she wears an incredulous face. "That seems really and truly ridiculous. Like seeing a lion in your front yard and poking it to see if it'll bite you."

Guilt lights up in my stomach. I'm putting people in danger. *Me.* It's my fault they're out there. Whether it's my Old Lucy impersonation or not doing enough to convince Pappap about what I saw . . . I'm to blame. Grammy says Pappap is doing his best to protect people from nonexistent mange-infected bears, but the thing with big teeth lurking in the lake is free to roam—and feed.

After school, Grammy insists on burying Snowflake's favorite toy and her extra collar since there's no body to inter. It's the first time I've dared to step foot into the backyard, and that's only because Grammy and Pappap are there. I can't quite decide if I'm being brave because there's safety in numbers or because I can run faster than they can, and that makes me feel worse about, well, everything.

Pappap fidgets as Grammy covers over the hole I've dug. Bob and Butterbeans sit together near the edge of the faux grave. Both look up at us under confused dogbrows.

"Snowflake was a good girl," Grammy says, tears on her face. "She didn't deserve to go this way."

"No, she sure didn't," Pappap said. "At least that dog lived a good, long life."

A million mean and terrible thoughts push around in my brain, fighting to convince me to say something. As usual, I stand there, lips pressed together to keep my feelings from flying out.

Grammy pushes herself to her feet and puts her arm around my waist. Bob comes around to lean against my legs, which is the only thing that stops me from shrinking away from Grammy. I feel less like family and more like a stranger.

Pappap stands with his hands clasped solemnly in front of him. He's wearing his good flannel and he's combed his white hair, which means he's probably heading back to Marley's. "Hain't no reports of animal attacks since Tuesday," he says. "Whatever it was that took Snowflake was a fluke. Maybe it left the area. Gerry's planning to lift the alert tomorrow morning."

Every muscle in my body cramps.

When Grammy sighs and heads back into the house, Butterbeans at her heels, Pappap claps me on the back. Bob still holds me in place. Pappap stomps around to the front of the house. The rattle of his car backing out of the driveway sounds a minute later. I swear a low moan whispers up from the lake.

I fall asleep early, with Bob sacked out in my kneepit. I dream it really *was* a bear that ate Snowflake. I wake up at midnight, wondering if maybe Pappap's right. Maybe I really *didn't* see what I thought. Sleep is impossible after that, but the silver lining is that it's impossible to have nightmares since I'm staring at the ceiling, going over the moment Snowflake died again and again until daybreak.

SATURDAY MORNING IT all catches up to me—I nearly fall asleep in the shower. I'm camped out in my bedroom trying to concentrate on reading for my history class, fighting the urge to nap, when Grammy pokes her head in to say she and Pappap are heading over to the ferry office to deal with a delivery. I'm half-tempted to go with them, just so I'm not alone in the house, but I don't want to be with them right now either. I can't hear how wrong I am about the possibility of a monster in the lake—or get another pep talk about impersonating Old Lucy—even one more time.

I creep around the house when they go, checking door locks and window latches. Bob and Butterbeans slink behind me, Butterbeans growling and Bob alert and practically on point. Maybe it's the dreams I've been having. Maybe it's worrying whether Skeet will leave me another rat . . . or do something worse. Every sound has me jumping out of my skin. I can't even call Troy or Darrin. Troy's visiting his grandparents, and Darrin's doing some kind of volunteer thing with his dad at the hospital. Sunday is no different—the house feels like a jail, trapping me inside, afraid of what might happen if I step foot outside.

The only good thing: whatever rumors are circulating about Old Lucy or about me . . . it doesn't matter. I can pretend to live in a world completely devoid of controversy and trauma. At least for a few hours.

The rumor reprieve doesn't matter much: on both nights, when I do find a few moments of peace, I dream again of the sensation of sharp teeth, the smell of death.

~~~

I YAWN AND glance at my cell phone. Four a.m. on the dot on Monday morning. I'm too tired to sleep. Everything in my body aches to shut my eyes and let myself drift off. Everything except my brain. The house is silent—the kind of quiet as loud as a truck plowing into a brick wall. I swing my legs over the edge of the bed and sit, peering through the dim murk of my room. Everything is cast in grays, like the whole world has been leached of color. Bob rolls into the warm spot I leave behind. I pat the bed until I find his legs, then give his long toes a stroke. He grumbles in his sleep twice.

I tiptoe to the bedroom window and rest my forehead against the glass. My breath leaves a ring of patchy fog. Even through the haze, the lake is visible just beyond the crest of the hill. My stomach churns.

The dim streetlights of Devil's Elbow glow. I can imagine the neat and orderly streets spooling out away from the lake. A sliver of moon shines in the clear night. Beyond town, the vapor from the nuclear plant curls up into the sky like a ghost. The spare waves on the lake reflect white, then sink into inky blackness. Save for the faint sound of un-dulating water audible even through the window glass and the dog's breathing, the night is hushed and tranquil.

The nightmares, the unrest—it's nothing new. It happened after my parents died, too. My dreams then were always the same: I was alone. Completely and totally alone. I woke up screaming more than a few times, sure that no one would be in the house. Grammy dragged me off to see a therapist, even though Pappap insisted that I was fine and just needed time to adjust.

It's amazing that he hadn't actually uttered the words "Walk it off" or "Rub some dirt in it." He probably wanted to. I'm surprised he didn't say that to me after Tuesday's attack, especially since he forced me back to school in the morning.

Funny how Pappap is always the one who never wants to step in, to interfere—at least not when it matters. *Let things play out* should be tattooed across his forehead. It's an odd attitude for someone who was a cop nearly all his life. Aren't police officers supposed to step in when things go sideways, to put things right?

Darrin would laugh and say I'm fooling myself about what cops do—and, of course, he's not wrong. Pappap lied and interfered profes-sionally his entire life about Old Lucy. He takes action to make things how he wants them to be and how he thinks they should be, not to make things good or right. He lies and manipulates to make sure no one finds out about the impersonations.

I take a step back and wipe away the last of the condensation on the window. A short, sharp scream floats up from the trees. My gut flips, and my arms break out into goosebumps. I throw open the window. A gust of cool air rushes in, enough to shake some of the fog out of my brain. I brace my hands against the sill.

Despite the scream, it's still almost dead quiet. Too quiet. Anoth-er high-pitched shriek shatters the silence. There's someone out there, probably because of *me*. Because of all the rumors about Old Lucy.

My heart breaks out into a sucking gallop. Every drop of spit in my mouth dries in an instant, and my feet are cement blocks. I should wake Pappap, force him to call Sheriff Ramirez.

As if he would listen to a single thing I say.

And really, it's the middle of the night. No one's wandering the woods alone. The noise is something else. Something normal. Foxes, probably. My shoulders slump. Of course. I've heard those sounds my entire life. I slam the window closed and throw the lock.

But what if it's *not* a fox? Whether it's a lake monster or a bear or something else, someone could be out there. The chilly air from outside seeps into my bones. I don't want to be like Pappap, doing nothing to save people if there *is* something wrong.

I throw on a pair of jeans and a sweatshirt, shove a small flashlight in my pocket, and head toward the back door before I can talk myself out of it. Before I can remind myself of what might be waiting in the dark. Pappap bought a whole bear deterrent kit to complement his supply of bear spray after the attack. It sits on the kitchen counter, waiting for me to grow a spine.

I palm the special mace from the kit and lock the back door behind me, then sling the kit over my shoulder. My hands are clammy, no doubt reacting to my own stupidity. Fox, bear, monster, psycho boy. And here I am. Yet I can't bring myself to turn back . . . because maybe *this* is how I break the cycle of lies. At least I won't feel like such an awful coward.

The backyard crawls with sound. Every rustle of leaves or whistle of the wind off the water is startlingly loud, but I don't dare turn on the flashlight. Not yet. If Pappap or Grammy wake and see the beam, there'll be a lecture. Pappap will have a heart attack over my lack of common sense when it comes to my own safety—and no, the irony will not be lost on me.

It's time for me to suck it up and be brave. Rub some dirt on it. The breeze blows strands of hair into my eyes as I start down the creaking stairs. One step after another, that's all I have to do. My legs are stiff as pins. By the time I'm at the floating dock, standing in front of the boathouse, my brain feels like nothing more than a chewed-up excuse of taffy and raw fear.

Another scream emanates from my right. My legs shake.

Look around, I order myself. *Look for signs of a bear. You can handle a bear. Stand your ground, make yourself big.*

An unvoiced thought lurks just behind my eyes, along with the ever-present memory of sharp teeth tearing into Snowflake. *Look for signs of the monster.*

My muscles finally loosen just enough to allow me a few tentative steps down the trail to the left. I glance at the mucky water and pickerelweed only a few feet to my right, at the gentle waves and the shiny surface of the lake. The mace is ready in my hand, and I turn on my flashlight.

The arguments keep up a running monologue in my head—run back home or move ahead, could it be a bear or is it a monster, is someone hurt or is it Skeet messing with me—as I creep down the trail. Every shadow is menacing. Every waft of air that curves toward me is a fetid breath. I keep my eyes on the water. The farther I walk, the more my legs shake.

A few minutes later, the meadow appears. My stomach unknots enough to enjoy the cold air on my face and the smell of fresh green things growing everywhere. It's weird to be here without all three of the dogs pulling me along. My hands squeeze into fists. There will never be a moment I don't miss Snowflake. Never. And there will never be a moment I don't remember the second she died. But I will one day find a way to walk in the woods and be near the lake without feeling like ants are crawling all over me.

Today is not that day.

The brush rustles ahead of me. My slow walk stalls, and my breath stutters in my chest. I listen to the rush of the breeze in the trees, the lap of water on the shore. I listen for the sound of birds or peepers, crickets—just like up at the house, there's nothing. Only more of that whispering hush from the thicket.

A low moan stirs the night. It comes again. My heart slams against my rib cage.

I hide the beam of my flashlight against my shirt. If there's something really out here, maybe I can hide in the dark. I take slow and careful steps away from the water, to what I think is the far edge of the trail, until long, wispy branches brush over my head. My breath is forced, harsh. I'm so focused on being noiseless, on listening, it's a shock when my foot slides in mud right at the water's edge. Somehow I'm nearly flush against one of the weeping willows growing out of the silt.

I wince and forget about trying to be stealthy—my light swings around. One step in the wrong direction, and I'll be calves-deep in the swampy muck. I lift my foot out of the mud and shuffle sideways, back toward the trail. Everything looks so different in the dark—I could swear that I wasn't anywhere near the shoreline.

The disorientation freaks me out almost as much as the idea of being out here with the thing in the water. If it rushes at me—or if I *do* find someone out here who needs help? What if it really is Skeet? What if I freeze? What if I can't find my way back to the house?

The weight of what I'm doing knocks what little bravery I have remaining right out of me. Every bone in me screeches that I should run. I trip over a root, and the beam of my light swings wide.

It illuminates another weeping willow, a stand of tall grass spiked in the water, a fine mist of fog floating just above the lake. The beam catches something reflective, and then it's gone.

What *is* that?

I edge back toward the tree again and part the tall grass with the rim of my flashlight. The curved edge of a hiking boot pokes up through the hollows. And an ankle.

My gasp doesn't sound real.

A gray-blue pale leg that ends in nothing but a jagged, bloody stump of shredded meat gently bobs a few inches away.

The flashlight drops, and my scream breaks the night.

7

LEMON

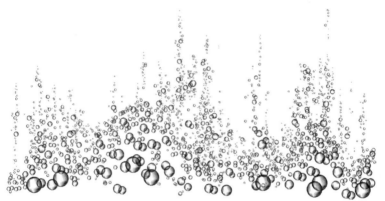

"**M**ERCIFUL HEAVENS, LEMON!" GRAMMY BUSTLES around the now entirely *too* cheerful yellow kitchen. The pink scarf wrapped around her hair flops with each step. Her bathrobe is tied tight to hide her flowered pajamas. Butterbeans thumps along after her, whuffing. The smell of coffee is strong. "What were you thinking? You could have been killed."

I slump in my chair, wrapped up in the same quilt Grammy bundled me in after Snowflake was killed. It feels like I'm bundled in a jinx. *Why* had I left the house in the first place? My conscience wanted to be clear. I want to be a better person than my grandfather, for sure, but now that our lake has become a slaughterhouse, bravery doesn't seem like such a smart choice. My hands clench and unclench. My fingers are so cold, like they'll never be warm again. The sound of that eerie moan swirls in my ears.

The back door slams open, and I jump. Bob barks sharply from the hallway and zooms into the kitchen a second later. Pappap strides in, a firestorm burning in his eyes. Behind him is Sheriff Ramirez. He isn't in uniform except for his brown duty jacket. The sheriff might have *High Alert* face, but he manages to give me a sad smile, which is the exact opposite of what I'm getting from Pappap. *He* looks like he might reach over the table and shake the life out of me.

"Shush now, Bob," Pappap says.

Grammy pulls a chair out from the kitchen table and shoos the sheriff into it. A mug of coffee is in front of him a second later.

"Thanks, Pearl."

She squeezes his shoulder.

Pappap takes the seat next to me. I stiffen.

Bob sniffs and stands guard in the doorway, his nub of a tail completely still.

The sheriff swigs his coffee, then taps his fingertips once on the table before seemingly gazing into my soul with Troy's eyes. "All right— let's go through this, if you don't mind."

Pappap glares at me.

I nod and try to avoid looking at him by focusing on the sheriff, who at least doesn't seem like he might be very happy to lock me in a closet.

My stomach is a cup full of glass shards. Who wouldn't be in shock after finding a random leg in the lake? I can barely remember sprinting back to the house and screaming my grandparents awake. Did the police cars arrive with sirens and lights? It's all just . . . gone. It's only after the sheriff and a bunch of officers went down to the lake with Pappap that I remember Grammy snapping at me and plying me with a cup of something scalding and bitter.

It's bizarre that death around here is immediately rewarded with hot beverages every single time, like there's a rule. Or maybe it's just bizarre there have been so many deaths.

"So walk me through what happened." Sheriff Ramirez digs a notebook and pen from his inside jacket pocket. "You woke up and then what?"

"I heard screaming. I thought maybe it was foxes, but then . . . you know, with what happened to Snowflake and—" My brain wants to spit out the whole story—Old Lucy, the thing in the lake, my grandparents' total lack of concern, bears, the rats and Skeet—but Pappap seems to see it in my face and nudges my ankle under the table. Finally, I say, "I heard that some kids at school had been at the lake the other night— you know, to see if they could find Old Lucy. I thought maybe they'd come back and gotten hurt."

The sheriff nods. "So you were concerned? That's understandable. Do you know the names of your classmates who were at the lake?"

Pappap's frown deepens. I can tell he's trying to figure out how this looks for Old Lucy. It's one thing for rumors to point to Old Lucy being involved in a killing—it's another entirely for there to be actual evidence. One thing attracts tourists . . . the other would likely drive the good tourists away—the ones who come here for fun and to spend money. Bob lies down in the doorway and rests his chin on his paws.

I shake my head.

"That's fine. What happened next?"

"I had bear repellent. I took precautions. I just wanted . . . I just wanted to make sure. I didn't think—"

Pappap lets out a sharp laugh. "That's the problem, hain't it? You don't think—"

Grammy's hands come down on his shoulders. "Ike, shush now." Butterbeans whuffs again from the floor.

Pappap's mouth snaps shut, and my stomach grates more glass.

"So you headed outside?" Sheriff Ramirez says as though neither of my grandparents has spoken.

Maybe I should try that sometime and see where it gets me. Probably grounded for life.

I take the sheriff through the next couple of minutes and through finding the leg, doing my best to keep it together—pretend that it happened to someone else, and I'm just telling a story that has nothing at all to do with me.

"So you didn't touch the leg or disturb the scene?" Sheriff Ramirez purses his lips.

Pappap sits up straight. "Now hold on, Gerry—you trying to say I raised my granddaughter to disrespect the scene of a death? You known me how long? And Lemon you known practically since she was born."

"That's not what I'm saying at all, Ike, and you know it. I'm being thorough, that's all. I'd ask Troy the same thing if he found part of a body."

Pappap harrumphs but keeps silent.

"No, I didn't," I say. "Er . . . disturb the scene. At least not on purpose. I did step in the mud nearby, so I guess maybe I did."

The sheriff nods. "We did see that. No harm, no foul."

"Did you . . . I mean, is there someone in the hospital missing a leg?"

"I'm afraid not."

Grammy clucks her tongue. Butterbeans groans.

"So you don't know whose leg it is?" A furry head butts against my ankle, and Bob gazes up at me. I scratch the heart-shaped orange spot on top of his head.

"We *have* been able to identify the, uh, owner of the leg."

"So . . . the rest of the body is out there?" I immediately regret asking. No answer the sheriff gives is going to be comforting.

"My officers did a search of the area."

"And?" The word comes out of me softly, but it lights up the entire kitchen.

Sheriff Ramirez shifts in his chair. His face takes on an uncomfortable expression, like someone is jabbing him with a pin. "Understand that I can't really talk about an ongoing investigation."

Pappap's mouth turns down. "Come off it, Gerry. There hain't going to be no real investigation." He aims his frown at me. "The upper torso was floating nearby, tangled in the outboard motor of a boat." He turns back to the sheriff. "You know damn well that Jenkins boy—"

"Jenkins?" An electric buzz shoots down my arms.

"Lemon, this is a bit of a sensitive situation." Sheriff Ramirez's dark eyes bore a hole into me. He waits a beat, completely poker-faced, before he says, "Whatever we talk about, I need your word that it'll stay between us."

My head feels like it's jangling around on my neck when I nod.

"It was Skeet Jenkins. Can you think of any reason he might have been out at this part of the lake?"

My hands go colder. I try not to think of the dead rat in the driveway and in my locker, but it's impossible. Those dull cloudy eyes stare out from my memory. "I don't know. Fishing, maybe? Hiking?"

"Uh, any other reason? Perhaps he might have been coming to see you? Maybe you two were planning to meet up?"

"Gerry!" Grammy explodes. Bob and Butterbeans leap to their feet and bark. "My granddaughter is a good girl."

"Or did you two have a fight?"

Pappap's jowls shake. "You best just tell it straight, Gerry. What hain't you saying?"

"There was a backpack in the boat. We found a map of the lake in it, along with Skeet's wallet. Your house is marked on the map."

Oh. *Oh.*

"What else?" Pappap's eyes narrow.

The sheriff returns his attention to me, ignoring the still-grumbling dogs. "Lemon, what is your relationship to Skeet Jenkins?"

"He asked me to the prom." My voice is barely a whisper. "But well . . . Troy and I are going." I slide a glance at Pappap, then add, "As friends."

The sheriff nods. "Was Skeet angry about that?"

It's as though I'm watching myself breathe and blink and answer questions from a million miles away. "Yeah, but maybe none of this has anything to do with me." My voice is squeaky. "You know how it is out here. People come to see if they can find Old Lucy all the time, just like the other night. Maybe he marked our house because it's not that far from where she's usually seen. Now that there's a monster—"

Pappap's knuckles go white, and I mash my lips together to stop myself.

The sheriff scribbles in his notebook. "Fair enough. I've been getting calls about it myself, asking about hunting expeditions for the lake. And it might explain why Skeet was armed."

"Armed?" Grammy cries. The pickup truck gun rack flashes into my head.

"There was a knife in the boat. In Skeet's backpack."

"What kind of knife?" Pappap says. "Butter knife? Machete? What are we talking about?"

"A small hunting knife. Roll of duct tape, too."

Grammy wrings her hands.

"Again, Lemon, I'll ask you to keep that information to yourself. Whether Skeet meant you harm or was looking for Old Lucy, we'll figure that out during the investigation. Nothing for you to concern yourself with."

I nearly laugh. Yeah, sure. "Okay, but . . . how did he die?"

Bob settles back into the doorway and raises his dogbrows at me.

"Hain't you hear me say he was caught in the outboard?" Pappap says. "It seems clear—the kid don't know his boating safety. No surprise. Ain't no one in that kid's family could find their ass with both hands."

"And you're sure?" I say. "You're sure it wasn't . . . something else?" Say a behemoth with giant teeth?

"The coroner will determine that for sure. Admittedly, it does look like you're right, Ike, but we want to be sure. *You* want us to be sure. And

I'm sure Skeet's mother will want us to do our best to get to the truth of what happened as well."

❧❧❧

PAPPAP WAITS A whole thirty seconds once Sheriff Ramirez leaves before turning on me with the full force of his righteous indignation. "If them fool kids are on the lake at night, you let them reap their consequences. I ain't raise you to be a fool. You can't be responsible for every damn body in this town."

Before I can stop myself, I say, "But . . . isn't the whole reason we impersonate Old Lucy to keep the town safe from ruin? What's the point of keeping the town going if we're just going to let everyone in it die? There's a monster in the lake, Pappap!"

His face fades up purple. "Don't you sass me, Lemon. You know damn well there hain't nothing out there but bears and maybe a couple of bobcats. When you're grown, you'll know the fine line we walk around here."

He's winding up for a long lecture, so I focus on a knot in the wood flooring and zone out while he rants. Grammy tactfully stays put, loudly washing dishes and murmuring baby talk to the dogs, although I wish she'd come sit next to me and act like a buffer. I tune into my breathing, on the tiniest bit of warmth returning to my hands, on the solid feeling of the floor beneath my feet. Every few minutes I have to remind myself not to let my eyes close.

Once, I'd been able to imagine graduating from high school and leaving town to avoid Pappap's diatribes. It's not the only reason I wanted to leave, but it was on the list. Now, the only possible reprieve I'll ever have is for Pappap to decide it's time to move to New Mexico for retirement after all.

Or if I kick my grandparents out of the house. The house *is* mine. At least I think so. Even though it's part of being the Old Lucy designee—the house and the ferry business—I don't think my grandparents can just hand me the keys. There's got to be legal stuff, and I haven't signed anything.

Then again, I didn't get a vote, either—and here I am.

I'm not ready to take over the business, even if I wanted to, and I'm certainly not ready to live in this house by myself. Not when there's a thing in the lake that apparently has a taste for human flesh—I don't buy the idea that Skeet got torn apart by a boat motor for a second. Maybe the monster did me a favor by getting rid of him, but in this case the enemy of my enemy is absolutely *not* my friend. Not when it ate our dog.

Not when it almost killed me.

Pappap paces the kitchen, waving his hands, ranting about my sacred duty to the family and town, until he abruptly stops. "I tell ya, Lemon—you're lucky to have me and your grandmother to take care of your messes."

Grammy snickers. "Leave me out of this, Ike. It's not Lemon's fault that a boy died in the lake."

Died in the lake? I'm happy for the unexpected assist, but Grammy makes it sound like Skeet just wandered out there and drowned, all on his own.

"Did I say it was? If she'da stayed in bed like she ought, none of this would have happened in the first place—that's all I'm trying to get at, Pearl."

Grammy turns off the water at the sink, turns around to face Pappap, and crosses her arms. "That's not even remotely true. The only thing that would have happened is *you* would have found the boy in the morning. And while I do wish that it hadn't been Lemon, it makes no difference. Dead is dead. And that boy still would have had a knife and a map with our house targeted on it."

"Ain't make a difference?" Pappap's face reddens.

I sigh quietly, but not quiet enough.

He whirls on me. "And you. Wipe that look off your face."

Grammy abruptly steps forward. "This is not going to fly, Ike. Leave Lemon be. She has a right to her feelings."

"But I could have done something," Pappap says, like he hadn't said anything to me at all. "Made it look—"

The urge is strong to just stand up and tell Pappap to shut up, to stop thinking of Old Lucy for once and stop being so selfish and gross. My feet won't move, though. I get a panicky feeling in my hands when I even think about telling Pappap to stop yelling, let alone any of those other things. He was mad enough when I questioned his sense of responsibility to Devil's Elbow. Instead, I glance out the window and wish to be anywhere other than here. The light is already starting to brighten.

"Look like what?" Grammy spits out. "Make it look like maybe it could have been an Old Lucy attack? And then what? You're not the sheriff anymore, Ike. If you tamper with a crime scene, that's not going to go well for you. And you heard Gerry—people are thinking about trying to hunt Old Lucy. That's one step away from people being genuinely afraid. That won't be good for tourism, so maybe just once we don't have to make all of this about Old Lucy."

Finally—someone talking sense. Pappap doesn't like it from Grammy any more than he likes it from me if the expression on his face is any indication. It looks like his entire head might pop off his body.

He sputters. "That *is* what all of this is about. We hain't live up here for our health, Pearl. The town needs us."

I allow myself to disconnect again. There's nothing new here, other than Skeet Jenkins's dead body and the possibility that maybe he'd been coming to hurt me, which Pappap seems to have conveniently forgotten now that the sheriff is gone. Pappap isn't inclined to believe anything I say about the actual monster living in our lake. He's not inclined to do anything to keep us safe—or anyone else.

The next person to die could be Darrin or Troy or their families. It could be Grammy. Tourists will be all over this lake starting next month. Little kids.

There's only one choice. I can't wait and hope the problem goes away all by itself. It's up to me to figure out what to do, and quick, or I'll be personally responsible for the impending summer bloodbath.

I know one other thing, too: I can't do this alone—so if I'm really going all-in, if I'm going to step up and defy Pappap for the greater good, I need to whip up some bravery—and I need help, which means the time for secrecy is over.

8

T R O Y

S CHOOL IS CHAOS. GIRLS CRYING in the halls. Guys pounding on
lockers. I half expect someone to shake a fist at the sky and yell,
Why, God, why?—like in the movies. Performative grief is wild.

Look, I'm not saying Skeet deserved what he got. Death by outboard motor is gruesome. Not sad about it, though, either. Dad filled me
in about what happened last night over breakfast this morning, swore
me to secrecy about the full story. Probably figured Lemon would tell
me anyway.

Dad caught me one last time before I walked out the door for school
this morning. "So, what do you know the Jenkins kid and Lemon? She
told me about turning him down for the prom, but I got a feeling she
wasn't telling me the whole story there."

"He left a rat in her locker," I told him. "Maybe another at her
house."

"How sure are you about that?"

"There wasn't a signed confession, if that's what you mean. It was him, though. A hundred percent."

Dad kept eyeballing me. I knew what he was doing—the whole *say nothing until they fill the uncomfortable silence* thing. As though the technique is a mystery to me. He coaxed a confession out of me about eating a batch of cupcakes he'd baked when I was six by staring me down. It's the last time it worked on me.

Finally, he said, "Keep an eye on Lemon. She'll need a friend—someone to look out for her. Be a good man."

Maybe he knows something I don't. Pretty sure he doesn't have a clue what's rolling around in my head: *I* might be why Skeet went after Lemon.

She told me to stay out of it after the locker rat thing went down. I said okay. Might have even meant it at the time. But then there Skeet was in the bathroom at school the next day. Me and him. No lie—he *smirked* at me. Said something about Lemon being a slut.

I had him by the throat in a second. Pushed him against the bathroom wall—not hard enough to leave a mark, but enough to make breathing tough. I'm not proud about it. No one talks about Lemon like that, though. *No one.* I let Skeet go, and he ran like a chickenshit.

Being a cop's kid . . . well, it's hard to get away with much. Thought for sure I'd come home to find Dad raging about me losing it on Skeet for a second. No one mentioned it, though. Not Dad. Not one of Skeet's dirtbag cousins. Not even Amelia. And if Amelia didn't hear about it, Skeet for sure didn't make it anyone else's business.

Except Lemon. He made it Lemon's business last night—and now the guilt is strangling me. Went out to her house to do who knows what to her. Probably because of me. She tried to make excuses for him when she called me, said maybe he was hunting Old Lucy, same as everyone else. Uh-huh. What was he going to do with duct tape? Hog-tie Old Lucy, leave her on the lawn of city hall?

Amelia's suddenly beside me at my locker. Her hair is slicked back, spikes of it fanning out behind her head like a halo. "Hey, how's Lemon?"

She's not the first person to ask. She *is* the first person to actually seem to really care. "Okay. She's staying home today."

"Well, yeah. Is it true she fed Skeet Jenkins to Old Lucy?"

"Where'd you hear that?"

"So what *did* happen?"

"Not *that.*"

Dad said the police were only releasing that *someone* died at the lake early this morning, nothing more. Hell, the bell hasn't even rung for homeroom yet, and everybody knows it was Skeet who died.

"I've heard at least a dozen different stories about what happened," Amelia says, like she can read my mind. "The funniest thing is that everybody seems to forget that that guy is a total twat, and no one likes him. *Liked*, I guess."

Two girls pass us, holding on to one another. "I can't believe he's gone," one says. "He was so nice."

"Case in point." Amelia jerks her chin at them. "You know he stole that girl's car once? They were at the drive-in a few towns over. He shoved his tongue down her throat and wouldn't stop pawing at her. She got out of the car—*her* car, mind you—and he just drove off in it and left her there." She shakes her head. "Selective memory. Anyway, apparently school administration is bringing in grief counselors to help everyone process the tragedy."

My phone buzzes. Text from Lemon to me and Darrin: *Can you bail on classes today?*

Darrin immediately responds: *Hell yeah. Just got to school—Troy, where are you?*

My first thought is that Lemon heard about the bathroom incident. She'll never speak to me again after this. I'm a dead man, all because I turned into a freaking caveman again. Still, if she wanted to tear me apart, she wouldn't invite Darrin as a witness to the carnage. I've got to tell her eventually. Just not today. Not while everything is still fresh.

My second thought is that Dad will find out I'm not in school, take away the Buick. Maybe punish me for life.

It's Lemon, though. She wouldn't ask if it weren't important.

I thumb back: *Meet me at the Buick, D. Where are you, Lemon?*

My house. Park down the access road, okay? Out of sight.

That's ... odd.

Amelia looks at me, looks at my phone. Lemon would say she's got *Suspicious* face. "Who's that? More bad news?"

"Oh, uh. Just ... Lemon. Checking in." I shove my phone back in my pocket. "Gotta run, Amelia. Left a book in my car. See you later."

I take off down the hall without waiting for her reply. Knowing Amelia, she'd decide to come with me if I told her where I'm going. She's nice enough. Just talkative. And nosy. The next corridor, the one that leads to the school entrance, is like an obstacle course. No one seems motivated to do anything but gather in knots or move in slow motion. A few more people are crying and pounding. It's Skeet's wake, I suppose.

Almost at the front door, one of Skeet's cousins steps up—Vern is his name, I think. He's got that Jenkins look about him, like he's trying to be tough while figuring algebra in his head. He grabs my arm. Leans in, expression mean. "You tell that little bitch to watch her back."

My hands clench. "Little bitch?"

"You know who I'm talking about," he sneers. "Skeet told me about her. Said she was a tease. Probably the reason he was out at her house last night. She probably promised to—"

"Finish that sentence, and I'll end you."

Even I flinch at the hardness of my voice. His face loses some of its bluster, like he's not too sure I won't take a swing. I'm not sure either. Dad's voice is whispering in my head, *Protect what you love.* This, though? Not what he meant. I'm pretty sure of it.

I take a deep breath, keep walking. Shake out my hands. Outside, people are still hurrying through the parking lot toward school. It's turning gray outside, rainy looking. Seems appropriate for the vibe of the school. Darrin slouches against the Buick. I give him a nod, unlock the door.

"Hello to you, too, sunshine," he says. When we're both in the car, he adds, "So what's the urgency? I nearly shit myself when Lemon of all people asked us bail on school." He pauses. "Your dad's not going to arrest her, is he?"

Once I'm behind the wheel, I say, "Why would he arrest her?"

"Are you fucking kidding? My sister barreled into my bedroom this morning at the ass-crack of dawn to inform me that Ike chopped Skeet into tiny bits over who the hell knows what—my guess is the rat thing—and that Lemon helped."

I swing out of the spot and head for the exit. "And you believe that?"

"Our Lemon? No. She's been a little on edge lately, but not in that special homicidal way. Ike, though? Maybe. You know as well as I do that he's positively unhinged, especially when it comes to Lem. I heard three other variations from Betsy before I even took a shower today. Apparently, there's some guy who works at Magic Monster who's been missing since last week—Ike allegedly killed him, too. Betsy didn't know why. I guess no one gave her a reason, which is weird since she's in everybody's business almost as much as Amelia. Queen of the middle school gossip, that one."

I pull out of the lot. "I'm about to say something way off the record, yeah?"

Out of the corner of my eye, his face crinkles in confusion, but he nods. I tell him what Lemon told me—and what Dad said.

His mouth drops open. "That's . . . well, hell. And they only found Skeet's head and his foot?"

"More or less."

Darrin hoots a laugh. "More of him, or less of him? I wouldn't have expected a pun from you when you're so obviously pants-shittingly full of anxiety."

I glare. "I'm fine. And don't be saying that kind of crap around Lemon. She's upset enough without you making body part jokes."

"Calm down, King Kong. You started it. So . . . think Ike's at the house?"

"Doubt it. He'd probably report us to the truant officer."

Darrin cracks stupid joke after stupid joke about what Ike will do if he finds us with Lemon during school hours until I tune him out. Let him get it out of his system. Ten minutes later, I pull onto Lemon's road. Pines on either side seem taller than usual. Gloomy. More dangerous. Between the wildlife around the lake acting all crazy, what happened with Snowflake, and now Skeet's death—feels like a killing ground out here. Even Darrin shuts up. We drive past Lemon's house. Her grandparents' car's not here. Still, my palms are an oil slick. Like Mr. Z *and* Dad are waiting to jump out of the trees and bust my ass for not being in school on a Monday morning. And that's the *least* bad thing that could happen.

I pull off about a quarter mile down, park on the side out of sight of the main road. Even darker back here . . . hushed.

"Is that wildlife warning still in effect?" Darrin says when we're out of the car. He's barely louder than a whisper.

I shake my head, walk toward the road. Something out here's tweaking my nerves. Can't say what it is exactly. Feeling of being watched, maybe. Could be an owl. Could be a bear. I don't want to find out.

We're at Lemon's front door in a few minutes. She flings it open before I can knock, pulls us inside. I hug her. No reason. I just do.

"Jesus, Ramirez," Darrin mutters.

Lemon hugs me back, real quick, then lets me go. She's dressed all in navy, jeans to sweatshirt. Makes her blue eyes bluer. Bob appears, licks my hand.

"Doing okay?" I say.

"I'm so sick of that question," Lemon says. "Grammy wouldn't leave me alone this morning. I had to force her out the door with Pappap."

Butterbeans waddles into the living room. Looks at me, looks at Lemon, then sways over to Darrin and plops at his feet.

"Your grandparents'll be gone for a while?" I say.

"Yeah. Something about estate planning," Lemon says.

Darrin touches Lemon's shoulder. "So what's the plan today?"

Lemon's eyes widen, and she shoots me a glance. "You didn't tell him?"

Darrin steps over Butterbeans and sits on the Zieglers' ugly gold couch. "Oh, he told me about Skeet. You wouldn't believe the stories spreading at school. It's a masterpiece of malarkey." Butterbeans jumps up next to him.

I shove my hands into my jeans pockets, lean against the door. Lemon must get annoyed with me for hovering—she points me toward Mr. Z's beat-up old recliner with the duct tape patches. I perch on the arm.

I'm debating whether to tell her about Vern Jenkins when Darrin says, "Cara texted me this morning, too. I had to talk her out of canceling going to the prom. She'd heard you stabbed Skeet with a fork after—"

Lemon's mouth twists. "Seriously? But I didn't even know Skeet was out here until he was—" She catches her breath. "Until after what happened to him. Why does she think I stabbed him?"

"Does it matter?" I say. "You know how it is. People talk, then forget about it when something else happens."

Darrin's grin comes with an eyebrow waggle. "With the sheer volume of scandals Amelia seems privy to, the *next thing*"—he uses air quotes—"is only a few hours away. She and Betsy would get along great. I should introduce them."

"Speaking of which," Lemon says, "did you give Amelia my phone number?"

We both shake our heads.

"She texted about ten minutes ago," Lemon says. "She said she's sorry I'm going through this and asked if I need a friend to talk to. No one has my cell phone number except you two and my grandparents."

Darrin says, "If she can find out about Aurora Hinkle's pregnancy test, she can dig up your phone number. The girl clearly has skills. I never asked what she's doing next year for college, but I bet she's going to be a reporter. Or a private investigator."

"I suppose." Lemon settles into Mrs. Z's rocking chair. Bob shadows her, paws her leg until she rubs the orange spot on his head, whispers something into his ear. To us, she says, "It just feels strange."

Darrin sits forward. "Right. Well, not to take the fun out of this, Lem, you've got me on the edge of my seat. Why are we skipping school and hiding the car up the road?"

She immediately fidgets, gnaws on her top lip.

"So . . . I have to tell you guys something. I need you to . . . well, I need you to not be judgy, okay?"

"Need I remind you that you are the turd of my heart," Darrin says. "The turd of both *our* hearts."

My hands start to sweat, sure the next words out of his mouth are going to come too close to telling Lemon how I feel about her. When he doesn't say anything at all, I almost pass out from relief.

"Uh, thanks." Lemon scratches Bob behind the ears. "That's sweet, but I'm serious." She twists slightly to look at me. "To start with, I've been lying to your dad. And so have my grandparents, about Old Lucy and about what happened last night. And that's just to start with."

Darrin laughs. "Why, Lemon Ziegler! You are turning into quite a saucy fucking delinquent! First you lie to the sheriff, and now we're playing hooky."

"It's not like that." She chews on her top lip again. I want to take her hand—just so she knows it's okay. Whatever it is. I don't, though, and she says, "Look, I think maybe the way to do this is to . . . I want to show you something down at the boathouse. And I'm asking you to trust me. No questions—not for the next fifteen or twenty minutes. Doable? We'll talk about anything you want afterward."

Darrin raises his finger. "Uh, Lem, you don't have the rest of Skeet's body stashed out there, do you? That is totally outer limits."

"What? No. Why would I—you know what? Never mind." She makes a sour face. "Just . . . we're going out to the boathouse. Don't make a lot of noise, though, okay?"

The look in her eyes has me on alert. "Are you—"

"Hey, you said you'd give me twenty minutes."

Whatever this is, I want to fix it. I want to jump into action and . . . I don't know, something. I push myself off the arm of the chair, nod.

She nudges Bob out of the way and stands. "Oh, and you have to promise me—I mean it—that whatever I say to you or show you stays between us. I don't care if someone tortures you. You don't know anything, now and forever. This is a life or death situation."

That's . . . *huh.*

She walks into the kitchen. Darrin glances at me again. I shrug. There's nothing else to do but follow her. The dogs trail after us, silent, watchful. Lemon stands near the back door, quickly thrusts the bear mace at me. "You take this."

She peers behind me at Darrin, passes him a canned air horn. He must give her a look because she says, "Humor me." She pauses. "Keep an eye out for anything odd or unexpected or out of place, okay?"

I shove my hands and the mace into my jacket pockets. Least Lemon won't see I'm shaking. It's the last shred of dignity I have. She's freaking me out—I admit it. I've got Lemon's back, no matter what, but what if she *does* have Skeet's body out there? Never occurred to me that any of the crap going around at school could be true. I'm thinking through all the things that might be waiting in the boathouse—Snowflake and Skeet hanging from the ceiling, a live bear, Mr. Z—when Lemon takes a quick breath and marches into the backyard.

"Don't let the dogs out," she calls over her shoulder.

Rain hasn't gotten here yet—the air is thick, sticky. For all of that, my palms are slick with sweat. Lemon pounds out to the rickety stair-case out back of her house. It's like someone's got a gun to her head almost—like she's got no choice. Everything feels unreal. Like a fun house that's nowhere near fun. I scan the trees, the yard, everywhere. But Lemon, she keeps going, down the stairs, steady.

She's dead silent as she leads us onto the floating dock. Takes a second to get my balance—the wooden boards shift under my feet. She fiddles with the clasp on the boathouse door. Darrin's probably just as nervous as me—he's breathing hard behind me. I know none of the things I'm imagining are behind the door. Dad says you never know about people. I know Lemon, through and through. Still, it's like some-one's peeling my skin off, layer by layer. Too much oxygen is stinging me, begging me to run.

The door squeaks as it swings open. Lemon steps into the darkness. The smell of exhaust and stale water's on me instantly. Dim light glows from outside, invading from under the shack and around Mr. Z's boat. Enough to see shadows, but that's about it.

I rub my damp palms on the inside of my pockets.

"Are we taking Ike's boat out?" Darrin says quietly.

"He would kill me," Lemon murmurs. Softer, she says, "He might anyway. Close the door, okay?"

The door clicks shut. It's almost like being in a tomb. Lemon flicks on the single bulb that hangs from the ceiling. Barely lights the pails of rags, gas cans, the oxygen tanks in the corner. Mr. Z's fishing boat is bobbing in the water. It's an old white bucket with a pristine engine—I don't need the light to see that. Been out here a million times since I was a kid.

Lemon squints at the water lapping around the boat. I swear she looks scared. A wave of panic rushes through me. She runs her palms over the knotty wall boards. A door springs open, one I never noticed.

She reaches in, pulls out a gray, wriggly pile of something. It sparkles. Are those teeth?

Darrin releases a high-pitched squawk. "What the hell is that?"

She shoves the bundle at me. Slimy and cold, whatever it is. I fumble with it, try not to squeal. A snout emerges from the pile. A latex snout. It's a face—short, pushed-in nose. A line of ridged nodules pop up from the big nostrils, stretch between black plastic eyes. Shades of pink and purple and gray. I peer at Lemon, about to ask her what it is. At least until I remember we promised no questions.

Her forehead is all drawn up, eyes on me. I can tell she's waiting for me to say something. I sniff the latex, immediately regret it. "Smells like the lake and BO."

"That makes sense." Lemon reaches into the closet, pulls out another piece of latex. Stegosaurus-esque plates run down the center.

"Kinda looks like that blurry photo of Old Lucy," I say. "The one your grandparents keep at the ferry office."

"That also makes sense." Lemon takes a deep breath and screeches at the top of her lungs. Damn near shakes the boathouse.

Darrin startles, takes a step back. Nearly falls off the walkway. He steadies himself. Lemon grabs his wrist, pulls him back from the edge. His eyes are hubcap-wide. "You *did* see Old Lucy, didn't you? You made the monster call perfectly."

Her fingers tighten on the latex in her hand. "That's because I *am* Old Lucy."

No way I heard *that* right. "Sorry—what?"

"It's all a hoax. It always has been. That sighting we had a week ago?" Lemon's words are rushed. "The one where Billy Voorhees claims he fed Old Lucy? That was me. It was my first time running a sighting by myself. He saw *me*. In the costume."

Darrin opens his mouth—Lemon cuts him off. "My grandfather taught me how. He's been impersonating Old Lucy since he was in his twenties. He took over from his dad—my great-grandfather—who took over from his uncle, who took over from his dad. My family has been keeping the legend of the Lake Lokakoma monster alive since, well, since there's been an Old Lucy."

My brain doesn't compute a word. I hear it, but it doesn't make sense. Maybe she's joking. I give her back the latex head, try to process. She tucks it and the other piece back into the closet. My hands still have that slimy snail feeling. "Are you fe—"

"No questions," she reminds me.

I nod, reach out, and squeeze her elbow. Yeah, sure. I did promise.

She gives me a small smile. "It's not like we've been doing all of this to be mean or to get one over on anyone," she says. "It's more like an economic thing—tourists come to see if they can find the monster, and they stay and spend money. It keeps the town from dying like everywhere else around here. And I'm the one who will impersonate Old Lucy for the rest of my life, or until someone else in the family takes it over. Yeah, my grandparents have the ferryboats, and that's how they make a living, so I get what you're thinking, but that came later. Like mostly because my grandfather wanted to have more control over the boat traffic on the lake."

The tension in the boathouse, man. It's a lot. It's radiating off Lemon like she soaked in it. I don't know what to do with my hands, so I cross my arms over my chest, lean against the boathouse wall.

"I know you're probably both really mad right now, but there's this whole thing about keeping it a secret and—well, I needed you to understand before I tell you the next part."

"The next part?" Darrin chokes.

There's a next *part?*

"Yeah, the part about lying to Troy's dad," Lemon says. "When Snowflake died. It wasn't Old Lucy, obviously—and it sure as hell wasn't a bear. I wanted to tell the truth, but Pappap wouldn't . . . well, I'll get to that later. And Pappap insists that Skeet got killed by an outboard motor, but I don't think so."

A prick of something—don't know what it is—starts at my feet, travels up my legs. Whatever she she's about to say, it's not going to be good. My palms are getting sweaty again. I swipe my hands against my jeans. "So who killed Snowflake and Skeet?"

Lemon looks me full in the face. Her eyes are brimming with wonder and terror and tears, even in the dim light. Even the air has an awful, thick smell to it that goes beyond the funk of the latex, the staleness of the water.

"Not who—*what*. A monster. A real one. It's huge, and it's got huge teeth. My grandparents think I'm hallucinating—they think I imagined it. But first Snowflake, and now an actual person. One that I *know* of anyway. So yeah, I need . . . I need someone to know that this—" she shakes the latex in her hands "—is a lie. I need someone to believe me. There's a monster in the lake, a real one, and it's not going to stop. What happens when the tourists get here? I mean, I can't just do *nothing* and let them line up to be sacrificed."

Can't take my eyes off her. I half expect her to tell me the tooth fairy is real, too. Then again, I never believed in the tooth fairy. Never even thought it was a possibility.

"Will you help me? Please?"

Finally, Darrin shakes his head like he's waking from a dream. "Lemon, what the fuck are you talking about?"

9

LEMON

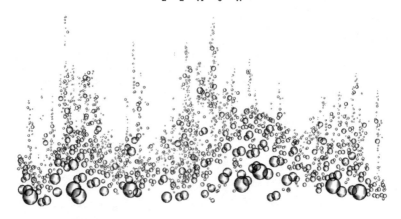

EVERY BIT OF AIR AND hope and faith I have in Troy and Darrin whooshes out of my lungs like the boathouse has fallen down directly on top of me. Tears sting my eyes. My tongue presses against the tip of my incisor as I close the door to the secret panel. Maybe it should have been obvious this wouldn't go well. People don't love being lied to—especially for years at a time. Pappap's drummed it into my head that you can only rely on family—and maybe that's because when you lie to family, they still have to love you. Friends don't.

That thought makes me want to hurl myself into the water and let the monster come.

When I turn back toward Darrin, he's grinning maniacally. "This makes so much sense." He jabs his finger at Troy. "What did I tell you? I *knew* there was something fishy about all this Old Lucy business."

Well. That's something. A tiny bit of hope squeaks back into me.

I peek at Troy. He doesn't look like he wants to scoop me up and commit me to the nearest mental hospital—but he also doesn't seem as eager as Darrin to jump on the reality wagon.

I'm trying to come up with something to say when Troy blurts, "Really, Lemon? Are you *sure*?"

Does he think I'm *lying*?

Darrin is practically bouncing like a little kid on Christmas Eve. "Of course she's sure. She's the worst liar in the entire world. What was that bullshit at lunch last week?" He raises his voice to a falsetto and says, "I guess I believe Old Lucy exists, too!"

"Good point," Troy says, one side of his mouth edging up. "Not what I mean, though. You're sure you want us to help? Neither of us knows anything about . . ." He gestures to the water, then touches my wrist. "Are you—are you okay? This is a lot for one person."

I shush him, but my chest feels lighter than it has in months. Is it possible that they *both* believe me? Relief is a spilled jug of water inside me, filling in the little pockets of self-doubt.

"Lemon, Jesus," Darrin yells. "You're the center of the most successful hoax of all time!"

My smile is genuine when I say to Troy, "We can deal with my personal trauma over all this later. For now there are some things we need to talk about."

"Wait. Pretending to be Old Lucy—that's on you, like, forever?" Troy says.

I nod, and he immediately has *Concerned* face. Maybe he'll hug me again like he did in the house. I wouldn't mind. Getting a Troy-hug isn't all that out of the ordinary, but it would be extra comforting just now.

"So how are you going to deal with that when you go to college?" Darrin asks.

"I'm not *going* to college, but that's beside the point—"

"But you *have* to go to college. How else are you going to be a veterinarian?" Troy interrupts.

"They don't let you just offer medical treatment or surgical intervention to living things for the fun of it," Darrin says. "It's not something you can learn online. People are picky about that. I asked my mom."

"Yeah, I'm aware." My face gets prickly. Talking about this is so much harder than I want it to be. "There aren't any decent animal science undergrad programs around here. If it were just the sightings and the keeping the gossip going, maybe I could manage, but Grammy and Pappap expect me to take over the ferry business, too. Can we please get back to the monster?"

"No way you don't become a vet," Troy says. "Since we were six, you've known. Rescued that mouse from the stray cat. I may not know what I want to do—but *you* do."

The tight smile on my face locks in the tears. "It doesn't matter what I want or don't want—this is my life. It's been decided. It's final."

"What about other family? Your cousin Will? Your uncle?" Troy says. "Couldn't they do it? Do they not know? About Lucy, I mean."

It's nice that Troy is trying to fix things, but he needs to stop. I just want them to listen. Okay, no—I want them to accept that there's nothing that can be done, because talking it to death is like jabbing me with a flaming fork over and over again. "They know. Look, could we drop this? We have more important things to worry about right now."

Darrin's head bobs his agreement.

"Right. The monster on a killing spree." Troy's voice cracks a little on the last word. "Can't we tell my dad about Old Lucy? Tell him everything?" There's a hopeful light in his eyes. He just doesn't understand. When I don't respond immediately, he adds, "If your grandparents don't believe you, my dad might. He'll know what to do—or find someone who does."

I let out a huffy laugh. "Pappap would . . . I don't know what he'd do, but it would be bad. He'd find a way to lock me in the house until I turn thirty. He might do that anyway if he finds out I told both of you. Plus, if any of this gets out, Pappap and Grammy might get jailed for fraud. The business would go under, and they'd lose the house. Between Old Lucy being a fake and the lake having an actual hungry monster ready to eat through the populace, there'd be no reason for tourists to come here at all. Devil's Elbow would end up like every other town around here—dead. Old Lucy is just something that's always belonged in the family, and it's got to stay that way."

"Now that me and Darrin know . . . guess that makes *us* family, huh?" Troy's smile is everything good in my life at this moment. It is cotton candy and puppy breath and snow days and . . . just everything. I throw myself at him and hug him hard enough to feel his heartbeat.

Darrin laughs and joins the pile. It's like being inside a cocoon of blankets.

I reluctantly break the group hug. "Does that mean you'll help me come up with a plan?"

"Well, yeah, of course," Darrin says, suddenly fixated on the water all around us, "but should we get the hell out of this boathouse? We can brainstorm anywhere. There's a man-eating creature with a yen for high school boy meat—and mine would be a tasty treat. Not to mention we should get away from your house in general. If Ike finds us here, it goes way beyond his usual fear we're going to steal your virtue. He may very well peel off our skin and hang our dicks from the flagpole."

"Vivid." But now the nerves are crawling over my skin, too. "We *should* go. I only brought you down here because I didn't think you'd believe me without showing you the Old Lucy costume. I've only seen the monster around the bend—you know, over near the willow trees, but anything could happen. It's a big lake, but it's a big monster."

Troy's mouth goes slack for a moment. "When you put it like that . . ."

I push back the door to the boathouse and glance back over my shoulder. "And it goes without saying that this is between us, right?"

Darrin makes a choked, strangling noise.

I whip around, my whole body tense, sure sharp teeth will sink into my skin any second.

It's Pappap who is about to tear into me, though. He stands outside the boathouse, a storm brewing on his face and white hair blowing in the breeze. "Lemon Bethany Ziegler, you are in serious trouble."

It's as though a spell has been broken inside me. I can feel myself shattering.

"We're all in trouble, Pappap." Spilling seventeen years' worth of secrets and having my two best friends by my side has given the words I've wanted to say to Pappap permission to unleash—and suddenly I'm ranting, arms stiff at my side. "Me. You. Troy. Darrin. Everyone who lives here. Every single tourist who's going to look for Old Lucy this summer."

"Hain't no need to make a scene now." Pappap's gruff voice is low and dangerous.

Darrin and Troy have the sense to hang back, but I take a quick step toward Pappap, who doesn't move a muscle.

"Don't you get it?" My voice carries over the water, returning to me even louder than I imagined it might. "Someone has died. A person. Our dog before that. You and Grammy can try to gaslight me all you want—it wasn't a bear that ate Snowflake, and it wasn't an outboard motor that tore Skeet apart. I didn't imagine *anything*. Someone has to be the adult here—and if it's not going to be you, it's got to be me."

"You best not forget who you're talking to, miss." Pappap's stubbly jaw is set, eyes narrowed. His focus doesn't shift even a little bit—he's laser centered on me, angry as I've ever seen him. Angrier than he was about me wandering around in the middle of the night.

"Can't blame Lemon for telling us," Troy says. "She almost died, too. She's scared for the town."

This time Pappap's gaze slides over my shoulder, icy. "Troy, this hain't none of your business. You think you got something to say, but I tell you now that you don't."

The reality of what's happening is catching up to me. People listen when Pappap talks, me included. He's used to it. He tells me what to do, and I fall in line. I don't know what he's capable of when things don't go according to plan.

He's *got* to be cognizant that he can't hurt Troy and Darrin—but I don't trust that he won't find a way if this goes any further. If he believed there was a monster, I wouldn't be shocked if he accidentally-on-purpose served them up to it.

And that's when I remember where we are—and what *could* happen. Darrin has it right—this is the last place we should be hanging out. There's nothing but water and tall grass around the boathouse. Water and tall grass that could hide a monster.

Troy and Darrin must be thinking the same—the tension behind me is palpable, and I doubt it's because they're wondering what kind of match I might have lit by yelling at Pappap.

There's this thing you do with animals when you want to calm them down when they've got their hackles up. I turn slightly so I'm not directly confronting Pappap anymore. I slouch and gently say, "I'm sorry you feel it's a mistake to involve Troy and Darrin. I am. Let's go back to the house so we can talk about it, okay?"

If I thought I could get away with rubbing the tips of his ears to calm him, I would.

Pappap's lips purse, his face wrinkling up, but he doesn't reply. Instead he pivots and stomps off the floating dock, up the rickety stairs to the backyard. This is uncharted territory for me, this extra-seething version of my grandfather.

I turn to mouth *Sorry* at Darrin and Troy. Darrin winks and follows after Pappap. He's trying to be all cavalier about it, but it doesn't escape my notice that he's nearly jogging up the risers. He may not realize he has just as much to fear from Pappap.

Troy puts his hand in the small of my back and nudges me forward. He stays behind me all the way up. He's steady, as usual. When we reach the yard behind my house, he mutters, "It's okay, Lem, we've got you. No matter what."

Maybe it's because his dad is the sheriff now, he *does* seem to understand that there's peril in the lake *and* in my house.

Pappap's left the back door open, which I suppose is a good sign: at least he didn't lock us out. Darrin waits by an Adirondack chair in the grass. I step into the kitchen first. Pappap furiously whispers to Grammy in the mouth of the hall that leads back to the bedrooms. Butterbeans sits at Grammy's feet, but his head hangs, eyes up, like he knows someone's in trouble and thinks it's him. Grammy glances at me, but it's impossible to read her face.

Whatever Pappap's saying, my arrival clearly signals the end of the conversation—she sits abruptly at the kitchen table and twists her salt and pepper hair over her shoulder. Pappap puts his hands on her shoulders and stares at us. His spine stiffens. Grammy folds her hands in front of her.

Bob pads into the kitchen from the living room, takes one look, and heads back out to where he came from. I don't blame him.

"I'm going to say this once and only once," Pappap says. It's so quiet in the kitchen that even the refrigerator appears to have stopped humming. "There hain't nothing in that lake. *Nothing.* Maybe you did see something, Lemon. Coulda been a sturgeon or a snakehead got thrown in the lake, got real big. Not big enough to kill a human, though. So there hain't going to be no more talk about man-eaters in the water unless we're talking about Old Lucy."

Darrin says, "It's really interesting—"

I wince, and Pappap says, "Son, you ain't wanna finish that sentence." I swear his hand twitches toward where he used to wear his gun belt.

"Pappap, come on," I say, mainly to get his attention off Darrin.

"You're awfully lippy today." He gives me a harrumph before coolly assessing Troy and Darrin. "I may not be sheriff anymore, but I can make damn sure you get hauled off to jail faster than you can blink. Bury you in a cell on some trumped-up drug charge until you die. So maybe you want to remember that if you get tempted to tell another living soul about Old Lucy."

It's not unexpected, not entirely, but it's still shocking to hear him say it aloud.

Grammy gasps and slides away from his grip. She staggers up from the chair. If I'm shocked, Grammy is *furious*.

"How dare you say that to them, Ike. How *dare* you. You've known them their whole lives and—"

"Pearl, now let me handle this."

Still speaking softly, I say, "This isn't the time to be threatening the guys who have no reason not to out us to the entire town."

Pappap takes an angry step in my direction, but Grammy cuts him off, scowling. They're hissing back and forth at each other when I turn to Troy and Darrin.

We've been around each other's yelling parents, but this is something else entirely.

This world of mine that has been so carefully crafted is disintegrating, and they don't have to be here when everything unravels and lands squarely at my feet.

"You should go," I say to them. "I'll handle this."

Troy scans me, uncertain. "I don't want to—"

"No," I say. "It's not even noon yet—he'll be yelling all day." I even manage a small smile when I say, "Save yourselves. I'll text you later."

Darrin peeks at Pappap out of the corner of his eye. "Crazy day, Lem."

"Yeah, now get moving before they stop arguing."

He snickers and makes for the living room. Troy stays put, though. "I don't like leaving you alone in all this."

"You're not. I promise." I do the same as he did to me on the stairs— herd him with my hand at his back.

When Darrin opens the front door, Pappap shouts, "Where do you think you're going?"

"Oh, Ike," Grammy snaps. "They're loyal to Lemon, and you damn well know it."

I give Troy and Darrin a quick hug and shove them out the door.

10

TROY

Mr. Z's kicked me out of the house a lot. More times than I can count. You know your friends long enough, that's how it goes. This is a first, though—Lemon's the one doing the kicking.

I get it. Mr. Z's beyond *mad* at us. Like scowling, wrinkled, powder keg *pissed*. Makes me want to race home, pack a bag, grab Lemon and Darrin, get the hell out of town. I don't care where—anywhere is better than here. But I see where Lemon's coming from. If we bail, and Mom or Dad gets hurt—or some kid from school—it wouldn't feel too good.

My hands are locked on the steering wheel of the Buick. I'm focused on the black road ahead. Darrin's too excited about finding out he's now part of a grand conspiracy—and oblivious to Mr. Z's threats. He cackled all the way back to his house, wishing it wasn't too late to add *Monster Hunter* to his list of yearbook activities. I'm all-in on helping Lemon with what's settled here in the lake—but I'm a realist. I'm betting this isn't going to be the adventure Darrin's hoping for.

I sit in my driveway, clamped onto the steering wheel, for fifteen minutes. Even if I'm not going to abandon the town to a catastrophe, still feels like I'm abandoning Lemon. Like I'm failing her.

Finally, I slide out of the car, head into the house. It's warm inside. Dad's on our worn couch in the living room, still in uniform, elbows on his knees. A notebook and pen top a mess of files spread out next to him. His laptop's on the wooden coffee table. He leans back.

"Hey, Dad."

"Hey, yourself. Aren't you supposed to be at school?" he says, real casual.

My brain shifts into overdrive, looking for an excuse. "I threw up, came home." My words tumble into each other.

Not entirely untrue. Vomit's been churning in my stomach for an hour now at least.

"Are you okay?" He's still on alert—different now, but still. Bad timing. "Are you sick?"

"Nothing serious. Probably something I ate." My voice is strange, a little too high-pitched. At least I can blame it on my stomach. "I just want to go lie down."

Dad nods. "Lemon wasn't at school, was she?"

"Uh-uh." It's like I'm edging up to the rim of a cliff, sending over a shower of rubble. Definitely dangerous territory.

"Did you hear anything at school about what happened?"

This morning at school, before Darrin and I took off for Lemon's house, feels like three years ago. I've got bigger problems than school rumors, but I say, "Yeah. Everybody knows it's Skeet who died."

Dad mumbles under his breath. Louder, he says, "So much for keeping things under wraps until we can get some answers."

"Makes you feel better, no one has the right story."

"What are they saying?"

"A lot of it's about Lemon and Mr. Z. Heard that one or both killed Skeet."

He rubs his chin, heaves a sigh. "That probably came straight from Skeet's mother. She's not taking things well. Look, if you hear anything else, let me know, okay? I released more details to the press, but until the medical examiner makes her final determination about how that kid died, there's likely to be all sorts of things said. The Jenkins clan isn't exactly known for their cool heads."

Already got a taste of that this morning.

Dad says, "I put a deputy on the mother's house to make sure she stays put, doesn't do anything stupid."

Like I'm not already sure certain death awaits us all. "You really think—"

"Nothing would surprise me when it comes to that family. It's why I'm glad Lemon stayed home today. I called Ike Ziegler and told him to watch his back, but you know him."

I nod, head back to my bedroom. Yeah, I know Mr. Z.

Death by outboard motor probably looks a whole hell of a lot different from death by monster teeth. Really, it doesn't matter—to everyone in Devil's Elbow or to the Jenkinses. Mr. Z probably isn't thinking about Lemon's part in all this, what it means for her. Normally I'd say people around here know better than to break into the Ziegler house or mess around with Mr. Z in any way. The man's got a reputation. He's also probably got guns stashed everywhere. But like Dad said, Skeet, his cousin, his mother, and the rest of his relatives are unhinged.

Even beyond that, though, Lemon's still in trouble. Skeet's death will get blamed on Old Lucy. Happens often enough when pets go missing, when there's a death on the lake. Can't remember a single proven instance, though. Not even close to it. No bite marks. No evidence at all. I don't know what the medical examiner might dig up with Skeet. If it points to an Old Lucy attack, a real one—might be more people than ever at the lake. Butting their heads into things. I want to think Lemon

wouldn't go into the lake in the Old Lucy costume unless it was safe—
that Ike wouldn't make her. She *could* be shot.

Hunted.

Hairs on my neck bristle. Luckily Dad's still in the living room—no
one to notice my rubber-legged lurch up to my room. No matter what
happens, Lemon's in trouble.

My bedroom desk chair creaks under me when I collapse into it. I
swear I don't blink for forty seconds. Instead, I'm blindly staring at the
movie poster on my wall.

Thinking about Lemon in pain. Lemon dying. All because of her
family's weird hobby.

If Dad wants to keep Lemon out of sight because of Skeet's family,
it might mean the prom's off the table. Or special precautions for the
prom . . . which gives me an idea about a tux. Wonder if anyone makes
tactical formal wear?

My phone buzzes. Lemon's face blinks up at me from the screen.

"Hey," she says when I pick up. "I just wanted to say I'm sorry for
everything today. You know, with Pappap. And the Old Lucy stuff, too."

"Not a problem. Why are you sorry about Old Lucy?"

"Not telling you about it sooner, for starters."

"Yeah, but you have an excuse." I kick off my shoes, nudge them
under the desk.

"I guess. But I never really thought much about it until I'd already
told you how much it puts you and Darrin right in the middle of a lot
of crap. Not just in the middle of me and Pappap, which is bad enough.
You could really get killed."

I laugh. "Funny, I was just thinking the same about you. My dad's
even nervous about it."

There's a pause. "You told him?" She is pure panic.

"No, no," I say quickly. "He's worried about Skeet's mom and the
rest of the clan getting stupid because a few people think you might
have killed Skeet."

She's silent for a few beats, then her whispered, "For crap's sake," comes over the phone. "You know, I was prepared to be relieved, but now I'm just freaked out again. Thanks, I guess?"

I groan. "Sorry. If it makes you feel better, Dad's got someone on the force keeping an eye on Skeet's mom. Wasn't going to say anything, but you know Skeet's cousin? The one with the ratty chin beard? He threatened you this morning."

"Oh, great. So everything just got more complicated. Faaaantastic."

I laugh at her sarcasm. "Just . . . promise you'll be careful, okay?"

"Same to you. I really *shouldn't* have dragged you and Darrin into this." I can hear the tears behind her voice. She clears her throat. "Too late now, I guess, but don't let me get you into a stupid situation where things could get out of control."

"Speaking of out of control, did Mr. Z finish yelling at you already?"

"You're not going to believe this, but he hasn't said much to me at all. When you and Darrin left, he gave me his standard death glare, told me I'm grounded, and then he and Grammy shut themselves up in his office. That was like an hour ago. They're still arguing."

"What are they saying?"

"I have zero idea. I retreated to my bedroom. There's safety in not being where the cranky old guy is."

"There's also safety in *not* being alone."

There's another silence—this time heavier. My palms feel like I'm holding sun-fried rocks.

"I really love you guys," she says. "You and Darrin."

My heart damn near snaps out of my chest. I know she's talking about *friend* love. Still, it's so close to what I want. So close.

"We love you, too. You know that." The *I love you* lodges under my tongue. It nearly chokes me not to let it rip out of my mouth.

"I *do* know that. I just wanted you to know how I feel is all. Dealing with the monster, with Pappap, this crap with Skeet's family . . . would be . . . I don't know, impossible . . . without you. But especially dealing with the monster. It's not like we learned about marine life extermination in biology. You said it yourself—you and Darrin don't have a background in any of this, and neither do I."

"So how do we come up with a plan?"

"I don't know. I'm not going anywhere for the rest of the day, that's for sure, so I'm going to get an hour of sleep if I can, then dive into the wilds of the Internet to see what I can find. I'm thinking maybe we should look into how invasive species are handled. There's that whole thing in Florida where lionfish somehow got in the coastal waters there."

"Oh, right. You made us watch that documentary."

"My point is that people deal with getting rid of unwanted wildlife all the time, on land or in water. We should be able to find something that worked that we can use."

Finally, something I can actually *do*—instead of sitting here, worrying. "I don't know what Darrin's doing, but we can definitely help."

"Yeah?"

"I'll call him. He's got access to all sorts of databases through his mom. Doctors maybe don't need to know about monsters, but there could be something. And I took that workshop last year on library research. Between the three of us—bet we come up with something."

"Do you—" The last word comes out strangled. "Do you think you'd be able to sneak out of the house tonight? Like maybe one in the morning?"

I pull the phone from my ear, give it an incredulous squint. Lemon was wandering around outside last night—that didn't work out so well. With the Jenkinses possibly lurking, it sounds doubly bad. I don't want to look like a coward. I don't want to upset her more. Definitely don't want to let her down, though. Finally, I say, "You really want to risk getting in more trouble when you're already grounded?"

It's the safest of the things that could go wrong. That's messed up.

"What's Pappap going to do—ground me harder? It'll be easier to go over all the stuff we find in person, so I'm thinking maybe that playground with the weird slide. It's secluded, so no one will see us. It's not near the lake, so no monsters. And it's not like I'm known for nocturnal field trips."

"So that wasn't you hiking around the lake in the middle of the night, finding Skeet's body?"

"Oh, right. Still—maybe that's better. No one would think I'd do it again."

We hash out the details. Lemon clicks off. I put my phone on my desk before opening my laptop. Sneaking out is the last thing I want to do. Lemon's Lemon, though—when she's got her brain wrapped around something, it's hard to get her to make a turn off course. Can't let her be out alone. She's right about one thing—with all three of us working on the problem, finding a solution feels doable. It doesn't stop my legs from feeling wobbly again, though. My body and my brain—they aren't in agreement.

DARRIN AND I pull up to the playground in the Buick just before one o'clock. Lemon's already waiting, all in black. The only reason I can see her is she's sitting at the end of a long pink slide. It's meant to be Old Lucy's tongue—the top of the slide has a plastic cutout of Old Lucy's face. The googly eyes make it look sinister, even without the dreary clouds. The quarter moon filters through in ragged tears, casts deep shadows everywhere.

I park in the darkest part of the lot. Darrin pops his door open. Looks back at me.

"She really refused to let you pick her up?"

I nod. "Said that Mr. Z would recognize the sound of the Buick, know something was up. Wouldn't let us meet her down the road, either. Wouldn't even tell me about her plan to get here. She said it'd be safer for us that way."

"Mr. Z's stubborn, but he's got nothing on Lemon." Darrin's surprised laugh echoes quietly. "Don't tell her I said that. She'll castrate me, and I'm kind of fond of my giblets." He glances around. "Besides, Dad has a nursing shift at the hospital, and Mom got called in for an emergency. Running into them at the hospital won't exactly help keep this rendezvous secret."

"You keep talking shit about Lemon," I say, "and your parents'll be the least of your problems."

He laughs. "Just get me home by three in the morning, okay? I had to bribe Betsy to keep her mouth shut. That girl drives a hard bargain. I think she's been reading our mom's books about negotiation." He swings out of the car. "I guess it's better than her reading Mom's anatomy books. The way she looks at me sometimes, it's like she's wondering what my liver looks like."

"She's fourteen. I don't think she's homicidal."

"Uh-huh. She *likes* you. You're lucky you're an only child." We're halfway across the macadam, the park so murky it's hard to tell where the grass and macadam meet, when he says, "Hey, I never did ask—how'd *you* get out of the house? I thought your dad would've had your house locked up tighter than a bank. Remember when Skeet's mom sent out her battalion of flying monkeys to break all those car windows around the mayor's house because she was pissed about her taxes?"

"Dad's working tonight. For all I know, he's the one watching the Jenkins place."

"You're not worried he might be watching Lemon, too?" He peers into the trees that line the field around the playground.

"Nah. Thinks Mr. Z's got it covered. He doesn't know the full story. Plus, I unplugged the router at our house. The surveillance cams Dad has on the house don't automatically shift to wireless. They don't record more than a few hours' of data. We'll be home before anyone notices."

"What, no silent alarms? Your dad's getting sloppy."

Lemon's pale hand waves, interrupts the gloom. She walks toward us. In the glow from the single security light, it's as though she's underwater. All shadowy and dim, almost a blue cast on her. I don't notice until she's closer, but her smile takes up her whole face. We meet near the seesaw shaped like Old Lucy's tail. She pulls us in for a hug, notebook still tucked under one arm.

She must have showered again before she came out—her hair smells extra sweet. She pulls away. It's like being set loose in the cold. I shiver, even though the air is warm enough.

Darrin laughs. "Better watch it, Lem—if Skeet's mom really is stalking you, she might start rumors about you herself. My favorite of everything I've heard is that you keep Old Lucy as a pet in your boathouse and have been training the old girl to kill." He pauses. "You do kind of keep Old Lucy in your boathouse, come to think of it."

"Wish you could tame the other monster," I say.

"We've got one monster too many," Lemon says. "Two if you count Skeet's people."

"I wonder what a group of monsters is called," Darrin says. "It's got to be alliterative, like a caravan of camels or a gaggle of geese . . . maybe a misfortune of lake monsters."

That at least makes Lemon laugh.

"So how'd you get here?" I ask her. "I know you didn't steal your grandparents' car."

"Are you kidding?" Darrin says. "Lemon is a first-class badass. She probably flew here on her giant ba—"

"I took Grammy's bike, thank you very much. Leave my balls out of it." She sticks her tongue out at him. I smirk, glance over at Darrin—it's clear from his face he's thinking about his giblets comment. "The roads are pretty dead this time of night, especially on a Monday . . . or, I guess it's Tuesday now. I can't keep the days straight." She adds, "Anyway, I figured it would be okay. No one would see me and immediately rat me out to Pappap." She leads us over to the bench with the spiky purple back, throws down her notebook. "Plus, I ducked in and out of drive-ways, through the trees. I wasn't actually on the street too long. I even stopped a few times to listen, make sure no one was out there with me. Skeet's relatives aren't exactly known for their grace. I figured they'd be pretty clumsy in the woods."

"That explains your ninja ensemble," Darrin teases. "Looks like you're taking fashion tips from Amelia." He slings himself down on the padded mat in front of the bench. "So talk to me, oh, ball-less turd of my heart. What'd you find?"

She grins and folds herself down beside him. "I want to save mine for last—and stop calling me the turd of your heart. It's creepy. What'd *you* find?"

He salutes her. "I started thinking about whales that get stranded. A few years ago a beluga whale got stuck in some river in France."

I shrug, find a patch on the mat, too. At least if we're low to the ground, we make a smaller target.

Don't feel eyes on my back, though. Or anything out of the or-dinary. Only the light wind brushing through the pines, the sound of crickets. The buzz of the security light.

Just because I don't notice anyone watching doesn't mean no one's out there, though.

Lemon nods. "I remember the whale."

"They fed the thing to lead it where they wanted it to go. Like a trail of tasty, fishy breadcrumbs. We could do something like that."

"Where do we want it to go?" I say, sliding my eyes over the tree line again.

"There *is* a creek that runs off the lake," Lemon says, "but there's zero chance a thing of this size could travel in it. It's too shallow. I don't even know where the creek dumps into. A river maybe? Or the Atlantic, eventually, I suppose."

"Okay, not a great option to move the monster, then," Darrin says. "But what if we want to kill it? Poisoned fish, maybe?"

"What if something else eats the poisoned fish?" Lemon says. "I don't want to poison the whole lake. That's madness."

"We're forgetting something," I say. "We need to figure out what this thing is."

Darrin says, "Does it matter?"

"Might," I say. "You want to kill a mouse, right? You bring in a cat. Or snakes. You wouldn't try grasshoppers or ants. Or slugs—you can kill 'em with salt. Pepper, though? Won't do a thing to them. Know your enemies, so you know their weaknesses."

Wonder what Vern Jenkins's weakness is. Doubt salt *or* pepper would work on him.

Lemon smiles again. Her eyes go big. "That's . . . kind of brilliant, Troy. It gives me an idea. I saw some paperwork Pappap had a couple years ago, like before he retired—he said he was buying underwater cameras for the station. Something about rescue supplies. I don't know why it stuck in my head, but . . . do you think maybe you could, uh, liberate the camera from the station somehow? Temporarily, of course."

Big order. But hey, it's time for big ideas. "I'll try to figure out how. No promises."

Lemon grins. "Yeah, of course. And maybe if we can catch it on camera, Pappap will have to believe me. That's a good—"

Darrin winces. "My ears are ringing."

She frowns, steals a glance toward the trees. "Is that like a Spidey-Sense thing? Like we're being spied on? Did you just feel—wait, there it is again."

A short, sharp jolt, like being rear-ended in a car—except the ground rolls. The light on the pole flickers. Two more lurches, and the lights go out entirely.

"Fuck," Darrin says. "It's aftershocks. It's got to be."

Lemon's already scrambling off the ground. "Grammy and Pappap will wake up for sure. I have to get home."

"Let me give you a ride." I hustle after her. Weird noises float out of the woods. Something rustling. Could be one of the Jenkinses—could be a bear. Dad said earthquakes shake up the wildlife. If I get eaten by a bear tonight, it won't matter what Vern Jenkins is doing or if Dad wakes Mom, calling her to check in. Now's not the time to take chances, though.

Lemon shakes her head, keeps moving. "No way. Pappap can't make life any *more* hellish for me, but—"

"Okay, okay, go," I say. I'm not going to waste time arguing—doesn't mean I'm going to listen to her. Amelia said something about bears swimming fast, but Dad drummed it into my head that bears *run* fast too. I don't care if I get caught or if Mr. Z sees me—or if Darrin gets snagged creeping back into his house. Well, I do care, but we're going to stealth tail Lemon home. She doesn't have to know. "Just text me—so I know you made it."

Darrin cracks up. "This is very touching."

I flip him off in the dark.

She pulls Mrs. Z's old-lady bike from behind some bushes. It's too dim to see—I'm sure Lemon's making a face at him, though. "I don't know whether to be happy or sad about the earthquake. At least maybe I might not be *the* topic of conversation tomorrow, but neither will Old Lucy."

After I see Lemon turn into her driveway without being run off the road by Vern Jenkins or an angry bear and then dump Darrin at his house, I'm halfway home before it hits me—why Lemon doesn't know whether to be happy or sad. If no one's talking about Old Lucy, Mr. Z might insist on a monster sighting. Lemon can't go back in that lake—not with a monster swimming around, chewing up people. I need to get that underwater camera so we can identify what we're dealing with, find a way to kill it. Fast.

11

L E M O N

D ECIDING WHAT TO WEAR HAS never been much of an issue for me. I'm either wearing the Old Lucy costume, or I'm wearing jeans. But this morning in the shower I got to thinking about what would be waiting at school. If Troy isn't exaggerating—and that's not something he does usually—it might be a hostile environment, to put it mildly. There's a quote I saw once, something about clothes being the armor you use to survive reality. And now, as I'm standing just outside the doors of *Devil's! Elbow! High!* it's a relief that the idea was floating in my brain as I was getting dressed. I'm still in jeans, but they're a nicer pair. It's not like I'm more conspicuous or like I'm wearing anything fancy, like Amelia, but everything is comfortable and makes me stand a little straighter. And even as people are passing by, whispering or not whispering about me and Skeet, the words don't take root for me. It's not about how I look—it's about how I feel. It's the first time I've really understood the power of wardrobe. It didn't even bother me when Pappap refused to acknowledge me this morning as I was leaving the house.

Come to think of it, that's probably why Amelia *does* dress the way she does. To hear her talk, she's a professional new kid, and that can't be fun. She's always wearing something that makes her noticeable, but it's more than that. It's the way she *wears* her clothes. She's never unsure or awkward, even when she's blabbing about the French teacher's ill-advised attempt to pick up an underage girl in the LucyMart.

I take a long breath and push it out, then follow a bunch of girls from the astronomy club in through the front door of the school.

Principal Showalter is standing to one side of the hallway, right in front of the Old Lucy mural, arms crossed, eyes narrowed. He sees me and doesn't react—it's safe to assume rumors about me or news of the Jenkinses' vendetta haven't reached him yet. My inclination is to keep my head down and plow through the masses to get to my locker, but a revenge-minded cousin of Skeet's might be afoot. Snippets of conversation zoom all around me. I pick my way around the hall, careful and deliberate.

". . . hear that she was definitely sleeping with Skeet. Danetta said that's why . . ."

"No, I mean, what if Lemon has actually trained Old Lucy to do her dirty work? Remember when her dog died? Maybe it was a test, and . . ."

". . . felt the quake, too. Shook me out of bed. I almost landed on my cat."

". . . don't know what Skeet saw in Lemon anyway. She's like a gawky, dorky tree."

It all just . . . bounces off me. *Armor.* I have a new appreciation for Amelia.

I make it to my locker without incident. Troy nudges my shoulder a moment later.

"How'd it go?" he says.

"It was a near miss. The lights were on in the kitchen, so it was good I left my bedroom window unlocked. Probably about thirty minutes after I got home, my grandmother peeked in on me, and that was that. I'm assuming you made it home without being made?"

He nods. "No problems at all."

"What about Darrin?"

"What *about* Darrin?" Darrin ducks behind Troy and comes up on the other side of me. "Not that I don't—"

The announcement system squawks on. "Lemon Ziegler to the counseling suite, please."

The entire hallway descends into dead air for at least a full five seconds. Every face seems to swing in my direction.

"Are we next?" Troy says. "Maybe Mr. Z managed to get us in trouble after all."

With a certainty I don't feel, I say, "I'm sure it's nothing. They're probably trying to figure out why I haven't been in to talk about my college plans."

Troy immediately breaks out into *Concerned* face.

"Yeah, I doubt anyone knows yet that we're planning a murder." Darrin gives me a half smirk.

I shush him. "Like I need more rumors around here."

"There's a bright side," Troy says. "At least it's keeping people talking about Old Lucy."

He has a point.

The counseling suite is in the next hallway. For reasons that have never been explained to me, an enormous papier-mâché Old Lucy is mounted to the wall outside—and it's not the happy pink-slash-purple version that everyone else in the town has adopted.

This one has pointy fangs and a barbed tail, with an almost salmon-and-gray colored body. It's a strange cross between Old Lucy and the real monster.

I shudder, even in my clothes armor.

The receptionist points me to an office at the back of the suite. Inside is a man I've never seen before. He's thin, with dark hair and a bushy mustache, wearing a navy blue suit and striped tie that's slightly askew. He doesn't stand but gestures to the chair perched in front of the desk.

"You must be Lemon Ziegler," he says. "I'm Alex Masters."

I sit. The office is bare. Just a desk, a chair, and a filing cabinet. The staff usually have photos on their desks, lots of files and pens. Maybe one of those inspirational posters, like the *hang in there* cat.

"I'll just get right to it. I'm a grief counselor. My colleagues and I will be calling many of your classmates in over the next several days, but I wanted to start with you since you were involved in the tragic accident." His voice is warm, and he's gazing insincerely into my eyes, like he wants me to think he can see into my very soul. I've been through grief counseling, and all he's doing is making me aware that he picked the wrong job.

"Accident?" I say, trying hard to keep my tone neutral.

"Mr. Jenkins's unfortunate passing. It must be very difficult for you."

"Oh, right. Yes. It is very sad." I fidget in the uncomfortable chair.

He studies his fingernails for a moment, then focuses on me. His expression seems to shift between concern and irritation and back again. "I want you to understand that I recognize it might be tough to talk to a stranger at a time like this. I assure you that whatever you say stays between us. This is a safe space." When I don't reply, he says, in the voice that I typically reserve for wounded or nervous animals, "Why don't you start by telling me about who Skeet was to you."

There's something so off-putting about him. Maybe it's his fakeness, maybe it's something else. It's not exactly that I want to be rude to him—I just don't want to talk to him. Getting in trouble by refusing probably isn't the best idea ever, though.

"He asked me to the prom but I'm going with someone else," I say, squirming.

He nods. "He must have been very fond of you."

"Fond? I don't think that's—" I'm about to say something that isn't very nice about Skeet but stop myself just in time. That's when it hits me—Mr. Masters seems like he's trying to pry information out of me. I'm sure of it. Carefully, I say, "Yeah, I'm sure Skeet had feelings for me of some sort."

"How have you been doing since his death?"

"Sad," I say again, mostly because I can't think of anything else *to* say. I can't tell this guy that I'm not thinking of Skeet at all, or that I've got other, more pressing, things happening.

"Hmm, okay." His mustache twitches. "Let's talk about your home life. Your records say you live with your grandparents?"

Oh, God, this is going to go on forever. He fires dozens of questions at me about Grammy and Pappap, about their business, about the lake and our house—even my sleeping habits, which is pointless and weird. By the time he releases me, I feel like I've told him my life story, or at least a very sanitized version. He even asks about Old Lucy and whether I've ever seen her.

I don't like it.

The halls are deserted when I emerge from the suite. Teachers are always going on about not having a budget for class supplies—Principal Showalter would have been better off spending money on pencils for class than that bargain-basement grief counselor. I swing into the next hall; Mrs. Stempfel's class has just started. Amelia abruptly darts out of the next doorway, clutches my wrist, and tows me over to her.

"What are you doing?" We're squeezed into a corner, door hinges digging into my shoulder.

"Are you having a good time today? Because it doesn't seem like you're having a good time." Her red hair twists back from her hairline—it's pulled into a ponytail on top of her head, and it's teased into a poof. Her hair is more unusual than her clothes, for a change of pace. She's wearing all black, of course, but the only slightly unusual thing is a mesh shirt over a camisole that shows a lot of skin. I wouldn't wear it, but I admire her armor anyway.

"That's why you nearly tore my arm out of my socket? To ask me how I'm doing? Shouldn't you be in English class?"

"Yeah, so should you. So what?" She leans in closer. "Let's get out of here. Today is not going to be a good time for you, so why bother sticking around for it?"

"Because someone will notice if I'm not here—and I'm already in trouble with my grandparents?" I want to stuff the words back in my mouth. She doesn't need to know.

"What—because of this Skeet thing? I know none of the stories are true, so what'd you do that that your grandparents are mad about?"

I smile, hoping it'll distract her. "How do you know none of the rumors are true?"

Her mouth pinches for a moment. "Gee, because I've *met* you? You're a cool girl. Way too cool to have anything to do with someone named Skeet, for crissakes. I'm supposed to believe you've been sleeping with him? Please. It's boring around here, but I'd have to have *nothing* else to do. Now Troy, on the other hand—that's a different story. I could see a girl risking life and limb to get down with—"

"That's not the way things are with me and Troy. You know that."

"But you're going to the prom."

"Yeah, as friends."

"Okay, fine." Amelia gives me an entirely not subtle once-over, and I'm instantly self-conscious. "But just out of curiosity, what are you wearing to this friendly, lake monstery prom? That's the true measure of how you feel about him, you know?"

"I haven't bought a dress yet," I say stiffly.

"Are you kidding me? You've only got a few weeks."

"Prom is more than four weeks away."

"I don't know how to tell you this, Lemon, but there are things like alterations and then you have to buy shoes and . . . and . . . what if all the good dresses are sold-out already? You'd have to factor in delivery time for dresses you buy online."

"I guess, but—" I'm about to say something snarky about not having time to care about prom dresses when saving the town is so much more important, but I manage to stop myself.

"But nothing. Look, this is an even better reason to skip school today. There are a few dress shops in Wilkes-Barre that aren't completely unfortunate. Better than those wedding-cake looking pastel monstrosities for sale at the shop in town." Amelia scans the hallway. "Troy said you're grounded, so I can guarantee that I'll have you back before the school day's over—and I'll even hack into the school's server later and erase the absence from your record. It'll be like it never happened."

Well, that's one way to get my attention. My eyes widen. "You can do that? Wait—is that how you find out everyone's business?"

"Seriously? All I do is listen when people talk." She grimaces for a moment. "You could almost say it's my job." She brightens and grins at me. "So what do you say? Are you in or are you out? Come on, I drove today and everything. My car's in the lot."

"You seem awfully anxious to get me into your car."

"I just want you to look good at the prom."

"Why do you care? You barely know me."

"So what?" Amelia jangles a set of keys I hadn't noticed. "You think I need to have made mud pies with you when we were still in diapers to be friends?"

I've never really hung out with anyone but Darrin and Troy. It's hard when you have secrets like mine, but it's also pointless when the two of them have always been enough. We've always kept our little circle just us. I do *like* Amelia—or at least I understand her a little.

"No, but . . . what if you're trying to kidnap me?" My mouth tries not to smile.

She snickers and mutters, "It's not me you have to worry about."

"What?"

"Okay, fine. I saw that cousin of Skeet's this morning. I want to say his name is Cleetus, but it's probably not. You know, the one who's been running his mouth about making you pay for killing his family? He brought a knife to school. I think it's a good idea for you to be elsewhere."

When she says it like that, my will to stay crumbles. Being *elsewhere* seems like a great idea. Wilkes-Barre, the moon, another universe.

"Shouldn't you report it to Principal Showalter? What if he hurts someone?"

"It's covered, okay?" Amelia gives the hallway one more look and tows me quickly around another corner. "Stay near the wall and move fast. If anyone stops us, we're just heading to the bathroom. Got it?"

I laugh morosely as she dashes down the corridor. It's almost like being at my house, taking Darrin and Troy out to the boathouse for the Old Lucy reveal, except there's a slightly smaller chance of being consumed. By a monster, anyway.

She beelines for a sleek black car when we hit the lot. She's parked a few rows from Troy's Buick. Her car beeps to unlock when she thumbs the fob, and she's so quick that we're halfway through Devil's Elbow before I even think about texting Darrin and Troy to tell them I'll be gone all day. Inside, the car is immaculate. It smells brand-new. The dashboard is all digital, with buttons I've never seen before. I know how to drive, but Pappap's car is practically an antique. It has roll-down windows. This car looks like it could fly.

"Nice car," I say.

"My dad's."

We have to drive down Front Street to get to the bridge that leads out of town. From behind the tinted windows of her car, I feel safe enough from the possibility that someone might see me—someone that could report me to my grandparents. Still, when I spot Danetta Harvey's dad power washing the sidewalk outside his pizza shop, I duck down. In the shop window hangs a new poster advertising the Lake Monster pie.

"I'll never get used to how totally enthusiastic everyone is about this lake monster stuff," Amelia says. "I heard someone had an Old Lucy–themed wedding a few months ago. Who does that? And this prom theme. Yikes. I mean, you seem kind of above all of it. You barely talk about Old Lucy at all, when everyone else is stark raving obsessed."

Warning bells are going off in my head. Grammy and Pappap's Old Lucy rules flash at me. Carefully, I say, "It's just that I live at the lake, so it seems less strange. Old Lucy's all around me, all the time."

"Don't get me wrong—Old Lucy is a nice idea, but all cryptids and legends and lore are nice ideas. Have you ever heard of the Loveland Frogman?"

I shake my head and sink farther into the unbelievably soft leather seats.

"It's this human-sized frog thing, but it allegedly walks around Loveland, Ohio on its hind legs and plays with a spark-emitting stick. People started saying they saw this thing as far back as the 1950s. Usually hiding under a bridge. The frogman," she adds dryly, "not the people who saw it."

"Naturally," I say. "But I'd expect to find a frog under a bridge."

"Sure, but a four-foot-tall frog with a sparkly wand?" She slides a sidelong glance my way.

"Okay, fair."

"The best part of this story is that in the early 1970s, a couple of police officers claim they saw the Frogman. One even says he shot it— and he's got the corpse of this thing in his trunk. Only it turns out that it was just this huge iguana missing its tail. And then in 2016, the cop who says he got the drop on the Frogman admits the whole thing was a hoax. People keep having these Frogman sightings, but it's all wishful and magical thinking."

"What are you saying? That you think Old Lucy is a hoax?"

She shrugs, keeps her eyes on the road. "Maybe."

I keep asking questions, but for being a talker Amelia never says much. I thought maybe she lived this glamorous life on the road, but she says she mostly does odd jobs for her dad when he travels around and sits around eating crappy food while waiting for her dad to get moved to a new job. And she won't say anything at all about her mom. No wonder she's always up in everyone's business—her life sounds sad, in a very different way from mine. The way she dresses makes more sense than ever.

She looks at her dashboard and groans. "We need to make a quick pit stop for gas. Gird your loins—this town is an armpit."

She swings the car down the off-ramp and into some little town I've never even heard of. The street is all cracked asphalt. It looks like there used to be shops lining the road, but now it's mostly dilapidated brick buildings with boarded-up windows. Dying weeds sprout from the edge of the broken curbs. I picture what Devil's Elbow might look like after years of neglect and lost jobs—the Lucy-licious Fluff and Fold falling down around itself. The Magic Monster shop gutted, reclaimed by concrete and leaves and tree roots.

There's a mini-mart on the corner that looks like it's still in business, and a gas station with two pumps across the street. The awning over the pumps has one bent pole, giving the structure the look of a spider with a broken leg. Despite the threat, Amelia parks underneath. She's out of the car in a second.

Some scrawny guy in a T-shirt with a stretched-out neck slouches against the gas station hut. He stares at Amelia, but I'm not sure he actually sees her. He has a vacant look in his eye. He twitches, takes a step toward the car, then sags back against the wall. He does it again and again until I'm sure he's working up the energy to rush the car. It's some relief when Amelia shoves herself back into the driver's side minutes later.

"This place gives me the creeps," she says and races back to the highway on-ramp.

"Why'd we even come here?"

"It's the only gas station I know of that's close to the highway, so we could get in, out, and back on the road. This town is such a piece of crap."

"How'd you know it's here?"

"My dad was stationed not far from here for a few weeks."

"Here? Why?"

She shrugs. "I don't know. He said it was some kind of staging operation."

Staging? I'm about to ask her what that means when she adds, "It used to be a cute little town back in the 1960s. Dad said it's mostly drug labs now—this part of the state is perfect for it. Midway between New York and Philadelphia, close to highways. Nothing else to do for money."

Pappap's voice comes floating back into my head. "What we do keeps Devil's Elbow a nice town. Hain't no use pretending like it wouldn't shit the bed if it weren't for the tourists."

Now I see what he means.

I watch the decaying farms roll by, the fields bare, and wonder what they're actually producing—if anything. It's depressing. Not just because this place used to have people who cared for it living here, but because I suddenly feel more trapped in Devil's Elbow than I ever have.

We pass a sign for Sugar Notch when Amelia flips on the radio, scans through the stations, frowns, and clicks through to the Wi-Fi to stream music instead. It's not long before Wilkes-Barre's downtown stretches out in front of us. I'm so used to Devil's Elbow and its bright storefronts and everything Old Lucy that I forget what normal towns look like. Buildings with more than two stories. Big hospitals and hotels. And two shops side-by-side that do nothing but sell prom and wedding dresses. Not one of these places has a lake monster illustration anywhere near it. It's glorious in a way that makes me feel like I can finally breathe—at least until I think again about what's waiting for me back home.

12

LEMON

A SURPRISINGLY STRONG HALF HUG IS not what I'm expecting from Amelia when she drops me off at Devil's Elbow High just before it's time to catch the bus home.

She doesn't seem like a hugger. Neither am I, except with Troy and Darrin. That's what happens, though—she hugs me. It's not even awkward.

"Troy is going to lose it when he sees you in that dress," she says as I'm climbing out of her car. "It was freaking made for you." She grins. "This tall, pale blond thing you've got going on is Amazon-esque. Perfect for the dress."

"You sound like Darrin—the number of times he's referred to me as an Amazon or as Stretch over the years is, well, a lot."

Amelia's shoulders bounce with her sarcastic laugh. "No, if I were Darrin I'd probably also add in a cheesy line or two and ogle your boobs under the guise that he's just kidding. He's kind of a horn-dog. That dress would be wasted on him. I'm glad you're going with Troy."

Not that her observations about Darrin are wrong, but she and I haven't been friends long enough for her to say stuff like that. In my most even tone, I say, "Okay, first of all, Darrin's a good guy, so lay off. And second, Troy and I are j—"

"Yeah, just friends." The corner of her mouth ticks up in the most maddening way. "You've said that like eight hundred times today."

"But it's true." I slam the door shut harder than intended. At least consciously. It's all just part of the noise of people scrambling in the parking lot, hurrying to leave. That's when I notice one of the Jenkins brood—some first-year kid, arms crossed over his chest—glowering at me from near the entrance to the school. I stiffen.

Amelia lowers the passenger side window. "Take this in whatever spirit you like, Lemon, but maybe put some time into reexamining that. I'm pretty sure Troy's into you—and if you saw the way you two look at each other, you'd be wondering if you're in denial, too. And when he sees that dress, and you all prettied up, and you see him . . . Yeah, you're going to forget all about being *just* friends." A moment of wistfulness passes over her face. "I hope I get to witness it."

I lean into the passenger side window, elbows on the track. The first-year is still within eyesight, and he doesn't let up the glare for an instant. "I'm about a hundred percent sure that's not going to happen for me, but why do you *hope*—are you going somewhere?"

She shrugs. "I never take anything for granted—my dad could pick up and go any minute, and it sounds like his group might want to wrap things up here pretty quick. Don't worry, though—I won't leave town without making sure you have your dress."

Honestly, with the way Skeet's family has decided I'm to blame, it occurs to me that I might not even get the chance to wear the dress. Whether from one of the Jenkins kids mowing me down, or the monster in my lake catching up with me, it's not looking good.

"You really don't mind keeping it?" It's insane to have a completely normal conversation amid all these threats, but hiding in a corner isn't an option. "It would look pretty weird walking into my house with a big prom dress when I was supposed to be here all day."

Hysterical laughter bubbles in my throat.

"It's the least I can do." She presses her hands to the steering wheel. "Look, I should go—and so should you if you don't want your grandparents to know you cut school."

I watch her rocket out of the lot. Her fancy car barely makes any noise. When I turn back toward the school, the first-year who was staring is gone. I shiver and beeline to the bus.

When I get home, Grammy's bustling around our yellow kitchen, hands sticky with dough. Her hair is pulled back in a bun that sits like a donut on top of her head. Butterbeans is lying next to the refrigerator, eyes constantly on her as if willing a glob of dough to break off and land at his feet. "Come on out and help me with dinner when you're settled."

"Is Pappap here?"

She shakes her head and offers a smile that tells me she knows I'm thinking about him ignoring me this morning. In the grand scheme of things, it barely registers as a problem.

I nod at Grammy and head back to my bedroom. Bob prances around my legs, little tail nub wagging. I give him a few good scritches behind the ears and a peck on the orange spot on top of his head but shoo him away before I close the door behind me. Some secrets are meant to be kept from *everyone* in the house, although Bob isn't equipped to tell.

Even on my phone screen, the dress is prettier than anything I've ever seen. Dark pink with an almost filmy silver overlay that drapes so you can't tell there's a high slit up the leg. The banded waist gives me a shape I didn't know I could have, and the low V-neck shows off a lot of me, but not in an obscene way. Pappap won't like the dress, but I could wear a potato sack and he'd think Troy and every other guy in the vicinity would be waiting to ravish me. I would never have tried it on, but Amelia insisted. She was right then, and she was right in the parking lot—it's like the dress was made for me.

Maybe she's right about other stuff, too.

And maybe she's not.

I key in Troy's name on my phone. He picks up on the second ring. "Missed some drama today," he says.

"What—was everyone all up in arms about the grief counselors? Did they call you and Darrin in to talk? What did you think?"

"That's not what I mean. Half the police forced busted in on the school today. Took Vern Jenkins out in handcuffs."

"Which one is Vern?"

"Skeet's cousin—the one who always wears the muscle shirts."

I feel like maybe I should gasp melodramatically for effect, but it's just one more very unsurprising thing in this string of complications that my life has become. It *does* explain why that first-year Jenkins kid was staring me down in the parking lot.

"Was it weapons-related, by any chance?" Is this what Amelia meant when she said she had it covered? She *does* seem like a go big or go home kind of person.

He chuckles. "Let me guess—Amelia knew the second it happened?"

"I think she might have *made* it happen."

"How do you figure?"

"Just something she said today. Doesn't matter. So what happened with the arrest?"

"Not sure. Dad's not home yet. Don't know if he'd tell me the whole story anyway. Least no one seems to be talking about *you* much anymore—everything thinks Vern killed Skeet and framed you."

"Oh, great. Skeet's mom and the rest of the family must love that. So no one thinks Old Lucy had anything to do with it?"

"Haven't heard a lot about that, either. At least not from the usual sources. Grief counselors were asking a lot about Old Lucy, though.

Pretty bizarre. Danetta's telling people they even said she should avoid the lake so she wouldn't be reminded about Skeet being killed. That sound right to you?"

"Not that I'm a full-on expert, but when I was seeing a grief counselor after my mom and dad's accident, my therapist said he wanted me to confront my grief, not hide from it."

"Huh. These counselors seem less about that."

"The guy I talked to was a thousand percent the least sincere adult I've ever met."

He huffs a laugh. "How was your field trip?"

"Amelia said to get a silvery-gray tie for your tux."

I can picture us together now, him in black, his shoulders all broad. Me in my new dress. Just like that, the idea of kissing him pops into my head. I try to push it away, but it won't dislodge from my brain. In fact, that's *all* I'm thinking about now. Like whether his lips are soft. How solid he is physically. Other things that have me wondering if I'm having a nervous breakdown. I examine the phone in abject horror. Amelia's a little puppet master, planting ideas where they don't belong.

"I have to go help my Gram, Troy," I say. "I just wanted to let you know I'm still alive."

"Let's keep it that way," he says. "Least we don't have to worry about Vern."

The way he says it isn't all that comforting. There's an entire unhinged Jenkins family ready to annihilate me. They obviously believe I killed Skeet or had something to do with it—but the reality of the situation is that they're mad at me because Skeet had the emotional intelligence of a slice of bread. I went out of my way not to hurt his feelings when I said no to him about prom—but guys like that think girls don't have the right to refuse anything.

Grammy's pressing dough into a deep pie dish when I reach the kitchen, still brooding. Bob's prancing behind her. "How was school?" she says.

"So . . . no more silent treatment?"

Grammy's eyes cut to me. "I was never the one not talking to you—plus, do you not remember me asking you to come help me with dinner when you got home? That's talking."

I give her my most sarcastic expression, and she laughs.

"You already know your grandfather's not too thrilled with you right now."

"But *you're* okay that I told Darrin and Troy?"

I sit down at the kitchen table, and Bob rears up to put his front paws on my shoulders. He gives me a lick up the side of the face. Way more comforting than the way Troy ended our conversation, and more comforting than Grammy's face at the moment, which hovers somewhere between worried and thoughtful.

She smooths a strand of hair back with her forearm, sprinkling more flour over her housecoat. "Let me ask you something. Do *you* feel as though you *shouldn't* have told them? Do you think the family secret is in any way more likely to be exposed now that Troy and Darrin know?"

"No, of course not."

She smiles and nods. "Because a burden shared is a burden lightened, right? And that goes double for whatever you may or may not have seen in the lake."

"Do you . . . do you believe me about the lake?"

The wrinkles on Grammy's face deepen. "I don't think you're lying, Lemon. There just hasn't been any proof. That's beside the point, though. What I think may interest you to know is that other people outside the family have known about Old Lucy."

My spine abruptly stiffens. "What? But—"

Grammy holds up her hand. "Would you get the pot pie filling from the counter?"

The total normality of what we're doing after my grandmother telling me everything I know about the family rules around Old Lucy is wrong has my head pulsing. Any minute the walls are going to start bleeding glitter—my reality has come apart at the seams. My attempt to process what she's said is useless, because all I can do is goggle at her, mouth gaping like a dying fish. It's the unbreakable rule: no outsiders; trust no one; blood is thicker than water. My legs don't even register walking over to the counter, but here I am, zombie-stepping over to where the filling sits.

Grammy's brows draw together. She wipes her hands on a towel and quickly takes the bowl from my hands, then sets it on the stovetop. The back door is cracked open a smidge, and a cool breeze blows in, sending up the scent of damp greenness to compete against the scent of roasted vegetables that hangs in the room. Even that seems out of place amid the buzzing of my brain.

Grammy pops the pot pie crust in the oven and pushes me back into the chair. She sits opposite me and folds her hands carefully on the table in front of her.

Her mouth purses like she's going to say something—she does it a few times before she says, "Your grandfather told *me* not long after we started dating in high school. And your great-grandfather's best friend and *his* family knew. They even helped make sure there were people at the lake for the sightings until they moved away."

"Are you kidding me with this?" I can't control my face, the volume of my voice, or even the way I smack the table. "Then why am *I* not supposed to tell anyone?"

Grammy smiles gently. "The longer your grandfather pretended to be Old Lucy, it got into his head that if you want something done right, you do it yourself. You know how he is—stubborn. Part of that is wanting to do things different from his parents, and so he conveniently forgot that he told me before I officially became part of the family. As for you, well, he forgets what it's like to be young and feel the responsibility of all this weighing down on you."

My jaw creaks open. "Weighing me down? But you said you were proud of me for getting to be Old Lucy."

"And I am. You and your grandfather are very different people, though. But maybe you feel like you want to do things differently, too."

"I didn't even know I had that kind of an option." I'm thinking a million different things, ideas swirling together so fast I can't pick one out to examine it. "Why are you even telling me?"

"Your grandfather's mad, honey. And I don't have to tell you that when he gets mad, he turns into a bully." She reaches over and puts her hand over mine, squeezes. She has surprisingly strong fingers—they're like thin bands of steel. "You've turned into a strong, smart young woman, like I always knew you would. I wanted you to know that Old Lucy is yours now—yours to do whatever you want with. It doesn't matter what Ike or anyone else says."

It's the way she says "anyone else" that catches my attention. And that's when I notice there are extra plates set out on the counter.

"Grammy, who's coming for dinner?"

She snatches her hand away, and her face pinches. "It wasn't my idea."

"And that idea that's not yours would be *what*?"

Grammy lays her palms flat on the table. Her entire body seems to fidget. "Ike drove over to see Bobby today—about you."

"Does he want Uncle Bobby to relieve me of my Old Lucy duties? Because if that's the case, he can have them—and he can deal with the monster in the lake, too."

Grammy squeezes her hands into fists. "Bobby's my son, and I love him. But I also *know* him."

"What's that supposed to mean?"

She barks out a sharp laugh. "I'm trying to tell you what it means. Look, he—he feels like he has skin in the game when it comes to Old Lucy simply on account of being a Ziegler, but he doesn't know what it's like to sacrifice for it. I just want you to be prepared for this dinner."

"Prepared? What, am I about to be tortured?"

"They'll say things to make you feel guilty, make you feel terrible—about telling Troy and Darrin, and about making a fuss about there being a monster in the lake. I'll be there for you tonight, but you also have to stand up for yourself. Don't rise to Ike's bait. He's good at riling you up. I know you think I don't notice, but I do." She lifts one shoulder and lets it drop.

I would almost give anything to hear that creepy low moan drift up from the lake so I have an excuse to run away. Even facing down Vern Jenkins with a knife sounds better than what's about to happen. After a few silent moments, I say, "Maybe I should go to Troy's for dinner."

"You *are* grounded," Grammy says, one corner of her mouth curving. "You may not like your grandfather, but you do have to abide by punishments while you're living under this roof."

"But you just said Old Lucy is mine—and that means this house is mine. I'm technically living under my *own* roof, aren't I?"

Grammy chuckles. "That's my girl. I'm not saying you're free to skip dinner . . . but I am saying that's the kind of thinking that's going wear Ike down." She pushes herself up from her chair. "Now why don't you set the table while I finish this pot pie. We're going to need sustenance to make it through in one piece."

❧❧❧

BOB AND BUTTERBEANS start barking an hour later, as loud as they had been the day Snowflake got eaten. Grammy and I exchange a glance. She turns off the stove, then washes her hands in the sink across the kitchen.

"Here we go," she says. "Remember what we talked about. You've got this."

I peek through the doorway into the living room. Shadows bob past the curtains at the front window. A few seconds later the doorknob jangles, and in comes Pappap, wearing his Ziegler's Ferry Tours hat with the smiling Old Lucy embroidery. He, on the other hand, is not smiling, especially when he catches sight of me. Uncle Bobby and my cousin Will are right behind him. That branch of the family has always reminded me of rodents—pointy noses and chins, with a quiet and sneaky way about them. Maybe I'm not being fair, since they voted me into impersonating Old Lucy just so they didn't have to be bothered themselves. Grammy has always said holding grudges is wrong, but she probably wasn't thinking about this particular situation.

Will barrels through the living room and knocks into Bob. "Our Midnight is much better behaved than this," he says in a voice that makes me want to hit him.

I whistle for Bob, who immediately quiets down and trots over to where I sit in the kitchen. "Maybe our dogs just don't like you."

Will looks my way and gives me his usual dismissive once-over. It's as though I'm being inspected for worth. Finding none, he glowers at me with eyes the same color as my own. "Were you not listening when we said that Old Lucy was a family secret?" he says. "This is not a group activity."

The desire to feel my palm slapping his face is almost too strong to stop. Instead, I clamp my lips shut to keep things I shouldn't say from flying out. Grammy's right—they are going to throw a lot of things at me tonight. I need to keep it together.

Will sails past me and gives Grammy a big hug.

Uncle Bobby slinks into the kitchen. "Heya, Lemon—hear you've been having a time." Oh, for crap's sake—he's pretending to be concerned. Like it's not completely obvious. He has zero acting skills. He rubs my shoulder, showing me his *Concerned Relative* face. "Dad says you can take us down along the lake where you say this thing jumped out at you. Can we head down there in a few?"

Where *I say* this thing jumped out at me. *Right.*

A fission of nerves pulls at me. The idea of being at the lake right now, out in the open, close to the water, exposed . . . it's not exactly appealing. All the threats in my life are coalescing, offering me up to man and monster.

Grammy pulls a pitcher of iced tea out of the refrigerator. "Can't we have dinner first? I don't want the pot pie to get cold."

"Don't worry, Ma," he says, grinning. "It won't take us but a minute. We'll see about Lemon's monster and be right back."

"*My* monster?" I narrow my eyes.

Will chuckles nastily. "You're the only one who's seen it, are you not?"

My teeth instantly slam together. It's tough not to stab him with the fork from the place setting in front of me. Maybe Grammy never should have mentioned Pappap telling her and my great-grandfather telling people outside the family about Old Lucy—or about Bobby and Will coming over to yell at me about breaking the code. It gave me a whole hour to stew about it, and now there's quality quasi-homicidal rage built up beneath my skin.

"You know what, Grammy?" I say, trying to project sweetness and light. "It's fine. They want to see where our Snowflake was killed, fine. I'll show them."

Her eyes widen, first at me and then at Will and finally at Pappap, who stands in the kitchen doorway. She has the good sense to be nervous based on my tone. I'll behave and play the game. I always have. But Pappap's smugness—he wears the expression like a mask—makes me hope the whole lake is teeming with murderous monsters so I can shove him and Will and Bobby into the water and be done with this whole thing.

Uncle Bobby skirts around the kitchen table and opens the back door. "Well, let's get this done, then."

The air outside is cool with a touch of humidity below the surface. Gray clouds hover low over the valley. They let me lead the way across the backyard and down the stairs, the boards creaking under our feet as we descend. A few birds squawk from the trees. The winds have picked up—enough to slam the incoming ripples in the lake against the rockier parts of the shoreline. My hair whips across my face. I haven't been down these steps since telling Darrin and Troy about the monster. All I can think about are teeth.

Big, pointy, sharp teeth, with strings of Skeet meat dripping off. I wipe my abruptly sweaty palms on the thighs of my jeans and scan the lake. It's rough waters, and I have no idea what that means as far as the lake monster is concerned. Suddenly, shoving anyone into the lake doesn't seem like something I want to do. I wonder how Troy's coming with borrowing the cameras from the station.

Pappap, Bobby, and Will are silent all the way to the bottom of the staircase. I stop short at the floating dock and peer around. No one's lurking in the trees, nor in the water, so that's something. The squat wooden boathouse jerks up and down in time with the waves. Will rushes past me to stand at the tall grass growing out of the muck at the edge of the lake.

"Dad, is the boathouse a little off-center?" Bobby says. "Did the earthquake knock it around a little? I heard you had an aftershock last night."

"Hain't nothing wrong with the dock or the boathouse," Pappap says. "You just ain't seen it in a while." It comes off like a dig at Bobby, but if it was meant that way no one reacts.

Bobby steps around me at the far edge of the floating dock and heads toward the door of the boathouse. He examines the hinges, like he knows what he's doing. He may have grown up in the house and used the boathouse for half his life, but there's being acquainted with something, and then there's having something deep in your soul. My grandparents' house—my house, I suppose—and this boathouse and this lake are anchored deep in me. I know every crevice and every chirr.

Pappap contents himself with staying where he is at the bottom of the stairs, almost next to me. "The Jenkins boy's boat was off to the left there, maybe a few hundred yards down the trail by the willows.

Another couple hundred yards down, around toward that marshy bit of land—that's where this business with the dog happened. Hain't nothing but a bear, I reckon."

I turn to insist it was *not* a bear when a quiet moan rankles off the water, just loud enough to hear over the wind and waves. I've heard that sound in my nightmares more times than I can count. I heard it the day the monster attacked Snowflake.

I heard it the night Skeet died. Pappap and Bobby are still yapping about the boathouse—neither of *them* seems to notice it, not even when it comes again, louder still.

Will, though, does. I can tell. He stands taller, straining to listen.

I take a half step back on the floating dock toward Pappap; he's still on the bottom step. The faint smell of rot hangs in the air.

"Pappap," I say, but that's all I get out before the boathouse rocks violently. The dock dips and throws me backward into Pappap's legs.

The sound of the boat banging against the sides of the slip is louder than my heart beating. Scrolls of water froth up and soak Bobby, now clinging to the boathouse door, from the waist down. Pappap brushes against me on his way to Bobby, and I seize his wrist. He shakes me off and keeps going.

Will sloshes through the tall grass. He doesn't react when I yell at him to stop, to get away—but he reacts when the dock, boathouse and all, lurches sideways on a lake that now seems to be boiling. The boards buckle, and the bow of Pappap's boat comes crashing through the front door. It would have skewered Bobby if he'd been standing where he'd been only seconds before. Will windmills toward him, sending up great arcs of water.

Then Pappap's in the lake, too.

The monster has come to introduce itself.

The thought is so absurd that it knocks me out of my stupor. A scream rips out of me. The dock is broken into pieces, and my feet are drenched. I launch myself into the water, fighting past chunks of wood. Will has almost reached Bobby. I stop to look for Pappap, but he's not heading in that direction. Instead, he's floundering toward his banged-up boat, now drifting in the choppy water. Part of the Old Lucy costume—the head piece, I think, drapes over the starboard side near the stern.

Of course Pappap is more concerned about Old Lucy.

I push down the dread screaming through my veins and turn back toward Will and Bobby. The stink of rot spikes. The water-slick skin of vast grayish jaws and that anvil-shaped head burst out of the lake and latch onto Will's arm.

His high-pitched wail even gets Pappap's attention. Pappap tosses the Old Lucy latex aside and dives below the surface.

I tear through the chop. Bobby's stabbing at the monster with a jagged plank. Blood foams in the water—Will's, the monster's, maybe both. My legs are hollow rubber, but I keep swimming, pulling with all my strength.

I'm going to die. That thing is going to eat half my family. It's going to eat me. All because Pappap refused to believe me. This is so stupid.

I'm close enough to see the monstrous teeth and the wrecked and bloody remnants of Will's arm flopping in the water. The monster screams—a sound as terrible as anything I've ever heard—and releases him. I snag the collar of Will's shirt and freestyle, one-armed, back to shore, sure at any second sharp teeth will crunch through the bones of my feet, just as I dreamed.

Will's body is completely limp. With luck he's just passed out from shock or pain and isn't dead. Of course I want my cousin to be okay, but all of this is going to come back on me in the end. Pappap will insist I didn't try hard enough to get him to believe me. Or worse, he'll—my brain shuts off to that line of thinking. Now isn't the time. I yank on the grass to get myself up onto solid ground. My soggy clothes weigh me down, make it hard to slide over the path, especially with all of Will's weight.

Grammy's suddenly next to me, helping me pull him from the water. Will's arm ends at the elbow, nothing there more than a gossamer of torn tissue, leaking blood. We get him to the other side of the trail, away from the lake. Grammy ties her kitchen towel just below his bicep, swearing incessantly—words I've never heard her use before.

I scramble to Will's other side and feel for a pulse at his neck. It's there, but not very strong.

Bobby and Pappap crawl out of the water about ten yards away.

"I'll call the ambulance," Grammy yells to them and heads back to the stairs.

Bobby skids to a stop at my side. He pushes me out of the way. Pappap takes me by the shoulders and nudges me behind him, even farther off the trail. They pat Will down, maybe looking for other injuries.

My throat is raw from the screaming and the wind and the water I swallowed. I should be feeling something—terror, sadness, some kind of mean-spirited glee—but there's a numbness now settling over me as heavy as a blanket. Mentally, anyway. Physically, the realization that I'm sitting on something sharp hits me. I shift sideways. There's a piece of busted-up dock, a torn chunk of pink latex, a couple shards of glass. There's even what looks like a hunk of metal broken off of Pappap's boat, and a weird cone-shaped metal thing the size a child's shoe. I set it all aside, in case he wants it.

Picking through the debris is at least a distraction from my alarming lack of emotion and the blood soaking into the ground.

Grammy flies back down the stairs a few minutes later, a quilt—the same quilt I've been wrapped up in twice now—in her arms. She smooths it over Will and tucks it around his shoulders.

Pappap pushes himself up and eases Grammy down into his spot. He glances at the lake, then back at me. He sighs and holds out his hand to me. Part of me wants to ignore him, like he's been ignoring me. There's a look in his eyes, though. Something I've never seen before in him: regret. I take his cold fingers, let him tug me up off the grass.

He pulls me close and slings his arm around my shoulders. He murmurs in my ear, "Hain't never seen anything like this. You have to understand—this is all—I thought you—I didn't see nothing like this coming. This is my fault. All of it."

13

TROY

A FTER THE EIGHTH TEXT COMES through asking how Lemon's holding up after Vern's arrest, I turn my ringer off. Half are from people
who called her a murderer yesterday. Trying to pretend they care
now is crap. They're probably just looking for dirt to spread around. I
go back to flipping through my college acceptance letters. Mom asked
me again today about making a choice. Right after school, too. Like she
couldn't wait until after dinner to make me miserable.

My phone screen pops on—this time from a number I don't know.
Let it go to voice mail, keep sorting letters. Got a pile of colleges I *don't*
want to go to, at least. That's progress. I should just throw *all* the letters
in that pile and be done with it. Definitely not making any decisions
beyond what I have anyway.

I wish a flash of inspiration would hit me. I owe it to Lemon to pick
a future. Show her I'm not some jerk who can't make up his mind.

It's Lemon's name that lights the screen a few seconds later.

"Bored already?" I ask first thing.

"Did your dad call you?" Lemon sounds breathless, like she's been running.

"About what?"

"My cousin Will got attacked in the lake. The ambulance just came and went. It's . . . it's bad, Troy."

I bolt upright. Acceptance letters go flying. "You're okay?"

"Yeah, but—can you go get Darrin and come over to the house? I want to talk through a few more ideas about how to deal with the monster. Pappap wants to hear what we've come up with."

"Mr. Z . . . wants me and Darrin . . . at your house." It's as though Lemon just proclaimed the sun is green—nothing about it computes.

"Don't think about it too much—just be glad he finally believes me."

"He's not going to try to feed *me* to the monster, is he?" It's a joke, but it doesn't come out like one.

"I doubt it. He's pretty freaked out. It's not every day you see your grandson get half-eaten by a monster that you were sure didn't exist."

LEMON ANSWERS THE door, both Butterbeans and Bob pacing the floor around her feet and panting. Lemon's hair is down, pushed behind her ears. Smear of mud down one side of her face. Behind her, Mr. Z doesn't look much better. The word *bedraggled* comes to mind. The frown on his face makes me think Lemon got it wrong—he doesn't want us here at all.

"Well, don't just stand there all day," he snaps.

"Have you heard anything about Will?" I ask when Lemon shuts the door behind us. Darrin's been quiet the whole ride over. He rubs her arm, gives her a smile. Thought for sure he'd be all over the place with excitement—maybe the fact that this is dangerous has sunk in.

Lemon shakes her head. "Grammy said she'd call."

"My mom's at the hospital again tonight," Darrin says. "Maybe she can find something out."

"Hain't no reason to bother your mother," Mr. Z says. "Pearl will call with news." He sinks into his battered recliner. Bob jumps up, wedges himself under Mr. Z's arm.

Lemon shrugs, nods to the couch. Not that being around Mr. Z is ever relaxing, but the air is so thick with tension it would be chewy if I took a bite. Darrin claims a spot farthest away from Mr. Z on the ugly couch. He doesn't even pet Butterbeans when the dog collapses onto his feet. That's when it hits me—Darrin's scared. Not worried, or even nervous. He's thoroughly scared. Guess I am, too, though I'm trying to be cool about it. I don't know if it's Mr. Z or the monster, but each minute that goes by, I'm more and more wired.

Maybe this'll even keep the Jenkins clan away from Lemon's house. Give them second thoughts that Lemon's to blame for Skeet, anyway.

I sit on the other end of the couch. My leg joggles up and down.

Mr. Z leans forward, elbows on knees. "Either of you boys have thoughts about what we're dealing with here? Lemon told me you been doing research."

"No, sir," I say. "The only person who's gotten a look at the monster is Lemon."

"Until today," she says. "Hey, any luck with the underwater camera equipment?"

"What's this now?" Pappap says.

Lemon swivels toward Mr. Z. "I had an idea to start looking at ways people control invasive species, but Troy said that might be useless if we don't actually know what this thing is—because if you want to kill something, you have to know what *won't* kill it."

"That's a real smart thought, Troy."

I bristle at the surprise in his voice. Don't know why—should be used to it by now.

"Right," Lemon says. "Because Troy *is* smart. A bunch of years ago you got some underwater . . . what are they called . . . ROV cameras for the station, so Troy's going to see if he can lay hands on one."

Mr. Z's eyes harden. "Steal one, you mean?"

"Pappap, do you want to listen, or do you want to start a fight?"

His frown deepens, but he doesn't say more.

I clear my throat. "Uh, no. No luck. I snuck a look at my dad's laptop—the equipment is there. It's just locked down."

"Like it *would* be at a police station." Mr. Z's jowls shake. "Fool kids. It hain't as fancy as the one I got for the station, but I got me a few of them fish cams last year so tourists could see what's under the water. Never could figure out how to hook 'em up. Would something like that work for what you have in mind?"

Darrin says, "Maybe. Are they motorized? Like can you control where it goes via an app or a remote?"

"They attach to a fishing line," Mr. Z says.

"It means getting close to the water, if that's the case," Lemon says, apprehension in her eyes.

"No way," I say, just as Mr. Z thunders, "You ain't doing no such thing."

"I'm not saying we have to go *in* the water." She tucks her hair behind her ear again. "And I don't want to—believe me. But . . . after we talked about it the other day, I got to thinking how we make it work. We have a few kayaks—"

"Forget it, Lemon. Your grandmother would skin me alive for even thinking about it. You hain't going anywhere near the lake."

"Can I finish?" She shoots him an exasperated look.

If it was tense before, it's more so now. Mr. Z's face is turning eggplant. Even Butterbeans is alert, swinging his thick head between Mr. Z and Lemon. It's weirdly fascinating watching her talking back to him.

"Anyway," Lemon says, scowling, "I thought we could get the kayaks out and maybe attach the cameras to the bottom somehow. The motorized ROVs could pull the kayaks out into the lake—and the kayak would act like a buoy to give us a visual of where the camera is located in the lake."

"How would we do that *now*?" Darrin says. "Without the motorized ones?"

"What about loading the kayaks onto the roof rack of the car, Pappap? There's that public dock over near Peter's Island. We could put one of the kayaks in the water over there and let it float. See what we can see. That should work, right?"

"How tight does your fish cam clip onto the fishing line?" I ask.

"I can't rightly say," Mr. Z says. "Why?"

I say, "If it's pretty tight, we could cast it out into the lake with a fishing pole from the stairs out back. Use a reel with a full spool—you can get, what, at least thirty yards out in into the water that way."

Darrin says, "I don't mean to state the obvious, but could one of the ferries go out with a cam attached to it? The ferryboats are big, so the monster would have to be King freaking Kong to outsize those, right? Please tell me the monster isn't that big."

"It's big, but not ferry big," Lemon says.

Darrin's visibly relieved.

"How many fish cams do you have, Pappap?" Lemon says. "Couldn't we do *all* of that—ferry, kayak, and reel?"

Mr. Z makes a noise in the back of his throat, then says, "Ain't happening tonight. Sunset's in about an hour—hain't none of you setting foot nowhere near that lake when it's low visibility."

Lemon says, "Well yeah, but we could cast from the stairs right now."

"Too windy," Pappap says, jaw clenched. "And the fish cams are over in the ferry office. I'll get them tomorrow. I hardly have no right to ask him, but maybe Bobby can help."

"You really think the hospital's just going to patch up Will's arm and let him walk out of the hospital tonight? And that Uncle Bobby's going to be okay with leaving Will after what happened?" Lemon says. "I don't think so. We're the only ones you've got, Pappap. And if you think I'm going to let you do it by yourself, you can forget it."

Mr. Z's face reddens again. "*Let* me?"

"Yeah, *let* you. I might not be able to boss you around right now, even if I am the Old Lucy designee—but Grammy can. I'll tell her if you shut me out. And don't plan on doing anything stupid because I'll tell on you for that, too."

Now Mr. Z's face has gone eggplant once more. Old man's going to have a heart attack.

"You want to pick your next works very carefully."

"I'm just trying to stop you from getting yourself killed." Lemon's voice is suddenly gentle. "Grammy would be really mad."

The room descends into silence. Darrin looks at me—I can tell he wants me to say something, break the standoff. Finally, I say, "Uh . . . shouldn't we maybe come up with some way to keep people away from the lake?"

When Lemon and Mr. Z keep eyeballing each other, I say, "We know there's a monster now—but the whole town has thought that for a long time. Shouldn't we, I don't know, try to stop people from coming out here? Especially if we're going to be launching cameras tomorrow? It might be hard to answer questions about what we're doing. Top of trying to keep folk from being eaten, that is."

Mr. Z sits forward. He still looks like he might explode out of pure fury. "Well, now, that's something I *can* do. Have to go make a few phone calls." He heaves himself out of the recliner. Bob barks at him as he disappears down the hall.

Lemon blows out a long, quivering breath.

Darrin laughs, though it mostly sounds like shock. "What the hell just happened?"

"Pappap's trying to assert his dominance," Lemon deadpans, then immediately cracks up. Bob hops off the chair, moves to Lemon's side.

He leans into her. "He doesn't like that I have any power over Old Lucy or anything else."

"Maybe he should have stepped in to stop you from being voted in as the family impersonator then," Darrin snarks. "Family never really sees you as you are—not when you're our age. They have this idea of you in their heads, and it's hard to get past it. If Ike had any idea who you are for real, he'd have known you'd boss it up about Old Lucy."

I grin. "He's obviously never done a group project with you."

"I don't know whether to take that as a good thing or a bad thing," she says.

"Good thing," I say.

"You get things done," Darrin adds. "You're just not obvious about it because you don't demand credit for organizing everybody."

"You make me sound . . . You know what? Never mind. I'll take it." She pauses, eyes wandering toward the hall. "I wonder what Pappap's doing."

"As long as he's not calling in a hit squad, I'm good." Darrin purses his mouth. "Ever hear of the Hollywood Star Whackers? We're not movie stars, obviously—I'm just saying that hitmen exist. It's a whole conspiracy."

"Of course it is," Lemon says, trying not to laugh. "Sounds like you're starting to believe in conspiracy theories a little more."

"Yeah, well, wouldn't you?" he says.

Now that Mr. Z isn't in the room, I relax. Start noticing things. A bloodstained quilt tossed in the corner. A pile of broken and twisted metal stacked on the floor behind the chair. Lemon sees me looking.

"It's stuff I brought up from the lake after the ambulance came," she says, quiet and serious. "Grammy will want the quilt—she made it. Do you mind taking it to the sink in the kitchen? I want to get it into cold water for a soak now that I'm thinking about it."

I snag it. "What's that behind the chair?"

"I thought it might be part of Pappap's boat. You want to look?"

She takes the quilt from me and heads out to the kitchen. Darrin follows. They're going back and forth about something, but it's not loud enough to hear. Pieces of Mr. Z's boat, huh? I recognize some bits— chunks of fiberglass and aluminum that used to be part of a hull. But not the small, metal, pyramid-shaped thing. I palm it. Weighs only a few pounds but it looks heavier. I take it out to the kitchen, crowd next to Lemon at the double sink.

"Can I borrow the sprayer for a second?"

She hands it to me. She and Darrin are debating the best place on the stairs to cast a line while I spray the mud off the doodad. With all that dirt washed away, small buttons emerge along the bottom. The buttons don't have any markings, but below them, a symbol's carved into the dull metal. It's hard to see, maybe a series of circles.

I pass the sprayer back to Lemon, squint at the symbol. "Hey, can you tell what this is?"

Darrin takes it from me, holds it up to the light. "Maybe it's a company logo." He shrugs, tosses it back to me.

"It's weird the way it—"

"The lake will be off-limits as soon as Gerry's office processes the paperwork," Mr. Z says from behind me. I jump, nearly the drop metal thing into the sink.

"How did you manage *that*?" Lemon says.

"Hain't nothing big," he says. "We can talk about it later. Right now, you and me have to go. Your grandmother called through—she wants us at the hospital."

I glance at Lemon. That doesn't sound good.

She switches off the faucet, shoves the quilt into the sink. "Okay, let's go. I just need a pair of shoes." She turns to me, squeezes my hand. Doesn't move for a few seconds—like we're holding hands. If Mr. Z notices, he doesn't say. Darrin does, though—he waggles his eyebrows at me.

"I'll text you guys later," Lemon says. "Sorry to rush you off."

"No big deal," Darrin says. "I'd call you the turd of my heart, but I know you hate it." He grins. "Let us know when you want to get the fish cams in the water. We want to be there."

Mr. Z's face gives away the fact that he'd rather twist off both our heads, but he manages to hold his tongue. Maybe Lemon's getting through to him after all.

❧❧❧

DAD'S PULLING INTO the driveway when I get home. He swings open the door to his cruiser, gives me a wave. I wait for him at the front door.

"I suppose you already know about Lemon's cousin," he says.

I nod.

"Busy couple of weeks," he says. "Now there's this business with the bacteria."

"Bacteria?"

Dad scratches his chin. "High bacteria levels in the lake. It's the damnedest thing. Ike called me a bit ago—guess he and Pearl stopped at the ferry dock this morning, said their water monitoring picked up some anomalies. He said he meant to call me, but then his grandson . . ."

Dad keeps talking, but I'm focused on the bacteria level thing. *This is Mr. Z's plan?* "What's that mean, though? High bacteria levels?"

"It means I had to call everyone and his brother to close the lake to traffic and fishing until the environmental folks can do some special testing." He opens the front door, lets me into the house. "I was going to put a wider alert out, anyway, see if I can get the Game Commission out to figure out what's causing the wildlife to attack. I bet my badge it's about the earthquake and aftershocks. Anyway, I still have some calls to make before I can kick off for the night."

"Why is bacteria enough to get the lake closed off so fast?" I lean against the wall in the mudroom, cross my arms over my chest.

"Bacteria's dangerous to people," Dad says.

"So are lake monsters."

"Yeah, but folks get nervous about bacteria because they fish out at the lake—they eat the fish. Old Lucy—they figure nothing bad is ever going to happen to them. Plus, tourist season starts in a few weeks. If it's not people looking for Old Lucy, they're fishing or hiking around the lake, going camping. But with luck, we can get everything taken care of before that's a problem." He pauses, looks at his phone. "Dammit, I'm going to have to call the Fish and Boat Commission and ask them to hold off on stocking the lake. You make sure you and Lemon and Darrin stay clear, all right? With the way things are going, it's probably some crazy flesh-eating virus floating around in the water."

"With how things are going?" A sluggish fog hits me. Being scared and tense is exhausting.

Dad frowns and heads into the living room. "What's next—swarm of locusts? Forty days of rain? It's like a curse has come to Devil's Elbow."

14

T R O Y

PRINCIPAL SHOWALTER SAYS EDUCATION WAITS for no man. Sometimes it does—holidays, first day of deer hunting season, big snows. Even got a half day off out of the earthquake. This bacteria thing, though? It's serious enough for a full day off. Text from the school said bacteria could affect the town's water supply.

At least I don't have to come up with an excuse to bail on school now.

Feels weird knowing the bacteria thing is total crap. It's for sure going to feed Darrin's conspiracy theory noise. I try to keep an open mind about anything being possible, but keeping secrets is hard—the whole *three can keep a secret if two are dead* thing. It's a surprise no one has ever taken Old Lucy public. Guess that's different.

My bedsheets are too hot. I kick them off, stare at the ceiling. Lemon texted from the hospital last night before I fell asleep. Will's not doing too good. Not that it's stopping Mr. Z from going ahead with the plan—said he told Lemon to cover for him with Mrs. Z and Bobby, since he wasn't at the hospital. He ran out to the ferry office, took most of the fish cams back to their house. Wants to be ready to look for the monster, I guess.

No text from Lemon this morning, though, about Will *or* when we're meeting up. Amelia messaged to say she heard something was happening out at Lemon's, asking if everyone was okay. That girl is on top of everything. My brain can't wrap itself around her and Lemon skipping school yesterday. Lemon's always been a rule-follower. Mr. Z is strict. Everything's changed now, not just for Lemon. Whatever—just glad Vern got his ass handed to him ... and Lemon *did* get a prom dress, one that I'm imagining her in right now, imagining pulling her close, the feel of her skin.

The thought of my hands on her won't do me any good. It'll never happen. Doesn't stop my brain from going there, though—until the lake monster intrudes, bringing with it an image of what Will's arm must look like.

Even though school's closed, I crawl out of bed and head to the bathroom for a shower. By the time I'm done, the smell of French toast cooking tunnels up the stairs. I throw on jeans, a T-shirt, my hoodie. Pick up the jacket I was wearing last night. Something clunks out of it, hits the floor. It rolls under my bed.

I grumble, get down on my knees to reach for it.

It's the metal pyramid thing Lemon rescued from the shoreline. Guess I must have shoved it in my pocket when Mr. Z came back into the kitchen last night. I sit down at my desk and turn the lamp on, look it over again. That symbol—it's still really hard to see. The pencil on top of my laptop gives me an idea. I rifle through my desk for a sheet of thin paper, hold it over the symbol. Scratch the pencil tip over the symbol until I can see the shape of it coming through. I study it, eyeball the metal piece, then sketch out what the symbol looks like to me—almost like a dog bowl with several thick, horizontal stripes running around the outside of it, continuing down into the well of the bowl before they hit the center, where another ring of circles bubbles up. Not much of an artist, but at least my chicken-scratch captures the optical illusion.

I text a photo of it to Darrin and Lemon, ask if they know what it is—Amelia, too, because why not? If anyone will be able to track it down, it's her.

Mom calls from the bottom of the steps, "Do you want breakfast, Troy?"

"You see school's canceled?" I say as I'm rounding into the kitchen a minute later. "You ever—"

A couple of old guys in navy suits in the middle of the kitchen turn to look at me. One's got a walrus mustache. The other—he's got a large square head topped by gelled-back hair. Looks like a motorcycle helmet.

Mom smiles, beckons me forward. She's underdressed in sweatpants next to the suits.

"This is my son, Troy," she says to them. To me, she says, "This is Agent Buck." She gestures to the guy with the mustache, then the other. "And this is Agent Mills."

Agent Buck offers his hand. I take it. Agent Mills shakes, too. Does that thing that screams *I'm a jackass*: squeezes hard enough to grind my finger bones.

Buck says, too cheerfully, "So, I've heard you all have had an earthquake in these parts over the last week or two. That must have been a real surprise."

"Yes, sir," I say. He looks familiar. Definitely seen him before.

"And now there's a bacteria problem at the lake," Mills says. "That can't be a coincidence."

"No, sir. Probably not." Who are these guys? "Where's Dad?" I say to Mom. Probably obvious that I'm fighting to keep the irritation off my face. These guys in my house are the last thing I want to deal with right now.

"I'm right here," Dad says from behind me. He sidles up next to Mom, nods to the agents. "You really didn't have to meet me here at the house. The station would have been just fine. Or I would have come to your offices. Not that I'm not appreciative of you coming out here."

"We wanted to meet right away," Mills says. It's like he's reading from a military thriller script, all urgent. "Seems as though a pretty big problem is brewing out at the lake."

"I didn't think it was big enough for the feds to be called in," Dad says. "I thought the locals would be taking care of things."

Feds?

"Just a precaution." Buck scratches his mustache. "We're part of a special department at the US Geological Survey that handles earthquake activity, as well as reports of unusual activity related to marine ecosystems. And when the medical examiner determined the Jenkins boy had died from a large animal bite, combined with everything else happening, we were alerted."

It takes real effort to feign surprise about Skeet—this is supposed to be brand-new information to me, at least as far as anyone who isn't Dad knows. And since when do guys from the Geological Survey dress in suits? Aren't they supposed to be scientists and big outdoors guys? I'd expect lumberjack boots and flannel shirts, not dress shirts and ties.

"Your bacteria readings were alarming," Mills adds, still coming off dramatic.

Mom says, "I didn't realize a small earthquake could shake things up so much, no pun intended."

Mills says, "You'd be surprised—it can change an entire environment in a second."

"Let's talk in the living room," Dad says. "Let my family have their breakfast."

Buck nods gravely, says to me, "Troy, your mother tells us you spend a lot of time at the lake because of a friend of yours."

Dad narrows his eyes. I can tell what he's thinking—there are rules about questioning minors. I turned eighteen two months ago, but he still thinks of me as a kid. I can't think of a reason not to answer, though.

"Yeah. Lemon's house is at the lake. Been friends since we were little."

Buck opens a notebook, glances at the page. "That's Lemon Ziegler, seventeen. Lives with her grandparents, Ike and Pearl Ziegler. Parents deceased. Her grandfather was sheriff of Devil's Elbow for thirty years. Ike's grandson, Will, is the one killed last night."

"Killed?" Now *that's* new information. "But . . . he made it to the hospital."

"I'm sorry to be the one to tell you this, son," Mills says, "but the boy passed early this morning. There were some complications from blood loss."

Lemon must be . . . I don't know what she must be. Sad, frustrated, mad. Things are complicated. Lemon cautioned Mr. Z last night against doing anything stupid, but agents poking their heads into everything— it'll probably fast-forward whatever dumb ideas Mr. Z's got if he thinks they might interfere with or find out about Old Lucy. He's gonna get himself killed. Maybe get Lemon killed . . . all because federal agents are now in the mix.

Finally, I say, "That's . . . sad news. Thanks for the update."

Mom's hands wash over each other. "Your father and I were going to tell you over breakfast. I don't know Will at all, but I grew up with Bobby and his wife. They must be devastated. And Lemon—I can't imagine how she's feeling. This is just terrible."

"Let's get moving," Dad says, all but herding the agents from the kitchen. Mills doesn't like it from the way his mouth gets all tight. My guess is he needs something from my dad, though—he lets himself be corralled.

Mom pushes me into a chair at the kitchen table.

I slide the blue placement out of the way, rest my arms on the table. "So what happens now?"

"With Will? I'm not sure. Lemon and her family have probably gone home, if that's what you mean. Bobby and Nan will have funeral arrangements to make. I doubt they'll have the funeral in Devil's Elbow—they live out near Lock Haven."

She brings a platter of French toast to the table, moves the ugly centerpiece out of the way to set the platter down. Hands me an empty plate and a fork. I was hungry when I smelled the toast the first time. Now, though? Lost my appetite. Shove a few pieces down my throat anyway—no telling what today might end up looking like.

The feds are still in the living room with Dad when I drift through on the way back to my bedroom. The talk is about the geography of the lake, nothing very interesting. Agent Buck looks up at me, gives me a nod.

It bothers me that I can't remember where I've seen him.

By the time I'm back in my room, my phone is flashing with text messages.

From Lemon: *Will died. I'm going with Grammy/Pappap to my aunt/ uncle's house for the day. Text you later.*

From Darrin: *About that symbol—call me. It can't be what I think it is.*

From Amelia: *OMG—did you find my speaker? A little cone-shaped metal one? I've been looking everywhere. Bring it to school tomorrow?*

When has Amelia ever been at Lemon's house? I'm tempted to text her back to ask, but it's Darrin I get in touch with first.

He picks up before the phone even rings, hisses, "What do you know about time travel?"

"Is this another conspiracy thing?"

"The symbol," he says impatiently. "It's related to time travel. Think wormholes."

"Wormholes? What do worms have to do with it?"

"For real? Worm*holes*. Have I taught you nothing? Basically a short-cut that connects two different points in space-time. *Time* travel."

"Again, I say . . . so what?"

The sigh that comes over the phone is full of pity for me for being oblivious to whatever Darrin thinks he knows. I nearly laugh.

Darrin says, "Ever hear the theory that the Loch Ness monster is really a time traveler?"

"No, but—"

"There are some people who think Nessie goes back and forth between current times and the Triassic period using wormholes, and that she's really a dinosaur. A plesiosaur, to be exact. It would explain why this fucking monster just randomly appeared in the lake."

"That's great, but what's the pyramid thing got to do with it, smart guy?"

"That's where I'm stumped." I can hear his frustration through the phone. "But if there are time travelers from the past, maybe there are time travelers from the future. Maybe it's . . . I don't know. Something future-y that some guy dropped."

He's completely serious.

"Future-y. Uh-huh. Amelia says it's a speaker."

"A speaker? Why does she know anything about this at all?"

"I texted her the rubbing. Thought maybe she could help. Says she dropped it out at Lemon's. Okay, not at Lemon's house, but at the lake. And if you say you think Amelia's from the future, I'm hanging up."

Darrin cackles. "Nah. She's kind of hot, but not in that *I'm a time traveling cyborg* kind of way. It's a bummer it's just a speaker, though. Is it a Bluetooth speaker for streaming music?"

"Didn't text her back yet to ask."

"Well, don't. Lemon finding a speaker with a wormhole symbol and Amelia saying she lost it at the same time is a little coincidental." I want to make fun of him for going all-in on being suspicious—but anything is possible. He adds, "I may think Amelia's low-key harmless, but you know me—I'm not one for coincidences."

"For once, I kind of agree." The sound of my fingers drumming on my desk is maddening, but I can't stop. "It would mean Amelia's been hiking around the lake. She seem like an outdoor girl to you?"

"Not so much. I guess we'll tell Lemon about it and see what she thinks."

"Might be awhile—Will died."

"Damn," he says, quietly. "Did Lemon text you about it?"

"Federal agents told me first."

A beat, then Darrin says, all incredulous, "Feds came to your house?"

"They're here now—downstairs with my dad. Know how you don't believe in coincidences? They're here to investigate the lake—something about the earthquake being the cause of everything." I lower my voice. "Including the lake monster."

"Wait—they know about the lake monster?"

"No, not like that." I run my hand over the top of my head. "They probably know about Old Lucy—least the fact that our town has a lake monster. And cause of death came back on Skeet—they know he was bit in half by an animal instead of chopped up by motor blades. And who knows what the hell Mr. Z or Lemon's uncle told the police about what ambushed Will at the lake."

"So what are you saying?"

"Dad always says government usually moves at the speed of a sloth. We probably have time before the USGS sets up. Having 'em out at the lake—doing whatever they're gonna do—might get in our way."

He pauses. "Maybe we should let them."

I pull back the phone and give it a look. "What if they kill whatever's in the lake?"

"Isn't that a good thing?" Darrin says, exasperated again.

"Yeah, but if it's public like that, everybody will say they killed Old Lucy. Then what?"

"Then Lemon can have a life is what."

"But you heard what she said," I say. "This town will go under. She cares about it."

"So you do, too—naturally."

I could live without the sarcasm.

"You want your parents and sister to live in a shithole?"

"You raise a good point. So what do you want to do?"

"I know where Mrs. Z has a hidden house key." Even saying the words makes my whole body itch. "I can be at your house to get you in fifteen minutes. What do you think?"

Darrin hoots. "Oh, you are living dangerously, Troy, and I'm not talking about the monster. Ike is going to literally murder you. Fuck it, come pick me up. If we're going to die, at least we'll die together."

15

T R O Y

T HE KEY TO LEMON'S HOUSE is under the flowerpot to the left of the front door—the one filled with purple pansies. Dad planted the same ones at our house a week ago. I've seen Lemon reach under the flowerpot a million times. Trying to talk myself into getting the key myself, though . . . even Darrin's trying to pretend like we don't have to do it. He's straightening the basket on the front of Mrs. Z's bicycle, wasting time. I sure as hell don't want to just walk into Lemon's house, but we need to get moving before the USGS agents make their move.

Finally, I slide the flowerpot over and take the key.

"Okay, so what's our big play?" Darrin says. "Explain it to me like I'm five. How are we supposed to magically solve this for Lemon before the feds get here?"

"Get the fish cams. Lemon said Mr. Z went out last night, brought a couple of them back here. Can't imagine they'll be too hard to find."

Darrin snorts. "And you don't think Ike's going to have our heads on spikes for breaking into his house on a random Wednesday, rooting through his stuff, and playing with his toys?"

"We have a key. Technically we're not breaking in."

"Yeah, I suppose."

"We don't have to do anything crazy. Cast a fishing line a bit from the stairs. See what we can see. And I think we can tie one of the kayaks to the top of the Buick—look at what's in the water near the public dock. Look at it this way: Mr. Z already signed off on the plan."

Like I'm totally calm. Like there's not an anxiety-sized hole in my stomach.

"Did you tell Lemon about the agents?"

"I texted her. Thought about letting it be—she's probably busy doing other stuff, taking care of her grandparents. It's got to be tough to lose a cousin."

"This is the very definition of being hoisted by one's own petard," Darrin said. "Ike really stepped in a pile of horseshit, and now Will's paying for it."

I shrug. I'm trying not to think about what happened to Will, all things considered. "You're stalling. We should just get this done—we promised Lemon we'd help. Have her back."

"I'm not exactly excited to potentially be monster chow, but I see your point. This is our chance. Your chance, too—be the hero and all that."

The words practically sparkle. I swear under my breath. Darrin always knows just how to get me. *Be the hero.*

Before I have a chance to talk myself out of it, I unlock the door and head in. Butterbeans and Bob aren't barking at the door like I expect them to be—Lemon and Mr. and Mrs. Z must have taken the dogs to Bobby's house with them.

Makes sense. Can't leave them home all day by themselves without someone to feed and walk them.

I pause by the wall of family photos just inside the door. Seen them a million times. Lemon in the first grade, hair in pigtails and a gap-toothed smile. A shot of Lemon, Darrin, and me in the second grade—in Mr. Z's boat. Mr. and Mrs. Z's wedding photo, the same for Lemon's parents. I barely remember them.

Darrin clears his throat. "Save your Lemon-scented fantasies for another time. I can smell them a mile away. We're on a deadline here, are we not?"

The fish cams are on the kitchen table, along with one of Mr. Z's fishing poles. Takes us about five minutes to download the fish cam app to my phone, connect everything, and set it all up. Neither of us talk much. I think about Lemon, though. How can I not? She's all around me in this house. Even a hint of her vanilla shampoo now and then. It's like she's in the hallway, about to walk into the kitchen and make me laugh. We've made cookies with Mrs. Z here. Lemon and I have worked through homework at this table. Talked about movies, made plans. All of us have.

"Jesus," Darrin says as I'm about to unlock the back door. "Your thoughts are loud."

"You already said that."

"Even Cara thinks you should just tell Lemon how you feel."

"Didn't ask for Cara's advice. Or yours. Let this go."

I swing open the door. The bright sun makes the shine off the lake almost blinding. It's not until we're at the stairs leading down to the floating dock that the full damage the monster did is visible.

"Holy fucking shit," Darrin says.

The boathouse is gone. The dock, destroyed. Pieces of them—the biggest about the size of flag—float in the water near the shore. The bow of Mr. Z's boat pokes out of a stretch of tall grass. Blood stains the shore and part of the path off to the left of where the dock used to be. It's not hard to imagine screaming, wood planks cracking. What *is* hard is imagining the size of the thing in the water. Lemon's described it a few times—at least what she saw of it. The monster has to be bigger than the picture in my head, though.

"Want to start over at the public dock first?" I say.

Darrin's shocked laugh drifts from behind me. "The farther from here we are, the better."

We find the kayaks on the side of the house, wrapped for over-wintering like they usually are around this time. Untying Mr. Z's knots to free them almost feels as intrusive as going into the house when no one's home. Some things you just don't mess with.

As we're carrying one of the kayaks to my car, my hands shake, trying to keep the hull steady. I'm a damn coward. I don't want to admit the state of the boathouse has me shook. Maybe only an idiot *wouldn't* be panicked. I don't know. Picking the less scary thing to do first—the public dock—feels like running away.

It feels like *not* picking a college because picking a future leaves my guts spinning. Not exactly, but not entirely different, either.

I toss Darrin the end of a length of rope from my trunk.

"You look like you're going to throw up," he says.

I shrug. "Let's just get this done."

We're both silent as we tie the kayak onto my roof and during the five minutes it takes to get to the dock. I maneuver around a few detour and closed signs. If Dad finds out I'm trespassing, well . . . he won't believe me that it's for a good cause. I have to keep reminding myself that this is all to help Lemon. Help the town. Can't believe this is what Lemon's been dealing with by herself. She's so much tougher than me.

The dock's down a tight, winding road. Pines loom on either side. Even though the monster's only been sighted on water, my palms start to sweat thinking of that thing rushing through the trees at us any second—crushing the car. Sending the Buick rolling, me and Darrin bouncing around with it.

My hands tighten on the wheel.

The sun filters through the pines in thin shafts of light. The dapples splatter over the road, almost like a welcome mat. Trees thin to reveal a small parking lot. I maneuver the Buick into the back spot where it's shadiest. Least that's what I tell myself. The reality is that back spot is farthest from the water. Doesn't help me if the monster *can* survive on land.

We're lugging the kayak to the dock when Darrin finally says, "I can't believe I let you talk me into this."

"It's just a normal day. We're hanging out."

"Yeah, and looking for a goddamn monster."

"At least maybe you'll get your proof that it's not an elephant."

He cracks up. "We could make a Devil's Elbow petting zoo if it *were* an elephant."

The dock is longer than the one at Lemon's—or that *used* to be at Lemon's. This one's not a floating dock—pylons are driven into the silt to hold the dock about two feet off the surface of the water. It's deep in this part of the lake. I've swum here more than a few times. Ten feet out, the lake bed drops something like forty feet. As a kid, I used to worry about the freshwater eels and the carp that live in the bottom. Imagined they'd bite my toes off or maybe pull me into the depths, drown me. Right now, eels and carp and Darrin's pet elephants would be the best-case scenario.

"You want to cut a length of fishing wire?" I hold out a set of snips. Doing something—anything—is better than being in my head right now. "Make it pretty long."

He scans the lake. "Lemon said we could just put the kayak in the water and let it go, but it doesn't seem like it'll float very far from the dock."

"I don't think either one of us wants to get in and paddle it out. Besides, I didn't bring an oar."

He gawks at me—and I can tell he's thinking the same thing I am. "What if we push the kayak out?"

"With what?"

He gestures at the trees. "Maybe we can find a long branch."

"I doubt there's anything just lying around that would be long enough to matter. I'll kick the kayak. Shoot it away from the dock. Maybe that'll help."

He snickers. "Finally, a benefit to being short—no one's going to be asking me to put my legs at risk."

I'm thinking about Will again.

It's weird knowing something hungry's out there. Knowing for sure. I'd always believed in Old Lucy the way you believe in gravity. Maybe you don't see it, but you know it's there. Gravity can kill you, too, but it's not actively malevolent.

The fish cam is finally secured to the fishing line, line is knotted to the kayak. Darrin nods at me, mouth pressed into a thin, tense line. I take the bow. Darrin takes the stern. I don't know about him, but I take careful, light steps to the end of the dock. Making footfalls that vibrate the water is a bad idea. Don't want to alert the monsters that there's a tasty meal waiting.

I hold my breath. We lower the kayak to the water. I freeze. Listen closely. Think of everything Lemon said about what she saw, heard. What she felt. All I'm getting is a light breeze, the sound of water lapping against pylons.

The kayak bobs in the water, clunks against the dock.

"I can go look for that branch," Darrin says. Can't take his eyes off the waves.

"No, I've got this," I say. "Keep a hold on me, though."

I lie down on the dock. Hang on to the edge and shimmy out, trying for as little movement as possible. I peek back at Darrin. He's already pale, horrified. He latches onto my shirt. Not sure if that's going to help much if the monster likes the look of my leg. Can't think too hard about it, though. I get a good grip on one of the boards set into the dock, swing my legs out.

"A little to the left." Darrin's voice is hoarse, urgent.

I shift at the waist. My foot connects with what feels like the kayak's hull. One deep breath—then a hard kick. Darrin tugs at me, frantic. Not sure if his silence is good or bad, but it doesn't matter: I contort myself to get my legs back on the dock, scramble away from the edge.

The kayak doesn't go far, but the wind is helping.

Darrin releases my shirt, blows out another breath. "Don't tell anyone, but I think I almost pissed my pants."

"Just think—we get to do it again back at Lemon's."

"Not with the kayak, though. Seeing the boathouse made my whole body pucker, but fishing off the steps will be way less fraught with peril." He pauses. "I didn't think about this, but how are we supposed to get the kayak and the fish cam back?"

"The water will eventually bring the kayak back to shore, won't it?"

"Maybe. It's a kayak, not a boat. What if the kayak turns over? What if it swamps and sinks?"

"Mr. Z will have one more reason to be mad at us then, I guess. If he makes a big stink, I'll take it out of my college fund. He can sue me."

Back at the car, I retrieve my phone from the seat, turn on the fish cam app. The video pops up murky. Not much to see—until I turn on the LED light attached to the cam. Clouds of dust turn the water murky in spots. Mostly it's just open water.

After fifteen minutes, Darrin says, "Think Skeet's family will lay off Lemon now that the coroner's report shows he was killed by . . . what did you say?"

"Large animal bite. And I don't know. Don't forget those rumors that Lemon is keeping and training Old Lucy to kill."

Darrin frowns at me. "Far be it from me to yuck anyone's conspiratorial yum, but no one in their right mind believes that."

"You think any of the Jenkinses are in their right mind?"

"Okay, fair." Darrin tilts his head to the side. "So how long are we going to sit here and watch?"

"I set the cam to record to my cloud account—we don't have to watch anything. Least not now." I glance up. Kayak's still upright. Looks like it's getting even farther away from the dock. Maybe floating toward Peter's Island.

"Out of all the places in the lake," Darrin says, "where do you think a fish that size would live?"

"What makes you think it's a fish? What makes you think it has a home? It could be a mammal—otters and manatees live in the water. They're mammals."

"Okay, fine, but otters also have a permanent burrow in the water. You know, home. Even the entrance is underwater."

"Been studying, huh?"

"Like you haven't," he says. "I'm surprised you haven't memorized entire books on animal science so you can impress our girl. Science is sexy and all that."

"Uh-huh." I give him a look. "Hey, I was thinking of sharks. Bull sharks and river sharks can live in fresh water. Or remember when there was that alligator loose in the river? It was, what, somebody's pet? It was only three feet long, but imagine if it had stayed lost for years? How big can alligators get? Sharks don't have a particular place they hang out in, but alligators build nests and burrow in mud."

I look up sharply, then down at my phone. I listen again, *really* listen. The shrill and cackling sound of bird song echoes all around me, but something is missing.

Darrin's eyebrows rise. "What?"

Can't quite put my finger on it—until I remember coming out here with Lemon and Darrin last year to fish off the end of the dock. Dad said the walleye were biting. Early in the morning, Darrin was all cranky about it being the butt crack of dawn. The thing about it—it was loud. Birds warbling, locusts chittering, frogs croaking.

My head pops up. Frogs. It's the *frogs*.

"Notice anything weird?"

Darrin shakes his head. "Should I?"

"Place should be full of chirps and grunts and clucks from frogs, but there's nothing. We've both spent a lot of time out here. You know what it should sound like. And there's been no fish on the screen—not one. Dad said the Fish and Boat Commission hasn't stocked trout yet, but there should be shad and crappies, schools of bluegills. Walleye. Even tadpoles."

"Can a single animal eat every fish and frog in or around the lake?" Darrin's voice is strangled.

"Might be a question for Mr. Z—he's the one who knows the lake better than anyone. He can maybe take a look at different parts when he goes out with the fish cam. If the fish are missing mostly from just this end of the lake—from here over to Lemon's house—maybe this is the monster's territory."

"Is that helpful?" he says.

"Maybe. USGS might be prone to giving up if they're looking in the wrong place—maybe we can do something to make that happen. You know, do something to direct their attention to another part of the lake while we're doing what we need to do."

Darrin's brows shoot up. "If you're suggesting we kill a couple of people and leave their bodies on shore over near the ferry dock as a distraction, I can't get on board with that. Homicide really isn't my thing. There are rules, you know? Laws about that sort of thing? I know you'd go out of your way to impress Lemon, but that's a line too far."

LEMON'S HOUSE IS exactly how we left it. Don't know what I expected. Can't take anything for granted now. Darrin was only joking about leading the USGS agents to other parts of lake. Still, he's not completely wrong about how far I'd go for Lemon. Stole a piece of chocolate from Lakebed Candies for her once when we were kids. Got in trouble for it, too, but I'd steal the whole damn store for her if it made her happy. The wind is gentler at the back of her house than it was at the public dock. My legs shake when I take the first step down the wobbly stairs. Part of my brain screams like a blubbering little kid. *What the hell are you doing? What the hell are you doing?* is on silent repeat.

I stop and breathe, realize I'm not as scared as all that. Not really. Dad told me once that each person only has so much fear. You spend it down, you're not as scared anymore. If that's true, I should be fearless. I'm not—but I'm not ready to jump out of my skin.

I take each stair, eyeballing the distance from me to the lake. I may not be scared, but I'm not suicidal. About a quarter of the way down, I stop.

Darrin's voice is choked when he says, "Good choice. Be a shame to deprive Lemon of a prom date after I worked so hard to make it happen." He hands me the fishing pole, fish cam already attached. "Too bad we don't have any bait. Maybe this would work better if we chummed the water."

"You really want to throw bloody chunks of meat down there? What if the monster never comes—you really think Lemon or Mrs. Z want to see rotting flesh after what happened to Will?"

Darrin shuts up. Probably shouldn't have brought up the idea of rotting flesh.

From where we're standing, the rocky lake bottom is visible close to shore. The trees overhanging the lake farther away cast long shadows into the water. The tops of the cooling towers from the nuclear plant on the other side of town are just visible over the treetops at the opposite end of the lake; steam clouds curl into the white clouds starting to roll in from that direction.

"Hey, did Lemon ever respond to your text about the agents?" Darrin says.

I shake my head. "Doubt messages from me are priority today."

"Right."

I get a good footing, cast the line. The breeze takes the line far out over the water. I lower myself onto the stair. Darrin sits one riser behind me. The fish cam app on my phone shows the same thing it did at the public dock: nothing much.

Hanging out on the stairs with a fishing pole feels a lot different from putting the kayak in the water. Doesn't mean I'm not keeping a close eye on the water, thinking about what could happen. When I can't stomach the scenarios I'm imagining anymore, I say, "So I take it since Cara weighed in about me and Lemon and that she's back on board with going to the prom as a group?"

"Yeah. She says she's got a dress—Old Lucy purple. Did you rent your tux yet?"

"I'm thinking about not getting one. Mom said she'd take me suit shopping instead. I don't have one."

Darrin snickers. "What did Lemon say about it?"

"Didn't tell her. Think she'd care?"

"Maybe. I'm just saying—maybe you want a tuxedo." A grin spreads across his face—the grin he gets when he's about to irritate the crap out of me. "It goes with the big movie cliché in your head, where Lemon suddenly realizes she's been in love with you the whole time. You sweep her off her feet, there's a sweet kiss set to swelling music. Flash forward twenty years to you guys and your kids cooing over your high school prom picture. You really don't want to be in a tux for that?" His voice rises to a falsetto. "*Oh, Lemon, Lemon, look at our sweet yellow-haired babies, Lemon, my love.*"

I twist around to punch him in the shoulder.

He rubs the spot, and in his normal voice says, "Besides, you don't want to look like one of the grief counselors who's been running around the school."

It clicks in my brain, just like that. I nearly drop the pole, lean to look at Darrin again. "The USGS agents at my house—think his last name was Buck—it was one of the grief counselors. *Knew* I'd seen him before."

"I think maybe you've got a touch of sun stroke, my guy." He flicks my forehead.

I bat his hand away. "Swear to God, same man. Same stupid mustache."

"Let's say I believe you," Darrin says. "If I were a conspiracy theory nut—and I am—I'd be making one very important connection right now: the grief counselors were making a big freaking deal about avoiding the lake. The guy I talked to was all, hey, the scene of the death will only prolong your feelings of sadness."

"You talked to one of them? I didn't know that."

"He didn't call me in personally, like they did to Lemon." He shrugs. "It was just in the hall. Between fifth and sixth period, I think. It was totally at random. He knew who I was—he said he'd heard I was a friend of Lemon's."

"Agent Buck mentioned Lemon to me, too."

Silence.

Darrin's mouth knots up, then he says, "Skeet died, what, less than twenty-four hours before the aftershock? Grief counselors were at the high school the day after—one day before Will was attacked and before the bacteria emergency Ike fabricated? You know what I'm going to say about coincidences." He nods toward the lake. "You want to bring the line in? Maybe cast out in a different spot?"

I reel in the line. Why not—we're not seeing anything on the app except more open water and the occasional piece of broken dock.

"So what do you think?" I say. "If the USGS agents want people to stay away from the lake, they don't need to pretend to be counselors. You're the self-proclaimed conspiracy nut. Make it make sense."

The line pulls.

"Let me think about it," he says.

I tug at the line, but it's not coming loose. On the app, there's nothing in the water. Maybe it's snagged on a broken chunk of dock. I slide down a step.

"What, may I ask, are you doing?" he says.

"I have to untangle the line."

"Have we learned nothing from last night? A safe distance is as far fucking away as possible from the water."

I hand him my phone. "Keep an eye on the cam—if you see anything I'll come right back up."

"I was sort of kidding about being a hero. Lemon's going to kick your ass when she finds out what you're doing."

My palms slick up the closer I get to the water. It looks calm. Rocks are still visible right near the shore. The tall grass is waving in the breeze—normal. I tug again at the line. Still stuck.

I reach the bottom stair, call over my shoulder, "Anything?"

"You're good. Crazy as a loon, but good. Proceed, dumbass."

I reach into the water. Cold as I would expect for April. The fishing line stretches taut. I follow it down until my fingers brush a hard surface. Yank lightly. Yank again.

"Troy. Troy. Troy. Back it up." Darrin's voice gets higher, louder with each word. "*Troy!*"

I jerk my head up. A swelling wave is zooming right at me. Darrin's scream is pure panic. I clamber backward, stairs digging into my back. He's got a handful of my shirt, ripping upward. My feet slip against the wet wood. Whatever's in the water—like I don't know—it keeps plowing. Darrin's momentum pulls me up one riser. It's enough to find my footing.

Darrin bellows, "Holy motherfucking shit!"

I flip over, hoist myself up, sprint up the stairs. Push Darrin to move faster. A deep groaning roars behind me. The staircase shakes more than normal. The sound of wood splintering blocks out everything else. Stink of dying things stuffs itself up my nose. I take the stairs two at a time, hoping like hell the wood doesn't fall away.

I don't look back.

16

LEMON

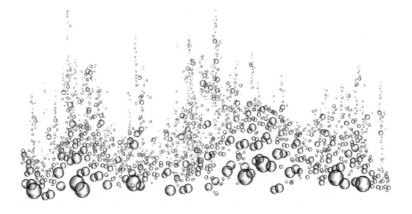

AN HOUR OF PAPPAP SCREAMING at me in the car is not my idea of a
good time. It's not my fault that my phone died while we were at
Uncle Bobby and Aunt Nan's, and I'm not to blame for not having
a phone charger with me at all times. It's not my fault that Troy and
Darrin's cell phone numbers aren't burned into my brain. And it's certainly not my fault that Pappap went berserk when I mentioned Troy's
text about federal agents stepping in to investigate the lake and then
insisted on speeding home right away.

It's not that I'm *not* concerned about the idea of agents snooping
around the lake to look at the earthquake and its impact, potentially
getting in the way of what we're doing to deal with the monster. I absolutely am. I wish I could call Troy, too, to get more detail about what's
happening. Pappap was on the verge of calling Sheriff Ramirez to demand answers until I reminded him it might look a little suspicious. It

was a miracle he put the phone down in a concession that I might actually be right. No one was more surprised than me when he apologized and hugged me—but he's been a jerk ever since. And worse during the car ride back to Devil's Elbow. He's convinced the agents are going to find out we've been faking the monster and expose the entire operation. He hasn't even stopped the car to let Butterbeans and Bob out to go to the bathroom, and now they're both whining and pawing at me, like I have control of the steering wheel.

I get Pappap's general irritation and Grammy's silence. I didn't talk to anyone for a solid week after Mom and Dad died, not even Troy and Darrin. Everyone deals with grief and guilt and disaster in different ways. I don't want to compare Snowflake's death to Will's, but there's just this awful, panicked dullness that catches you by the throat and throws you in a corner when you lose someone like that—and you see the moment they die. It slammed into me at the lake when I pulled Will to shore, just like it sank its hooks into me after I stopped screaming the day the monster ate Snowflake.

Pappap pulls into the driveway of our house. "Son of a bitch. What are them boys doing h—"

Screams punch through the open windows of the car. I know those voices.

"Stop the car! Let me out!" I yell.

"Merciful heavens!" Grammy says.

I throw open the door before Pappap comes to a complete stop behind Troy's Buick. My sneakers send up gravel as I skid onto the lawn and run full-out around the side of the house. Behind me I can hear Butterbeans and Bob zooming for their usual bathroom spot, but my mind is firmly on what might be happening behind the house.

"Lemon, now you wait," Pappap hollers.

The screaming gets louder with each step.

My knees buckle when I round into the backyard. Troy and Darrin stand at the top of the stairs—whole, from what it looks like. Troy's bent over, hands braced on his knees. Darrin has a grip on his arm. There's no blood.

I run, the thud of the blood in my veins pounding in my ears. Both of them screech when I barrel into Troy from behind. His head shoots up, and his eyes are wild. His face is green as cabbage. He catches me around the waist and reaches for what remains of the staircase railing.

"You scared me half to death," he says, before throwing his arms around me, too.

"*I* scared *you*?" The absurd thought of kissing him fills my head. Like really kissing him. Right here and now, with his chattering teeth and with Pappap probably right behind me. I wish Amelia had never put the idea of it into my head.

I'm snapped back to reality when Darrin hugs me from the other side. I squeeze back, but Troy's lips, kissing Troy, having feelings for Troy—it all still bounces around in my brain, a subconscious notion that never truly goes away. Darrin is pressed up against me, too. I still have no idea what happened. Mostly I'm too afraid to ask.

"Someone want to tell me what in the hell is going on here?" Pappap asks in a hoarse, angry voice.

Troy and Darrin disentangle themselves and start talking at once. Of course, the second I truly understand, my legs *do* give out. My butt hits the grass. Bob is on me a second later, licking my face. My lungs work overtime trying to suck in oxygen while simultaneously not letting Bob tongue-kiss me. Pappap starts swearing when Troy and Darrin get to the part about the monster seemingly chewing its way up the stairs after them as they ran. That's when my brain shuts off—it's just too much. Too much information. Too much terror. Too much shock.

I scratch Bob's ears and look at the steam from the nuclear plant drift into the clouds, ignoring the sound of everyone talking.

Pappap, Troy, and Darrin are still having a discussion—if you can call it that since it's mostly Pappap cursing and yelling—when Grammy urges me up off the ground. There are tears on her cheeks, and her wrinkled mouth is pressed tight. I unfold myself and let her lead me into the house. Bob and Butterbeans are underfoot the whole way.

Grammy gently nudges me into a chair in the kitchen. She fills the kettle with water and puts it on a burner. Butterbeans situates himself near the refrigerator and watches her bustle around the room.

"Grammy?"

She turns. She's still silently crying.

"Do you ever get the feeling that maybe we're being punished for lying all the time and manipulating people into believing in Old Lucy?"

Bob sits heavily on my toes.

Grammy finally swipes the tears off her face. "I used to think about that when I was younger—if what we do is inherently bad or inherently good. Whether people would be mad if they found out about Old Lucy. This family benefits personally. It wasn't always like that, of course. The ferry tours business came later, and maybe that made things simpler. Or cleaner, I guess. On the whole, though, I think we've done more good than harm."

"That doesn't answer my question."

"No, I suppose you're talking more about karma. I don't know the answer to that, but it hurts my soul that maybe Will paid the price. Or your parents, for that matter. A parent isn't supposed to outlive their child. And a grandparent certainly isn't supposed to outlive her grandbaby."

The back door opens, and Pappap walks in ahead of Troy and Darrin. Pappap's got *Angry Buzzard* face. A small pinch of too-late alarm kicks in—leaving them with my grandfather when he's in his feelings isn't the wisest thing to do. I really owe them after all this. I knew telling them about Old Lucy would involve them in ways that wouldn't be comfortable, and I knew asking them to help me deal with the monster might be dangerous. I still can't admit to myself *how* dangerous, even now.

Troy catches my eye and smiles. He's still a little pale beneath his normal color, but he seems . . . okay.

Sorry, I mouth.

He waves his hand and shakes his head.

Pappap kisses Grammy on the top of the head as he passes behind her. I'd expected him to stop in the kitchen to bawl me out some more, but he beelines into the living room.

"Will one of you hook up the feed to the big screen?" His voice is decidedly *not* angry despite his expression.

Darrin blows out a breath. "Yeah, I'm on it."

Troy hands Darrin a cell phone. "The codes you need to sync the phone to the TV are in the app version file."

Darrin edges around Grammy, but before he can go, I clutch his hand—and I take Troy's hand, too. "I didn't catch everything you did today, but thanks. You didn't have to, and I know that—and I want you to know that I know."

Darrin snickers. "What's that line—I only regret that I have but one life to lose for my country?"

"No one's losing—" That's all that comes out of me before my chin starts to quiver, and my throat goes thick. Because people *have* lost their lives over this. And he and Troy could have, too.

"Hey," Troy says. "None of that." He nods to Darrin, who slides his hand from mine and turns into the living room. Like he can read my mind, Troy says, "We can cry and think too hard about what could have happened later." He sits next to me and puts his other hand on top of our clasped fingers. "We're with you, Lem. A hundred percent."

The kettle whistles. Grammy flits about, collecting teabags and mugs. I keep hold of Troy until my heart starts beating normally.

"Hain't you want to watch?" Pappap bellows from the living room.

"Watch what?" I say.

"The footage from the fish cams," Troy says. "Don't know if the cam from down there," he gestures toward the back door, "caught any of whatever that thing is. The line was caught, and—"

"Yeah, I heard you say that." I don't want to hear it again. I *can't* hear it again.

"Maybe the cam from the kayak we set loose near the public dock is still running, though. Even if the kayak sank, cam should be okay. It's got a few hours' worth of battery life."

Darrin's still tinkering with the television remote, sitting on the floor, when I take my mug of tea out into the living room. Pappap's in his usual recliner, staring intently at the screen even though it's blank. Grammy goes to her rocking chair, Bob and Butterbeans keeping up with her, leaving me and Troy sitting close together on the gold couch. It's like he's holding me up, keeping me calm.

A second later, the television screen comes over blue-green-brown, and Pappap says, "Good job there, Darrin."

My eyes widen. I don't think I've ever heard Pappap say anything nice to either Darrin *or* Troy. It's certainly a complete vibe switch from the last hour or two.

Troy leans over and whispers, "We have an understanding. I'll tell you later."

They have an *understanding*? That's . . . unexpected.

"This coverage is from the bottom of your stairs," Darrin says. He says it like nothing even happened—perfectly calm. "Troy cast out once, and the line drifted back in after a while."

"When I was pulling the line back in, it got stuck," Troy says. "That's why I was at the bottom of the stairs."

"Something you fools won't try again because you hain't going nowhere near the lake, right?" Pappap says, practically growling.

"We're clear on that, sir," Troy says.

Darrin snickers and fast-forwards through the footage, which is mostly blank screen.

"Well, would you look at that?" Pappap hisses twenty minutes later.

On-screen, the cam picks up Troy's hand reaching into the water and tugging something invisible.

In the distance, a dark hulking thing darts through the frame. Just for a second. Troy wraps his fingers around the fishing line, probably.

The monster zooms into sight for a split second, and then the cam shakes and spins.

Troy sucks in a breath.

I want to look at him, but I can't take my eyes off the screen. Grammy's hand flutters near her mouth, eyes wide.

"Back that up some," Pappap says.

Darrin plays and rewinds it a dozen times. Each time, Pappap leans a little closer to the television. "Never seen nothing like that in my whole goddamn life," he says. "Didn't catch more than a glimpse yesterday."

The doorbell chimes, and Grammy bolts from her rocking chair. Bob takes up with a bevy of high-pitched barks.

We all look at each other.

"Darrin, you turn that off now." Pappap arranges his expression into something carefully neutral. Every word sounds like he's shouting. "Put on something else. Like we was watching a movie. Like everything's normal."

There's nothing normal about the idea of all of us sitting around with Pappap watching a movie on a Wednesday when it's not quite noon.

He puts his hand on Grammy's tense shoulder. His eyes shift around at each of us. When he's satisfied, he unlocks and swings open the door.

Two men in suits—I can see them through the screen door. The man in dark gray has wispy white hair swirled into an impressive comb-over and a pasty glow, and round wire glasses that make his eyes enormous. The other wears a suit that from here looks like the color of wet logs. His teeth and skin are so white I nearly blink against the gleam.

"Ike Ziegler?" the guy in the dark-brown suit says. His words are clipped, and Bob is still barking, with Butterbeans whuffing in chorus. "We're with the US Geological Survey. Sheriff Ramirez says you called in the report on bacteria? We'd like to find out more about the instruments you've been using, get some history of the lake. Is this a good time?"

Pappap doesn't say a word—he just stares at them.

"Shush, you two," Grammy says to the dogs. They grumble and back away.

The men peer through the door at all of us, expressions set into emotionless masks to match Pappap's.

Darrin's face is doing this strange, pinched thing. He's giving me laser eyes, like he's trying to convey something critical. I can't read him, though—he just looks like he has to go to the bathroom.

It's like we're all caught in some strange web of silence, except for the dogs.

"Oh, goodness, Ike," Grammy says, "let them in." She nudges in front of Pappap, who stiffly stands his ground. She ushers the two guys in. Bob and Butterbeans gather on either side of Grammy like sentinels. "From the US Geological Survey, you say?"

"Yes, ma'am," says the man with the round glasses.

Grammy turns to me. "Why don't you kids go outside and play?"

Play? Seriously? But I don't argue—anything to escape the awkward tension.

Darrin nearly knocks the agents over as he darts for the front door. The agents, Grammy, and Pappap jostle around, maneuvering past one another, while Troy and I follow Darrin. Darrin's pacing along the driveway, muttering to himself, when we make it outside. He motions us to follow and jogs toward Grammy's lilac bushes, lined up against the road.

"You know how you said one of the agents that came to your house looked like one of the grief counselors?" he says to Troy.

What?

Troy nods.

"I thought you were full of shit. But I've seen that white-haired dude—he was at the school, roaming around the halls. Also acting like a grief counselor."

"I'm sorry—did I just have an aneurysm?" I say. "What are you talking about?" I look back at the house over my shoulder, eyes falling on the agents' car in the driveway. It's black—sleek in a way that's expensive looking. Tinted windows. I know if I get a look inside, the car will be immaculate and smell new. "Oh my god, that's Amelia's car."

"*Amelia?*" Darrin's mouth knots up. "Tell me she's been at your house before."

"What? No. I mean, she knows I live at the lake."

"Amelia's *all* up in this," Darrin says to Troy. "I know it. She *has* to be."

"Up in *what?*" I say. "Is someone going to tell me what's going on?"

Troy and Darrin fill me in—every last detail.

Finally, I say, "Amelia *did* say her dad's with the federal government. And she did say his team was planning to wrap up whatever project they're working on really fast."

Darrin's eyebrows draw down. "So are they actually USGS agents, or are they something else? What do we know?"

"Not much," Troy says. "Marine ecosystems. Bacteria. Earthquake. Trying to keep the lake area clear. Bogus grief counselors. That's it."

"And maybe it has something to do with time travel?" I say. "Are you sure?"

"No—Darrin *thinks* the symbol looks like a time travel thing. We can safely leave that out of this, though, because yeah. That's too weird even for this screwed up situation. The speaker is Amelia's, for sure, but that's about all we know."

"Amelia's first day *was* the day after the earthquake," I say. "I'm going to go see if I can hear what they're saying to Grammy and Pappap."

"Uh-uh," Troy says. "What if they see you? I'll go."

"Oh, please. What if they see *you?* At least I live here. I can say . . . I don't know what I'll say, but I'll think of something."

Troy opens his mouth until I give him a glare. "Stay here," I say. "Act like you're *playing*, like my grandmother told us to."

Darrin chuckles.

I nonchalantly saunter over to the side of the house and peek through the living room window. Empty. The border of short orange marigolds that Grammy planted along the side of the house leads me right toward the back porch.

Voices sound from the backyard.

". . . like to evacuate you from the lake. I spoke to some of your neighbors, and they've all agreed. We'll relocate everyone to a hotel during our investigation. It shouldn't take too long—a few days at most."

"Hain't no need for that," Pappap says.

There's grumbling I can't make out.

Pappap says, "We've had outbreaks at the lake afore. Besides, Pearl and I have the ferries. We can't take the boats out of the water now— tourist season starts in weeks. I know the government hain't proposing to get in the way of a man making a living."

"We would be happy to assume the cost of the cranes to remove your boats, Mr. Ziegler."

More grumbling I don't quite get.

One of the agents says, "There's been an outbreak of this type of bacteria in the commonwealth—everything in or near the lake is at risk of contamination. We could take care of it tonight, have you all back in your homes and businesses in a few days. You have my word that no damage will come to your property. When we're done with our work, it will be as though we were never here."

"If it comes to that, we'll even pay you for the loss of business revenue."

The same as when Pappap closed down the lake with his bacteria story, they're trying to get us away from the water, too—what are they planning to do here that they're trying to avoid an audience? And what does Amelia have to do with *any* of this? I have to assume one of those guys is her dad, but what else?

I'm about to slink back to Darrin and Troy when I hear one of the agents say, "I understand your grandson had an accident yesterday— we're terribly sorry for your loss."

Something about the way he says it makes me clamp my teeth together.

"Thank you," Grammy murmurs.

"The medical reports didn't provide a great deal of insight into how it happened—"

"And just how did you get hold of the medical reports?" Pappap says. "I know my son hain't signed nothing to release private medical records to you."

"We want to be thorough," one of the agents says. There's an edge to his voice—it's as hard as Pappap's.

I dig my nails into the palm of my hand. This makes zero sense.

I scurry back to Darrin and Troy to relay the conversation.

"Right," Darrin says. "It sounds like a classic black ops situation. You always hear in conspiracy theories about the military sending in special teams to spread misinformation, do some dirty work, and then sanitize the field."

"Don't make this into something it's not," I say.

"It's not impossible," Darrin says. "Like there was this thing—it happened maybe a decade ago. Troops were deployed into Texas for military exercises. People started hearing it was a test run for declaring martial law and disarming people. The whole thing turned out to be a Russian misinformation campaign to rile up a bunch of backwoods schmoes. Black ops isn't unheard of, is what I'm saying."

"Call Amelia," I say. "Right now. Call her."

"And say *what*?" Darrin says. "Besides, you're the one who just spent a whole day with her shopping and being besties. *You* should call her."

"My phone died—remember? I didn't even have a chance to put it on the charger yet."

"I'll call her," Troy says. "Texted her this morning anyway. It won't be weird." He says to Darrin, "Have my phone?"

Darrin hands it over, and Troy pecks at the screen.

Amelia's voice comes over the speaker phone. "Well, Troy Ramirez. Thanks for finding my speaker."

"Yeah, sure. What is it anyway? The speaker?"

"They're just, you know, speakers. My dad got a pair in Japan."

"That's what the buttons do?" Troy says, locking eyes with me for a moment. "Connect to Bluetooth?"

"Among other things. Volume, Bluetooth, recording, navigation—it has out of this world, off-the-charts connectivity."

"What's the brand?"

If this was happening in person, Troy would have Amelia tied to a chair, shining a light in her face and demanding answers in some tiny little windowless room. I shiver. There's just been too much stress today—it's giving me the willies.

"They don't sell them in the US. I think they're a prototype," Amelia says, voice light. "Anyway, I was afraid Old Lucy or a bear might have eaten it. My dad would have been pissed. What do monsters and bears eat anyway? I bet lots of fish."

"What were you doing at Lemon's house if you're afraid of Old Lucy—or bears?"

"Oh, I didn't actually mean I was *at* her house. I was out hiking—just trying to get to know Devil's Elbow. I hiked *past* her house."

I've never seen her in anything other than forehead-to-toenails black. I think I would have noticed if she were marching along the trails near my part of the lake.

"Didn't know you hiked," Troy says, nodding to me like he can see the thoughts in my head. The idea freaks me out since I've been so intent on his lips for the last day or two. "Come out with me and Darrin sometime. We have a ten-miler planned."

Darrin scrunches up his face in confusion. He and Troy have never hiked anywhere in their lives, as far as I know.

"Yeah, maybe. It'd be fun to get to know you guys a little better. I really like you and Darrin and Lemon—you're nice."

"Speaking of nice, Lemon said you have a super nice ride."

I glance at the car again. An idea pops into my head. A very bad, very stupid idea.

She laughs. "It's my dad's. You know, government issue and all that. Anyway, will you be at school so I can grab the speaker? You wouldn't believe some of the stuff people are saying about this bacteria business. Like it's all a front for something. Or, hey... my dad's out right now, but maybe I can come to you later? Are you at Lemon's?"

It only vaguely occurs to me that I should be wondering how she guessed that, but I'm still staring at the car.

"Naw, Lemon's at her aunt and uncle's house," Troy says. "Why don't I call you tomorrow? Who knows the next time we'll have school—especially if it's a *front for something*, right?"

Darrin taps Troy's arm. "Ask her what she knows about wormholes," he whispers.

Amelia laughs, but it sounds weird—fake. "See you soon then."

The second I'm sure the line is dead, I say, "We should follow them. The agents. When they leave, I mean."

Darrin grins. "Why, Lemon, for a girl who thinks my conspiracy theories are crap, you are embracing the dark side. I like it. We have Troy's fine vehicle and, as I recall, nearly a full tank of gas. Let's hit it."

17

LEMON

S UNSHINE GLOWS DOWN ON THE road and makes everything glisten like gold. The sky is bright, robin's egg blue with wispy clouds streaking through. It's making me a bit nervous, truth be told, and it's hard not to get stuck on the idea that everything is about to go terribly wrong. I'm supposed to be keeping an eye out for any sign that the agents know we're following them, but my brain is firmly obsessing over the weather and the weirdness of my bodily reactions: I can feel my heart beating and the bones beneath my skin. I can feel Troy's Buick vibrating under my legs. And yet part of me is at the dock, still. Last afternoon after school. Hauling Will out of the lake. Watching Grammy tie a tourniquet on him. Hearing the ambulance wail its way into our driveway, even as the smell of rot from the monster hangs in the air. In the antiseptic hospital waiting room, about to see Will's surgeon walk through the doors.

And I'm still in my backyard. Today. Nearly crying with relief to see Troy and Darrin safe at the top of the stairs. Stopping myself from kissing Troy in a way that would have been so incredibly bad. It would ruin everything.

The Buick bounces over a spring pothole. Amelia's car—her dad's car, whatever—is still in sight down the street. What am I doing? Obsessing about Troy at the same time that I'm reliving the trauma of seeing my cousin half-devoured by a monster? I'm sick. Though I do remember reading about anxiety making people act compulsively.

Maybe I'm not sick, maybe my obvious angst about the disaster of my life over the last week or so is giving me the compulsive urge to kiss Troy. It's not like I thought about him like that before Snowflake was killed. Amelia just made me conscious of my reaction. I'm sure that's all it is.

Weirdly, knowing that I'm probably just having a trauma response doesn't make me feel any better . . . and it doesn't make Troy any less attractive. I inwardly cringe.

The car pulls off at the post office, right in front of the mailbox painted to match the Old Lucy colors my grandparents use at the ferry office. They both get out. I'm staring at the pale guy with the ultraviolet teeth, looking for any family resemblance to Amelia, and fiddling with the charging block for my phone and trying to logic my way out of sliding a glance toward Troy's strong hands.

"Seems like a weird time for a stamp run," Darrin says.

Troy parks on the next block. A woman from the mayor's office is putting up new flags on the light poles on the street—welcome flags bearing a likeness of Old Lucy waving jauntily. A light wind shakes the car, in turn sending down a shower of catkins that makes it seem like we're sitting through a green rainstorm.

"How long should we follow them?" Troy asks.

"Who knows. Pappap is thoroughly impressed with us, though," I say.

Darrin laughs. "I heard him through the phone when you called. It feels like we fell into an alternate universe where Ike isn't a cantankerous old jackass."

"Trust me," I say, thinking of how he's been acting all night and all morning, "he's still a cantankerous old jackass. You've just landed on his good side."

"For now," Troy says.

I nod. "For now."

I just won't look at Troy, that's all. I won't notice that way his muscles shift when he drives, or anything else for that matter. There are more important things to worry about.

Darrin says, "And I thought senior year was going to be boring. I did *not* have tailing federal agents and gathering intel to kill a lake monster on my list of things to do before graduation."

"I wish we didn't have to kill it," I say.

"Why?" Troy says. "Doesn't seem to mind killing anyone else."

"I don't know. I just . . . When we were looking at invasive species, I ran into an article about endangered species, and another about animals that used to be thought of as cryptids. You know, like the giant squid. People thought it was a myth, but it turned out to be real. What if it's . . . what if it's *that*? A cryptid?" I turn to Darrin and grin. "I'm turning into you."

Troy says, "If you were turning into Darrin, you'd propose that the government's stepping in to plant a monster where it shouldn't be— maybe test drive a monster the feds created as a weapon."

Both Darrin and I stare at Troy, open-mouthed.

"Well fucking done." Darrin slowly claps.

"Now I know I've spent too much time exposed to messed up conspiracies," I say, "because that doesn't sound all that crazy."

Nothing sounds crazy anymore.

The corner of Troy's mouth lifts. "No, suppose not. Anything's possible."

Darrin says, "Hey, they're coming out of the post office."

We all turn to watch them get in their car and drive past us, past the woman hanging flags. The car turns right one block down. Troy gets back on the road, and moments later he turns right, too. "This heads out to Nolan's Woods. What are they doing out that far?"

I lean forward, fold my arms along the dashboard, and rest my chin on my hands. I keep my eyes on the road, looking at the back of the black car, keeping an eye out for one of the Jenkinses following us, just in case. After a few miles, the road narrows. The trees loom tighter until a solid wall of pines and oaks block out the sun.

The car takes another turn. I sit up straight. "Oh, now *that's* interesting."

"So?" Darrin says. "It's another road."

"Seriously?" I say. "For someone convinced that following these guys is going to reveal the clue to a vast conspiracy, you don't seem overly concerned that they're heading out to the Bartel Camp. It's usually only occupied during hunting season—which it currently is *not*." I lay a hand on Troy's warm shoulder and shiver—he's so warm. I snatch my hand back, cursing Amelia for the eight billionth time. "Don't turn down the road. It's a private drive. It'll be a dead giveaway that we're following the car if you do."

"We're done with this then?" Troy says.

"What?" Darrin says. "No. We know where they're going, and did you hear what Lemon said? This isn't hunting season. We *have* to follow. You know where the camp is, right, Lemon? Can we get there on foot?"

I nod.

Darrin says, "Troy, pull over there—there's a break in the trees. It'll hide the car."

The Buick barely wedges into the space. Troy says, "Someone should stay here. Lemon, maybe—"

"Yeah, no," I say. "Do either of you know how to get to Bartel's? I've been out here with Pappap a million times."

"I'll go with you, and Darrin will stay," Troy says. He and Darrin trade a look. Darrin mutters something incomprehensible, but Troy glares and says, "Stop talking."

"Yeah, yeah," Darrin says. "Go. I'll be your getaway man."

"Be careful, okay," I say. "Text Troy if you see anyone else pull in. I'm leaving my phone here to keep charging. If my grandfather calls—or Grammy—pick up, okay?"

He nods. "At least try not to get caught, turds of my heart." His voice is light, but his expression says something way different. I shiver again, this time for an entirely different reason, and push out of the car.

A few seconds later, Troy and I run across the street and spring into the forest. The wind is heavier here. It bays like a wound-up dog. The branches shimmy above, but all that touches my face is a breeze and the scent of pine needles and dirt. Birds call out. In the distance, I swear I hear the high-pitched screech of a fox and maybe a roar of something bigger.

I swipe my hair back and force my feet forward. Troy pushes up a low hanging branch. I duck beneath it. We move fast, picking our way through the trees and brush. Troy gets in front of me a few times—and my brain immediately leaps back to thinking about him in the most inappropriate ways. It's like a plague—it won't leave me alone, like a song that's stuck in my head. If Amelia hadn't said anything, maybe I would have latched onto some other obsession. Randomly taking up shoplifting to relieve the tension of being near death all the time would be preferable to constantly mooning over my best friend. This is torturous.

A gleam of bare wood and glass shines through the trees ahead. I put a warning hand on Troy's arm. His fingers curl over mine, and my skin heats abruptly. He slows to a stop.

"Are we crazy for doing this?" I whisper. "Am *I* crazy?"

"Maybe. I'd be more worried if you decided to bail."

"Why?"

He sighs, gives my hand a squeeze before dropping his arm to his side. "Been friends for a long time, you and me. One of the reasons I've always liked you is that you give a crap. About everything. School, me and Darrin, your family. Even this town. If my dad told me I had to impersonate Old Lucy for the rest of my life, I'd probably tell him to shove it."

"You absolutely would not."

"Not in those words maybe. But you—look at all you're giving up to protect your grandparents and Devil's Elbow."

"Do I have to remind you that you and Darrin almost died today for the same reason?"

"Didn't do it for the town or your grandparents."

"Then why?"

"Because of you." He says it softly, almost too softly to hear. He leans in for a moment, but then clears his throat and straightens. "Darrin and me, both—you need us, we're there." He lightly punches me in the arm, all buddy-buddy, and gives me a grin.

It is the entirely wrong time to be having this conversation—not to mention my brain screaming at me about his lips—but my stomach drops into my toes. He thinks of me as a friend, and that's it. It's better this way, better to cut my weird, obsessive reaction off before I do something stupid that ruins our friendship, but the disappointment is sour in my mouth.

"Thanks," I say. "Truly—you have no idea how much easier all of this is because of you." I smile, too, trying to pretend there's nothing wrong beyond the fact that we're traipsing through the woods, chasing federal agents.

I jerk my chin at a sprawling log cabin that rises up among the trees ahead. It's a simple A-frame with a plain blue door and wide windows set around the house. A thin gunmetal chimney shoots up from the roof, but no smoke billows out. I tug Troy behind a tree, trying to clear my head so I can concentrate on doing what we came here to do. "Look. I don't see any lights on inside. Maybe there's no one there."

"No car, either. Maybe they kept driving."

"There's no other place to go."

"Car could be behind the house, or camouflaged somehow. They *are* federal agents—maybe they have some weird technology. Invisible cars."

"Okay, *Darrin.*" I snicker. He laughs, too.

The wind kicks up a shower of gravel and dust from the narrow driveway that leads to the front of the house. Even if there's evidence that cars had been on the drive, the wind would obliterate it in seconds.

Pappap's voice is in my head, telling me to be careful, to assume the worst—to assume that someone is watching. It's Old Lucy sighting advice, of course, but it still applies.

It's weird that Pappap doesn't like Darrin more; their combined paranoia is considerable. The sound of leaves blowing and birds squawking will cover the crash of anyone else in the forest with us or any noise coming from the house.

Still, these guys *are* with the government, like Troy said—they probably have access to next-level weaponry. Spy gear, maybe— cameras and motion detectors and such. Maybe they've bugged our phones, in which case they already know where we are. My palms start to sweat.

I kneel to sift through the brush and the carpet of debris on the ground and inspect the tree.

"What are you doing?"

"Don't you think there are probably cams? You know, surveillance? If the agents are here, they're not here by chance. There has to be something out here for them."

Strands of hair whip into my eyes, and I brush them back impatiently. We have no way to do a thorough search, not in a forest— equipment can be hidden anywhere. Stuff we've never seen before . . . or imagined. There might be a whole army of people in that house who've been following us since the second we set foot in the woods. I bite the edge of my thumbnail.

Troy abruptly whips out his phone.

"What are you doing?" I ask.

"I want to check something. It's windy, right? And there are no lights in the house. Don't know if you noticed, but there was a light pole at the junction road leading out to this place—it wasn't on."

"Okay—but so what?"

"So maybe the electricity is out. Could be an outage in the area. Might be good to know, right?" He chews on his lower lip, thumbing his phone screen. A giant smile spreads across his face. "This whole area's out. No electricity. Maybe it won't matter if there's surveillance equipment. No electricity equals no Wi-Fi—and no lights."

I flash a grin at him and dart behind a thick stand of trees, and Troy is right behind me. Now that he's thoroughly dashed my hopes, my brain is at least giving me some peace—I can concentrate on what we're doing. Branches scratch at my face, and the smell of dirt and pine pound at me with each gust of wind. I take a deep breath and scurry out of the trees to the corner of the log cabin. It's shadowed, but not dark enough to hide us completely. Anyone looking out a window can see. And it's not like we don't look suspicious, sneaking along the boards of the house.

A flutter of movement freezes my blood. I press back against the wall as hard as I can. It comes from the window, propped open a few inches, next to my head. I count slowly and silently to ten, lift my head from the wood, and peer through the edge of the screen.

At first I don't see anything at all, only a hazy purple darkness and the outlines of a low table. As my eyes adjust, the shapes of equipment become visible. Things that look like old-fashioned radios and more modern computer monitors, but everything is silent. Half a dozen of the cones I found are lined up on a desk next to the door. A man sits at a table, his back to the window. His elbows are planted, shoulders slumped.

I duck under the sill and motion to Troy to look. His eyes widen as he scans the window. "Not the agents we followed," he mouths. He looks again and dodges back abruptly. "Two other guys came in the room. One of them is Amelia's dad."

". . . about the motion detectors," a voice says. "It's those hicks at that lake. They aren't equipped to deal with this."

Troy takes my hand.

"Command said to wait." It's a second voice, muted. The man sitting at the table, maybe.

"What for? Does he think the yokels will get lucky and kill this thing by themselves?"

"Be thankful a lot of the people who live out there took us up on our hotel offer. And that everyone is marginally afraid of the lake because of this Old Lucy impersonation."

Does that mean . . . they know? About me, about my family? A wash of heat pours over me, like I've just been dipped in a vat of fire.

"That's two things Ike Ziegler did right. That and lying to Ramirez to have the lake roads blocked. We'd have had to simulate a bigger disaster to keep people away otherwise."

My eyes cut toward Troy.

"Yeah, but that still makes the Zieglers a pretty problem, doesn't it? That girl invited her friends to be a hot lunch. Ash said they were in the goddamn boathouse when she checked the scene. How dumb can you be?"

Who the hell is Ash?

A third voice, farther away and female, calls, "Dad, you should—"
Dad?

"I'm in the middle of something. Why don't you come in here and collect the tapes." The man pauses. "And then today? Those two idiots with the fish cams. We need to get these people out of the field."

There's a harsh laugh. "I know no one wants to deal with the mess of eliminating the family, but it would make things much simpler. Kill them, out them as grifters, whatever works."

"We stick with the plan."

"What plan?" I mouth to Troy, but my head is stuck on the parts about *eliminating* my family and me or telling our secret. I can barely breathe.

There's another flutter at the window. I peep over the sill and freeze. Amelia stares back; she immediately raises her finger to her lips, then presses her hand against the screen not far from my nose. Her red hair is parted in the middle, each side wrapped in a bun above her ears. From this close, I can see every freckle on her pale white face.

I kick Troy's ankle and tilt my head toward the window. He raises his eyes and recoils. Only my hand on his wrist keeps him from running.

A flash of light and a high-pitched hum blare from the window. I clap a hand over my mouth to keep a squeak back. The room descends into darkness again, and one of the men groans. "This goddamn place," he gripes. "The electricity grid sucks. Can't wait to get back to civilization. Maybe we should just nuke this whole town instead of just the lake and call it a day."

My eyes dart back to the window. Amelia is mouthing words to me: *Run. Go.*

A million questions come to me, with no way to get answers. It's dumb luck we even overheard what they said, dumb luck that Amelia hasn't given us away. I want to barge into the house and demand that these guys leave my family alone. Demand Amelia tell me what's going on. The urge of it holds me fast to the spot.

"Lemon, come on," Troy whispers.

Amelia's eyes blaze. She puts her hand on the screen again and mouths, *Go! Now!*

Troy tugs me back toward the trees, and I follow, numb with fear and anger and helplessness and disgust . . . but mostly anger. It's crap.

This is Devil's Elbow, not some place run by a dictator where people are disappeared for being in the wrong place at the wrong time.

Another electrical pulse surges behind us, a flicker on, a flicker off. The wind still tears at my shirt, at my hair, but the gusts have softened.

Troy swears and releases my arm. He's got serious *High Alert* face. "We gotta go. Get deeper into the trees. Can you lead us farther away, still get us to the car?"

I nod and stomp away from the house. I stew all the way back to the main road, almost surprised when we burst from the trees onto the paved lane. Troy watches me like I'm a bomb five seconds from blowing up in his face.

"You okay?" he says.

"No, but I—"

The nose of Troy's car juts abruptly into the road, and Darrin's worried face is behind the wheel. He clambers over the driver's seat to the back. "Hurry up. A bunch of cars just tore out of the driveway."

Troy slides behind the wheel. My butt hits the passenger seat just as he clicks his seat belt. He throws the car into gear. He looks in the rearview at Darrin. "Won't believe what just happened."

18

TROY

I USED TO LIKE TO DRIVE. Pick up Lemon, Darrin . . . randomly drive around 'til one of us figured out what to do. It's why I'm the unofficial driver whenever go anywhere. Now? The Buick's too conspicuous. Looking around for places to hide it—to hide *us*. Probably nowhere *to* hide—not with the setup I saw through the cabin window. Not with all the USGS agents—or whoever they are—know. With Amelia in the mix . . . the agents probably have the goods on every single person in town.

Lemon sits cross-legged on the seat next to me. Arms folded over her stomach, face stormy. Finally, she says, "I can't tell Pappap *most* of that."

Darrin leans over the seat. "Death threat, threat of revealing the Old Lucy secret, threat of destroying the lake, or something else? It's all pretty bad, and Ike is two seconds from losing his shit as it is."

She shifts to look at him.

"You saw how he was about me telling you two about Old Lucy and about how far back this goes. I think deep down he knows you'd never sell me out, but strangers? Strangers who could and would destroy everything our family has worked for in this town? I tell him that, and it's over."

"What do you think he'd do?" I'm gripping the steering wheel hard enough I can barely feel my fingers.

"He's already delicate because of Will dying," Lemon says. "We all are. But think about what he threatened *you* with—now multiply that by a million. He's just . . . in no condition to handle this."

I make a fast right into the parking lot of Hitchcock Organics, pull around to the back parking spaces. The Buick blends right in with the crappy cars some of the employees drive.

"Gee, Troy—have a hankering for tofu or something?" Darrin says.

"Trying to avoid agents finding us, smart ass," I say. "So what's our next move?"

Lemon slides my phone over the seat. "I'm calling Amelia." She dials, puts the phone on speaker.

"Oh, hey," Amelia says, all chirpy.

"Are you alone?" Lemon says.

"Nope," Amelia says, "but try playing around with navigation. I'm sure Lemon knows how to get there. The store's not very big—like maybe the size of Peter's Island."

Darrin glances at me and mouths, *What the hell?*

"Uh, okay," Lemon says. "First, thanks for warning us back there, but second, we've got to talk. Can you meet us somewhere?"

"Uh-uh. There's that test in Mr. Chismar's class tomorrow, so I should study for that."

Lemon pauses, looks at the roof of the car. "I'm assuming you're giving me hints since none of that makes sense, so I'm just going to keep asking questions."

"That's right, yes," Amelia says, all sweet. "But I heard he won't be posting the results until tomorrow night."

Lemon goes silent.

Amelia says, "For what it's worth, I think you have the right idea—but Chismar doesn't care. You know him, always looking for the easiest solution. Hard to argue him out of anything. He definitely doesn't play well with others. Anyway, I'll see you tomorrow. Oh, and tell Lemon I dropped off her dress. See ya!"

When the call drops, Lemon passes the phone back over to me. Her mouth is twisted. "Okay, did anyone understand that?"

"She's not trying to deny anything," Darrin says. "I don't know if that's good or bad."

"Probably good," I say. "If her dad knew she helped us, she wouldn't have bothered to . . . do whatever the hell that was. She would have just told us to go to hell, or not answered. So that means she's still helping us."

"But can we trust her?" Lemon cocks her head to the side. "She's been lying to us from day one."

"Maybe," Darrin says.

Lemon straightens in her seat. "What do you mean, maybe?"

"Yeah, she's obviously been extracting information for the agents," Darrin says. "For all we know, Amelia could be an actress—a forty-year-old pretending to be seventeen. I don't think so, though—she was obviously on your side today, and it seems like she's been relatively upfront with us—her dad does work for the government, exactly like she said. I assume that's true anyway. Men in black, right? It's not out of the question that feds can be doing secret stuff. I bet she's been dropping breadcrumbs from the very beginning. I'm not saying she's on our side, for sure."

"She might have even gotten Vern Jenkins arrested to protect you, if what she said to you the other day means anything," I say.

Lemon nods thoughtfully. "I'm more concerned about what Amelia said *today*."

"Her speaker!" I twist in my seat to face her. "What if she left it for us to find? Dropped it accidentally-on-purpose? Said the buttons were for navigation. Something like navigation, recording, and a few other things. And you heard her just now—try playing around with navigation."

Lemon leans toward me far enough that I can smell her hair. She says, "Peter's Island."

"Okay, where's the speaker now?" Darrin says.

"My house."

"Let's go then." Lemon's eyes blaze. "We can try to figure out the rest on the way."

❧❧❧

BY THE TIME I'm in the driveway of my house, jolting out of the Buick, we've come up with a few ideas. Whatever this speaker really is, we've got to play with the buttons near Peter's Island. Mr. Chismar teaches geology—so maybe that's a reference to the agents. The not playing well with others thing . . . Darrin thinks it means there's no use trying to play up to them, to compromise. Lemon's convinced Amelia's hint about Chismar's test grading means the agents won't do whatever they're planning at the lake until tomorrow night, which means we've got just over twenty-four hours to figure it out before everything goes very south. My stomach is a churning brick.

House feels dark, dangerous. Even the carpeting on the stairs is sinister. Like maybe there's a bug hidden in the corner. Don't know how much of what the agents know is because of Amelia playing spy, and how much might be secret surveillance on all of us—Darrin's idea—but I can't stop thinking about it. After I grab Amelia's speaker and head back down the stairs, I pick up a picture frame on the credenza in the living room, flip it over.

Work the back off the frame. Nothing.

Leaf through a pile of books; check the television, the remote controls, and the thermostat. A few other things. Everything's fine . . . as far as I can tell. Not like I can pry apart any of the electronics—my parents would be pissed.

Gee, Mom and Dad, sorry I destroyed the Roku. Thought the house might be bugged.

Front door clicks open, then shut. A second later Dad comes into the living room. His uniform is wrinkled. "What are Lemon and Darrin doing in your car?"

"Came to pick something up—heading right back out." Just seeing him makes me jittery. "Hey, you seen the USGS agents around anywhere?"

Dad eases into the armchair, peels off his sidearm holster—sets it down. Service pistol clunks on the table. "Thinking about joining the feds maybe? I grant you, it's more exciting than the police academy, but you'll need at least a four-year degree for that."

He seriously wants to have this conversation *right now*?

"What? Dad, no."

"Military service can be another route in for some jobs," Dad continues. He smiles at me, hopeful that I'm buying this. Can't he see I'm ready to jump out of my skin? "Secret Service, for instance." He pauses, his smile slips. "I never imagined you joining the marines, but you'd be a fine recruit. Do you some good to get that kind of discipline."

"No military, no feds, Dad. Bad idea. I have to *go*."

Dad gives me a look—his lecture look. *Great*. This is *no* time for this. "Son, you have no plans whatsoever for what's next. Aren't most of you kids dying to move away from home and be on your own? When I was your age, I couldn't wait to leave. Do all the things I couldn't do here, live in the big city."

"But you came back," I blurt. Crap. Last thing I want is to encourage this line of discussion—especially now. College can wait. Lemon and Darrin can't.

"Sure did. The fact is that I'm a small-town guy, and sometimes it takes leaving the place you grew up to know it. I had ambition and drive and a plan, but plans change. I love Devil's Elbow, and when you love something, you want to protect it. You know that. It's why I came back after I went to the police academy."

One thing we have in common: I love something, all right. I love some*one*. I wanna protect her. It's all I think about—finding a way to keep Lemon safe. It's what I'm trying to do now if he'd just *stop* talking.

"Dad, can we talk later?" I'm trying to keep the panic out of my voice. "I need to—"

"If you don't want to go to college," Dad says like I never said a word, "maybe a trade school. Be a plumber. I don't know, learn how to weld and be a welder. But pick a future." Dad fixes me with a stare. "This isn't about Lemon, is it?"

I sputter. "What? Why?"

"Your mother and I are *not* idiots. We're fully aware that you have feelings for Lemon."

"Dad, what? No, it's not that." The lie sounds stupid coming out of my mouth. "Look, they're waiting for me."

Dad's face pinches into a half smirk. "You're not saving the world today, I'm sure. I'm not going to pry, Troy. How you feel about that girl is your business, and I don't want to interfere. But it is my business if you're not making any decisions about your future because of her."

"Geez, Dad, come on." All the air goes out of me. Like both lungs collapse, catch on fire.

Dad snorts. "Let me tell you something—I've been your dad for eighteen years. You may think your mom and I are clueless, but we raised you. We have eyes. Can I make a suggestion? Something to think about while you're out with your friends?"

"Yeah, okay." Anything to end this conversation.

Dad mumbles something, shakes his head. He says, "Go to community college. You can live at home if you want, although that drive is a bear, especially in the winter. You take a lot of classes, figure out what you're interested in. Maybe do an internship or two. Transfer to a four-year college later. Problem solved."

For a second my brain short circuits. I forget about everything outside the house. Agents, monster, even Lemon. "That . . . that would be okay?"

"It's definitely okay. Your mother and I want you to take a step forward, and making a decision about what's next is a good step, no matter what that decision is. Just remember—anything is possible."

My throat goes tight. For the first time, that idea scares the shit out of me. Still, with all that's going on, I'll feel better if I can stay close, keep an eye out for Lemon. Stay home, going to community college. It's doable. If any of us survive, that is.

Dad gathers his gun and holster, stands. "Maybe we'll talk more this weekend?"

"Thanks, Dad." I hug him, wonder if it'll be the last time.

He pounds me on the shoulder, lets me go.

Darrin glares when I slide back into the car. "Take your freaking time, okay. We're not in any rush."

"Sorry—my dad got to me." What am I supposed to say? *Yeah, Dad, gotta go see about killing a lake monster.* Sure *that* would've rushed things along.

Lemon smiles at me, all soft-eyed and sweet. Puts her hand on my arm and squeezes. It's almost enough to make up for Darrin continuing to complain as I take the back roads to the public dock. What does he want? For the agents to figure out what we're doing? For one of the Jenkinses to happen to see Lemon in my car and start tailing us? I mostly tune Darrin out.

Even driving the back way, it doesn't take long until I'm creeping the Buick down the narrow road to the public dock. The sun hangs lower now, pines casting heavy shadows. Quiet enough to set my nerves on alert.

Lemon darts out of the car as soon as we're parked in the back corner. Second she does, my eyes jolt to the tree line, look for signs that anyone might be watching.

She calls over her shoulder, "Come on. I don't want to be here when it starts to get dark. There are spots around here where the monster can hide. I should know—I use them when I'm in the Old Lucy costume."

Peter's Island blares bright green, then turns golden all in a blink. The lake turns a few shades darker. The air smells crisp, with an undercurrent of dead fish and conifer.

"Any sign of the kayak?" I say, trying to keep my head on-task. Don't need to be thinking what I'm thinking: namely, with the light getting dimmer, it's like a horror movie set—complete with places for the monster to lie in wait. "Last we saw, it was about halfway out to the island."

The three of us stand all in a row at the edge of the parking lot, gawking at the murky water.

Darrin clears his throat. "Just for the record, I'm really wishing my Old Lucy-is-an-elephant theory would have panned out."

"Yeah, I'm sure that wouldn't have complicated any of this." Lemon shields her eyes, keeps looking. "Maybe the kayak floated all the way out."

Her face gives nothing away—this could be any other day, from her expression. She's steady, calm. Means she's probably freaking out.

She adds, "It was windy out by Bartel's—if it got windier here after you left, it could have been pushed anywhere." Amelia's speaker is in her hands. She turns it over and over, studying it. "Should I . . . just start pushing buttons?"

"Guess so," I say.

"Is it weird that I'm afraid you're going to push the wrong thing and trigger a global nuclear war?" Darrin says. "My mom showed me an old movie from the 1980s like that. It had something to do with playing tic-tac-toe. I don't know. It was weird. Carry on."

"And on that note." Lemon gives a nervous half laugh and shrugs. She pushes something, and I hold my breath.

Nothing.

"Maybe it's not what Amelia meant." Lemon stares at the speaker like it's going to give up answers if she just looks hard enough.

"Or maybe she lied to us," Darrin says, voice hard.

"Thought you said—"

"I know what I said." Darrin shoves his hands in his pockets. "Maybe I'm wrong—maybe she's giving us the runaround, keeping us from doing things that will actually make a difference."

"I've still got more buttons." Lemon shakes the speaker.

"Maybe it's just a speaker," Darrin says.

"Keep at it," I say. But now I'm imagining that Amelia, her dad, and the rest of the agents are over at Lemon's house, killing off Lemon's grandparents. Goddamn Darrin can't keep his thoughts to himself, pushing his paranoia into my head.

Lemon pushes two more buttons, nothing happens—except a flock of birds lifts off out of a weeping willow hanging over the water. Squawking aside, it's nothing earth shattering.

"Shit," Darrin says.

Lemon glances over at me, expression rigid. She bites her top lip. I know what she must be thinking—we're wasting time. I give her a nod. She presses another button.

A sound like the squealing of train brakes erupts. My head snaps up just as something cracks into the rocks at Peter's Island. Even from here I can see the churn of white water.

Lemon gasps, hits the button again. This time the sound coming from the island is more like a rasping, heaving bellow, like two ships smashing into each other. A grayish body that's got to be half the size of a Ziegler's ferryboat jerks out of the water, hits the edge of the island.

"Oh fuck," Darrin shouts. "Kill the shit out of it."

Another button hit, but the thing in the water surfaces farther away from the island. Another, and it screams, halfway between the island and the dock.

Lemon winces each time. She hands me the speaker—or whatever it is. "I know it needs to die, but that sound. I . . . I can't."

"Doesn't matter anyway." I pull Lemon and Darrin farther away from the water. Thing that size—probably can't reach us, but no luck-pushing here. "Don't think we're doing anything to it while it's in open water—maybe hurting it. That's all."

Darrin's practically bouncing. "Still, that's something. We can make it surface—we'll know where it is."

Lemon's mouth twists. "We have to go back to my house. I still don't think I should tell Pappap much of anything we heard the agents say—but I can give him this and tell him we think we have until tomorrow night."

"Okay," Darrin says, "but what if we actually find a way to kill the monster, and it doesn't matter? What if the agents annihilate the whole fucking lake and you and Ike and Pearl anyway? What if the agents really do tell the whole world that Old Lucy's been a fake from the start?"

Old Lucy will be dead. The town will die. I'll die, too, because I'll fight for Lemon with my last breath.

"You want to think that way, go ahead—but nothing's over until it's over," I say. "Let's go."

19

THERE MUST BE TEN DOZEN muffins cooling in Lemon's kitchen. Mrs. Z is at the counter by the sink, white mixing bowl in her hands. She stirs furiously with a wooden spoon while Lemon talks. The idea of eating anything makes me want to puke. Darrin, though, he's already a muffin and a half down.

"Merciful heavens! I invited that little redheaded girl right in," Mrs. Z says. Butterbeans stands guard at the back door, watching us. "It was right after Ike left for Marley's to talk to that friend of his. If I would have known, well . . . I don't know what I would have done, truth be told. The garment bag she dropped is in your room, Lemon—are you concerned that there might be another of her . . . hints in the bag? Or maybe a listening device?"

"I guess there could be," Lemon says, turns to me, Darrin. Bob pads down the hall from the bedrooms, circles her chair before picking a spot to lie. "You know, Amelia did say one thing the day we went . . ." Her face pinkens up. "Grammy, I'm going to tell you something, and I know you're going to be mad—but under the circumstances, can we back burner discussion for a day when we're not about to all die or be maimed or have our cover blown to the town or whatever?"

Mrs. Z stops stirring, puts the bowl on the counter. Props one hand on her hip. She narrows her eyes. "Go on."

"I skipped school to go to Wilkes-Barre with Amelia yesterday." Lemon stops, fidgets for a second, then stills. "We went dress shopping—for the prom. I . . . asked Amelia if she'd keep the dress so you and Pappap wouldn't find out I wasn't in school."

"Don't think I'm not keeping count of these transgressions, young lady." Mrs. Z squares her shoulders, grimaces. "You got out of a grounding once for skipping school. If you th—"

"Grammy, come on. Focus—we can do this later. Please?"

"Okay, so you have a prom dress." Her voice is flat.

"Right," Lemon says, carefully avoiding looking at Mrs. Z in the face. Can't blame her. "Anyway, what I was going to say is when Amelia and I were on the way over to Wilkes-Barre, she said that her dad didn't plan on spending much time on whatever he was working on here, so she might be transferring out of Devil's Elbow High School pretty soon—but she would leave my dress if she knew she was going to disappear."

"We already know that," Darrin says. "Not about your dress, but about her dad and the agents being done with their work pretty fast—like, tomorrow night."

"Right," Lemon says. "I'm trying to rack my brain for something else she said that day that means something and might be useful."

"Mrs. Z is right," I say. "Maybe get the dress bag, Lem—we can take a look."

Mrs. Z's eyes widen. "You will do no such thing—you're not supposed to see Lemon's prom dress before the big night."

Nice that she's assuming this is all going to go our way, and we'll all still be here by prom night.

Lemon's face goes even redder. "Gram, that's brides. We're . . . not getting married."

Darrin cracks up—I can see he's probably recalling his *sweet yellow-haired babies* crap.

"Shush, Darrin." Mrs. Z doesn't seem to know whether she wants to frown or smile, but the smile's winning out. She glances at me, winks. She *winks*. "You boys wait right here. Lemon, let's go see your dress."

I can't get over the wink. What was *that*?

"Do you think Lemon is the only one who doesn't know you're full-on in love with her?" Darrin says when they're down the hall, Bob and Butterbeans following them like it's a parade. "Because Pearl seems aware."

"So're my parents," I mutter.

"What's that?"

"Nothing. Look, I can't just sit here on my hands. We're on a freaking deadline."

"Call Amelia again," Darrin says. "Maybe she'll give you more clues."

I dig the phone from my pocket, dial her up on speaker.

A woman sing-songs, "We're sorry. You have reached a number that has been disconnected or is no longer in service. If you feel this is in error, please check the number dialed, and please try again."

Darrin stops chewing.

I copy Amelia's number from her contact page, paste it into the keypad. Try again.

"We're sorry. You have reached a number that has been disconnected or is no longer in service. If you feel this is in error, please check the number dialed, and please try again."

"Oh fuck," Darrin says. "What's that supposed to mean?"

I scramble out of my seat and call back down the hallway, "Lemon, we have a problem."

Her blond head pokes around her bedroom door. "Another one? How refreshing."

"Amelia's phone is out of service."

"Hey, Mrs. Z?" Darrin hollers from behind me.

"What is it, Darrin?" comes the muffled reply.

Lemon's eyeballs are boring a hole into me, mouth working like she wants to say something.

"Did Ike ever watch the other fish cam recording? The kayak camera?" Darrin asks.

"He couldn't figure out how to load it."

"Think he'd care if we watch it now?" he says.

"No, go ahead. I was going to suggest it anyway, especially after that thingamajig . . . You go right ahead."

"We'll be right out," Lemon says, ducks back into her room.

Before she shuts the door, I hear Mrs. Z say, "I daresay it's a daring neckline."

My eyebrows practically shoot off my face. Now is a thousand percent not the time for my brain to be on how Lemon looks in her dress—doesn't mean I'm not thinking about it.

Darrin's on his knees in front of the television with the remote when I step into the living room. "Phone?" he says.

I hand it over, take a spot on the ugly couch. Watch him get everything set up. Screen pops up grainy and muted blue. The bottom of the kayak is visible along the top of the screen. "Can you fast-forward until there's stuff to see?"

"We might miss a fast flicker of something."

"Yeah, but who knows how much footage we have to get through."

"Go ahead." Lemon steals into the living room, sits next to me. Bob's with her. Dog coils up in Lemon's armpit. "If we don't see anything fast-forwarding, I'll watch on regular speed tonight."

Mrs. Z bangs around in the kitchen. "Are you kids hungry?"

"No," Lemon says at the same time Darrin delivers an emphatic, "Yes."

My stomach grumbles. Not sure if it's hunger or fear. Haven't eaten since this morning—maybe it's both.

Lemon leans close to me. "Grammy agrees with me about not telling Pappap about, well, everything. She said he'll only do something ill-advised."

"But what about Old Lucy?"

She lifts one shoulder. "We can and should try to get rid of the monster ourselves in the time that we have, but if worse comes to worse, we'll have to let the agents destroy the lake—Grammy won't let anyone else die because of Old Lucy, and doing anything to make the agents go public about everything Old Lucy–related would kill Pappap."

"So . . . that's it then?" I say.

"No giving up. Grammy is sure we can figure out a way to deal with whatever happens."

"You're okay with that?"

"No." Her eyes rim with tears.

Darrin says, "Not to interrupt your lovefest, but you want to take a look at this?"

I glower in his direction, but he's not paying attention. His eyes are on the television, looking at— What is that? I lean forward, try to focus.

"Are those . . . claws?" Lemon swipes at her eyes.

Mrs. Z appears in the doorway, drying her hands on a towel.

"Looks like," Darrin says.

"Fish don't have claws," Lemon says.

"Bears do, though," I say. "Is it a bear? Not saying I'm back on the bear theory, but maybe this is random and has nothing to do with the monster."

"No, looks at the shape of the foot." Lemon clambers off the couch, steps over Darrin to get to the screen. She traces the outline with her finger. "Even if this was a bear with mange, like Pappap tried to gaslight me into believing at first, the shape is super wrong. This is more like a reptile. It's all scaly looking, but not like fish scales, and not like mange."

"We're back on the giant, man-eating alligator?" Darrin says. "There's a giant snapping turtle-alligator cryptid who allegedly lives in West Virginia. It's called the Ogua."

Mrs. Z says, "Are you suggesting the Ogua got lost and took up residence in our lake?"

Darrin cackles. "Trust me—it's the most sane thing I've heard today."

"Would you advance frame by frame?" Lemon says.

Darrin sobers, nods.

She's silent for a moment, then shrieks, "Stop."

"Jesus, what?" Darrin says.

Mrs. Z's hand flutters over her heart.

"Look." Lemon points to something dark on-screen.

"Those fingers?" I say.

"I think it's a flipper," she says. "A little like an otter. See how—"

"Oh yeah," Darrin says. "Otters have retractable claws, right?"

"How do you know that?" Lemon looks at him, incredulous.

"I was paying attention when you made us watch that otter documentary."

"No, really," Lemon says.

He shrugs. "Cara likes otters. But I doubt she'd be so crazy about the idea of an alligator-otter hybrid that's about to destroy the town like freaking Godzilla."

"And that's how you knew otters build burrows?" I say.

"Some of us have to work to win the heart of our beloved." He flashes me a grin laden with a billion things he'd like to say to Lemon to torture me.

Mrs. Z says, "Is any of this important? That it's like an otter?"

"It could be," Lemon says. "Otters can hold their breath underwater for long periods—they breathe air. Obviously it's not an otter, but if this thing is similar to an otter, that makes a difference to how we might have to hunt it." She takes a deep breath. "Keep fast-forwarding. See if we can follow where it goes." Pulls the rocking chair over, perches on the edge, hands braced on her knees.

Mrs. Z says, "So it really could be an alligator-otter hybrid?"

Lemon, Darrin, and I say simultaneously, "Anything is possible."

Not one of us sounds excited.

"Alligators breathe oxygen, too," Lemon says, "and can hold their breath underwater for at least fifteen or twenty minutes."

Mrs. Z's face pales.

The foot-flipper thing rushes off-screen, leaving only air bubbles swirling in its wake.

The footage advances in nothingness.

Darrin says, "Hold up." He pauses and rewinds—the kayak looks like it's flying through the water. "Okay, what the hell is this?" He jabs his finger at the screen.

Lemon says, "Peter's Island is coming up closer too quick—even if the wind caught the kayak, it wouldn't be moving that fast."

Everyone in the room can probably hear my blood pulsing as the kayak rushes closer and closer. Something bashes the kayak in half. Mrs. Z gasps, twists her dish towel in front of her. Lemon and Darrin lean in.

"Play that back," Lemon says. "Slow motion." Moments later she says, "Looks like a tail, don't you think?"

"How can you tell?" I say. "Even in slo-mo, it's just a blur."

"I don't know." She glances at me, face carefully neutral. "Just a hunch."

It hits me she's probably thinking about vet school. She's got all this knowledge she'll never get to use. I want to go to her, wrap her up in a hug—tell her everything's going to be okay. A lie told for love shouldn't count against me.

"Holy shit!" Lemon jumps from the rocking chair.

"Language, Lemon," Mrs. Z cries. "Language."

"Sorry, Grammy, but look." Lemon points.

A big, dark thing zips through the water, drags half the kayak with it. Seems to swim right into the rocky base of Peter's Island at full speed. The cam hits, then the screen goes dead.

Lemon's eyes are huge. "Whether it's part otter or part alligator or part Darrin's West Virginia snapping turtle thing—I think maybe we found it's hidey-hole."

My body nearly jumps out of my skin when Mr. Z comes barreling through the door, yelling, "Pearl!" Stops short when he sees us, grumbles, "I hain't like that this house is a hangout."

"Ike," Mrs. Z says, "the kids have some things—"

"Word's out about Will and that Jenkins kid," Pappap says. "People canceling hotel reservations left and right. Talk about mounting up hunting parties for Old Lucy, folk thinking they can solve things theyselves and save the summer."

I groan quietly. This complicates everything. "What about the lake closures?"

"Damn fools don't care. I didn't know what to tell them about Will—I've spent so long pinning every damn thing that happens on Old Lucy to keep interest up I couldn't come up with anything. It's different when it's all fact, not rumor."

Mrs. Z is back to wringing the dish towel.

"Any idea when people might try something?" Lemon says, but I can see the panic in her eyes. Darrin, Mrs. Z—we're all thinking the worst.

"Hain't no way it'll be tonight—they're all too scared to be up here after dark these days. At least they got half a brain. Between them feds being all shady and a real monster in my damn lake, it's right dangerous." He looks around at us. "Them feds you follow lead anywhere?"

Lemon blurts, "We might have figured out where the monster lives. I don't know if that's the right word, but . . . watch. This is from out at Peter's Island."

Darrin plays the recording back, side-eyeing Lemon.

"Well, I'll be damned," Mr. Z says. "You boys done good."

"Lemon's the one who spotted it," I say. "We just—"

"Team effort," Mr. Z says. "Damn good job."

I nearly pass out from the shock of the compliment.

Lemon says, "Uh, we did find out something else."

She very carefully tells Mr. Z about Amelia being involved, the speaker and what it does, the fact that we probably have until tomorrow night *if* we've actually figured out correctly what Amelia means. Leaves out the cabin, the death threat, the outing threat, and everything else, though.

"Ike, I think we need to call the agents." Mrs. Z's knuckles are bone white. "They said to call if we change our mind about evacuation—so let's change our minds. We can . . . we can tell them we've seen something in the lake. Find a way to tell them what we know without implicating ourselves. Let them kill it. We can rebuild Old Lucy's reputation. Maybe . . . maybe in a few years—"

Mr. Z's face turns into a thundercloud, but Darrin speaks first. "Rule number one in government conspiracy theories—never trust what anyone who works for the government or law enforcement says." He shrugs at Mr. Z. "Sorry, but that's just the facts."

"Hain't no need to apologize," Mr. Z says. "I was going to say . . . not *that* . . . but I ain't trust these folks as far as I can throw 'em, Pearl. They'll go back on their word, then throw us under the bus in a second. Throw this whole town under the bus. I've had the keeping of this lake for damn near fifty years—I don't mean to fail her now."

Lemon startles, shoots me an alarmed look. Between Mrs. Z going to pieces and going rogue and Mr. Z growing more determined to do who knows what, things are going downhill quick.

Mr. Z says, "Tomorrow morning I'll take a ferry out to the island with one of them fish cams, see what I can see."

"Not by yourself, you won't," Mrs. Z says.

Mr. Z smiles, pats Lemon's shoulder.

"I wouldn't dream of it. We have to be smart, but I hain't going out on the ferry without being prepared for a few different ideas I got. We'll get this taken care of ourselves . . . our way."

This is going from bad to worse.

"I'm going with you, right?" Lemon says.

I look at her out of the corner of my eye, willing her to back down.

"Now, I don't see no reason why you need to—"

"You put me in charge of Old Lucy, so it's my lake, too." Lemon's jaw tightens.

"Ike," Grammy says, "you know I don't want Lemon anywhere near the lake while—"

"I know, Pearl. That's why I'm keeping her out of it."

"Hey!" Lemon says.

"That's not what I mean," Mrs. Z says. "Lemon's right—we have to start treating her like an adult if we're giving her adult responsibilities."

Mr. Z sputters. "Lemon hain't no adult."

"*Lemon* is standing right here," Lemon says. "And she will be going with you tomorrow on the ferry." She crosses the room to stand next to Mrs. Z. They both cross their arms.

"I'm outranked, eh? I don't like it."

Neither do I.

20

L E M O N

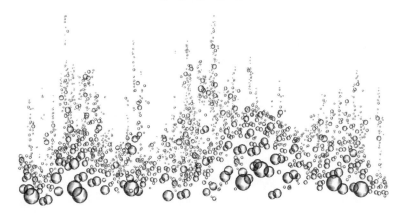

T HE HOUSE IS EERILY QUIET the next morning. The high school is closed again on account of the nonexistent bacteria. I fully expect to discover Pappap went out to the lake last night—when the lake was dark—just to spite me. But he's at the kitchen table, scribbling out what looks to be a list on a yellow legal pad. There's a half-eaten muffin on a plate in front of him, along with his favorite Old Lucy mug from the ferry tours merchandise shop. It doesn't mean he's been home all night, of course.

Pappap glances up, gives me a nod, and goes back to his legal pad.

He's probably still mad at me and Grammy for presenting a united front.

I stand at the back door and focus on the lake. Bob remains still asleep in my room. It's still so bizarre that there's something out there, something deadly and hungry, in a lake I've loved my whole life. Behind me, Pappap's chair scrapes against the floor. A moment later, his hand lands on my shoulder. He's standing close enough to smell the sleep on him. It's nice that one of us got some rest—I stared at my ceiling all night, dialing and redialing Amelia's now-defunct phone number and dreading daybreak . . . every now and then thinking about Troy in ways that are completely unproductive, occasionally wondering what Skeet Jenkins's family has planned for me or if they've moved on to their next imagined feud.

"You know I can't think of you as anything but a little girl," Pappap says. "I was there the day you was born. Just a tiny thing, brown fuzz all over the top of your head. Big eyes. Your eyes stayed blue as your mother's, but your hair fell out a few weeks later, grew in blond."

I've heard this story from Grammy, but Pappap's not the type to get all mushy or nostalgic. I keep watching the lake.

"Never told anyone this—not even Pearl—but I knew all along that Bobby'd make a poor choice for this legacy of ours. Your dad was the one. Smart as a whip. He loved this town as much as anyone. And your mother—hain't never met anyone more suited to the life. You're just like the both of them. That's why I didn't put up a fuss about Bobby and Nan voting for you to take over for me. I knew it were going to be you since right after the accident with your parents."

"Pappap—"

"Let me just say what I have to say. I know damn well you don't want this life. There hain't no one else, though—and I don't mean that you're the last resort. I mean that you're going to do a great job—Bobby, Nan . . . I'd have been worried. Even Will, bless him. Feels wrong to say it now, but it's true. I know I hain't never got to worry with you. You'll do the family proud, whether it's the ferry business or Old Lucy or keeping up with this house. I know, because you always done us proud. So don't be thinking that I'm trying to keep you out of what's happening because I ain't trust you—or because I think you're a kid. It's because I love you, granddaughter."

I bite my tongue to keep my sudden tears from overflowing. He presses a quick kiss to the back of my head and sits back at the table. I can hear it when he starts writing again. I stay still until there's zero chance of my voice wobbling or losing control of my face. He's never said anything like that to me. Ever. Pappap's always been this crusty old guy—even when I was younger.

I clear my throat. "So what now?"

I turn toward him, half expecting some kind of miraculous transformation to have taken place, but he's still my crusty old grandfather. He's wearing a ghost of a smile, though. Maybe that's the way he looks when he loves someone.

He gestures to the legal pad. "I been figuring out what we might need to head out to Peter's Island. I can pick up a few things at the hardware store and such when the shops open. I definitely want to stop at the butcher shop—pick up blood and meat scraps."

"Oh, right. Bait."

He nods. "By the way, your grandmother took Butterbeans and rode her bike out to the Devil's Elbow library with a load of muffins for them."

"She did make a lot of them."

"You hain't mind staying here and waiting for your grandmother, do you? I'll swing by when I'm done my supply run and pick you both up. Heaven forbid if Pearl hain't a part of this monster hunt, too."

This gentler Pappap is nice, but trusting what he's saying at face value . . . I don't know. He's a liar—we all are in this family. It's not like he's ever lied to *me*, though. It's usually that he's so blatantly and unpleasantly honest that's the issue. Still, the thought that he could be lying makes me hesitate to answer. It's this weird olive branch of sweetness offered just now that pushes me to accept it and offer it back. What can I say? I *want* to believe.

"It's fine," I say. "I need to take a shower anyway. Do you mind if we don't take Troy and Darrin on the ferry with us?" After how close they came to death yesterday on the stairs, I can't do that to them again.

"No, that's good—hain't no reason to put them in harm's way to-day."

I nod. "I was thinking, though—about later."

"Later when?"

"I'm thinking positively that we're going to be able to kill this thing, so we're going to have to somehow tell the agents that we did—and then they can leave and stop bothering us. So, what would you think about going to the press?"

His forehead furrows. "I thought we was on the same page about not telling any more folks about what we do out here?"

"No, not like that. It's just . . . the agents—" I cut myself off—the words *want to kill us and kill the town and tell everyone Old Lucy is a fake* are on the tip of my tongue. "Well, I assume there'll be some kind of proof that we killed this thing—a body, maybe. What if we have the news stations and the newspaper out here, and show them the body? The agents must be monitoring local media, right? So that'll be good for broadcasting to them that this is over—plus Sheriff Ramirez will know, and we can ask him to get in contact with them, too. They'll probably want the body for testing. Plus, maybe I can stage an Old Lucy sighting as soon as we can get the costume replaced. That'll get everyone in town talking."

Pappap chuckles.

"Make sure everyone knows the monster in the lake *isn't* Old Lucy," I finish. "I can spread a theory that Old Lucy was probably hiding until the danger had passed."

"Been thinking about this a little, huh?" Pappap says and laughs again. "Proof positive we picked the right Ziegler for the job."

I should be feeling good about the compliment, but the longer I ramble at Pappap, the less sure I feel about how successfully we can convince anyone that the monster is dead but Old Lucy isn't. But at least if we go public—like *really* public—the agents will have to back off. No one wants to kill off the nice people making noise in public. It attracts too much attention. And if they still try to tell everyone about Old Lucy being a hoax, well...I don't know how we'll handle that, but maybe we can fight it with an alternating conspiracy that the federal government is trying to ruin Devil's Elbow because they found oil and want the land for themselves. That should rile people up.

I inwardly groan. I *do* sound like Darrin.

❧❧❧

PAPPAP'S GONE BY the time I'm done with my shower, but my nerves are still rattling. I snag a muffin and head back to my bedroom. Bob's up, so I feed him a chunk. His little tail nubbin wags like crazy.

Every inch of my skin is a live wire while I dress for the day. I mean, what is the proper attire for monster hunting? Amelia would know. Then again, Amelia knows everything, apparently—and now she's unreachable. *She's missing* is what my brain whispers to me. She's missing, maybe because her dad found out she helped us. Because she's been dropping hints all along, even though we didn't know enough to catch them or understand what she was saying.

I don't know what to think, although I'm sure Darrin has a theory. My fingers itch to text Troy and Darrin, but if I do, I'll have to lie to them about my and Pappap's plan—and I just can't. It's better to avoid telling them anything at all until it's over. At least I'll know they're okay, but it still feels gross. Asking for their help and putting them in danger has been bad enough, but cutting them out now...especially Troy... it's making my stomach grouchy.

I thought maybe what happened in the woods yesterday on the way to the cabin would wipe out the feelings, but somehow, everything is magnified this morning. My prom dress hangs from the curtain rod above one of my bedroom windows. The garment bag is unzipped, showing just a hint of the gray tulle overlay.

Maybe I'll confess to Troy at prom. People are always saying it's the exclamation point at the end of our senior year—and everyone's all dressed up and feeling emotional. We'll be dancing, and it won't be all that weird to kiss Troy, even if he has made it clear he's not into me. He might never want to talk to me ever again after today, anyway . . . or maybe . . . well, maybe something else.

It would be a shame not to get to wear my dress.

I pull the top of the muffin off and take a bite. It's blueberry. Obsessing about *any* of this right now is not a good idea, even though it's much more pleasant than imagining the next few hours. I pull a pair of jeans and a T-shirt from my drawer and slip them on, push every feeling down until I can almost pretend this a normal day.

Almost.

Bob pads behind me, out the door, down the hall, and into the living room. I'm too nervous to sit, so I tidy. I reposition cushions. I fluff pillows. Straighten pictures on the wall. Rearrange the coffee table so it's at a perfect right angle to the gold couch. Center the area rug. I end up in the kitchen, unloading the dishwasher and washing the rest of Grammy's muffin tins and mixing bowls by hand. Anything to keep busy while I'm waiting. Bob's so annoyed with me that he curls up on the couch and falls asleep. I'm back in the living room nudging the curtains into perfect symmetry on either side of the front picture window when I see Grammy pedal furiously into the driveway. My anxiety edges up. She tucks Butterbeans under her arm, throws her bike down, and storms inside. Okay, angsty engaged.

Butterbeans wiggles away from her and lets out a few high-pitched yips.

"Where's your grandfather?" Grammy pants.

"What's wrong?"

I've never seen her quite so frantic. The wrinkles on her cheeks tremble, and her gnarled hands clutch the neck of her top. Her hair is coming down from her braids. "Is he here?"

"No, he said he went out to buy supplies." Pretending everything is okay is officially not working—my brain is screaming so loud I can barely hear Grammy over the din. "He's coming back to pick us up when he's done."

"I knew he was being too cheerful this morning. Flo Benscoter came into the library just as I was leaving and said she saw Ike at the ferry office, unpacking things from his car. Swore he was carting sticks of dynamite. I called, and he had the audacity to tell me not to worry. That fool is taking the ferry out by himself."

My heart throbbing is pulverizing my ribs to powder. "Dynamite? What is he trying to do?" I already know. He *knows*. About everything. I don't know how he knows, but he does. "Did you tell him?"

Grammy shakes her head. Her face is the color of rotting tomatoes.

The speaker. It's in my bedroom. I sprint down the hall and into my room, to the dresser where I put it last night. It's gone. I turn around, but Grammy's already behind me, Bob and Butterbeans sprinting after her, barking.

"He took the speaker," I say. "He must have overheard us yesterday."

She mutters, "That man just can't leave anything alone."

"Okay, let me think." I push my fingers against my forehead, but nothing comes to me. That's not true—one thing does, but I don't want to even consider it. Swear words pop in my head like big bubbles full of toxic gas. A few more seconds, and I say out loud, "I'll call Troy. He'll come and get us, drive us to the ferry office. Maybe we can catch Pappap before he goes out."

"There's no time for that, Lemon." Grammy hustles through the living room, both dogs following.

"Then . . . okay, I'll ride your bike down to the public dock. If he's heading out to Peter's Island, he'll see me. I'll take my phone and . . . where's the air horn?"

"No, absolutely not." Grammy whips open the door and hurries out. "I'll go."

I run after her, slamming the door before the dogs run out. "I'll be faster. Maybe call the sheriff—tell him Pappap's violating the lake closure order. That'll get a fast response." I wrestle the bike out of her hands.

"Lemon, no." Grammy tugs at the bike, and I yank back. "Oh, I'm not going to argue with you. You're as stubborn as he is." She throws her hands up.

"Then just give up and let me go," I yell.

She scowls and orders me to wait before rushing into the house like she's on fire and needs water to put herself out. When she ducks back outside, she shoves my phone and an air horn into the front basket. She adds, exasperated, "Just . . . okay, go. I'll keep calling Ike and trying to talk sense into him."

I take off, peddling fast as I can. The smells of the lake crowd into my nose—resinous pine, the muck of fish—as I get closer.

I lean the bike against a tree when I hit the dock and tuck the phone into my jeans pocket. The air horn is cold in my hand. I don't hear the buzz of the ferry engine, but I pound down to the edge of the public dock and eye every inch of the lake, trying to see everywhere—keeping watch for the monster and for Pappap. The blood is clanging around my body so fast I can feel it pulsing in my feet. Just then, a chugging reverberates over the water. I can just make out the stern of a boat at the edge of Peter's Island. Pappap took the smallest vessel—a trawler. I have to go with Grammy on this one: he *is* a fool.

I blast the air horn, three times quick in succession, and wave my arms. I'm about to set off the air horn again when my phone rings.

"Lemon, hain't you got no sense? Go home."

"I could say the same, Pappap," I yell. "Take the trawler back or I'll jump up and down on the dock. Vibrations attract notice underwater, don't they?"

"It ain't safe out here."

"What have I just been getting at?"

"Dammit," he hollers through the phone. "Wait right there. I'm coming to get you."

The trawler pulls away from the island and moves in my direction. I step back from the edge, stomach still roiling. The boat rumbles closer and closer until Pappap sidles the engine and drifts up to the end of the dock. He shoots a withering glance my way. He bellows, "Come aboard then."

I catch the mooring line he tosses to me and reel the boat in close enough to jump on. "What do you think you're doing?"

"Me?" Pappap's voice takes on a tone of overly dramatic wounded innocence. "You're the one keeping secrets. I give you a chance this morning to tell me what I overheard in my own damn house, and you don't say a word. Where is your sense of family pride? Your sense of loyalty?"

I approach the helm as he comes about back toward the island. "You only said that stuff to me to get me to tell you about what the agents said?"

He grumbles, "Now hain't the time to get all—"

"Forget it," I snip. "Grammy says you have dynamite on board. What kind of stupid thing are you planning?"

Pappap huffs. "Ain't nothing stupid about it. I took your metal doodad, and I'm going to make sure I know where that damn monster is. Draw it to me. I got the chum from the bait house to help. I'll blow that monster up good and proper."

"Uh-huh. Why'd you have to do that alone?"

"You may not think I like you overmuch, but hain't no way I'm putting my wife and only granddaughter in the way of a man-eater when it just killed my grandson." He arcs the boat to starboard slightly, jaw set.

"Right. So what happens if you can't kill the monster single-handed?"

"You made sure I hain't single-handed anymore," he says sourly.

"What's Plan B, Pappap?" I grip the helm's doorframe. "Come on."

"I'll wait for it to settle back into its den or its . . . whatever it is . . . and blow up the island."

My eyes bug out. "You're going to *what?*"

"Won't do you no good to make faces at me. That's what I'm doing. It's the only rational thing—if that thing's living at Peter's Island, I'm blowing up Peter's Island."

"*That's* rational?" If I make it back to shore, my grandparents and I are going to have a talk about logic and trust, because none of this is okay. If I've got to give up my entire future for this crap, Pappap's going to have to try harder not to kill himself or the infrastructure that makes impersonations possible. What am I supposed to hide behind if the boulders are gone? If this is Pappap's plan, why *not* let the feds destroy the whole lake?

I shake my head and keep an eye out—a wave that looks weird, a flash of mottled gray, that awful, strangling moan. There's nothing, though. Just us, the trawler, the water, and Peter's Island, now almost close enough to touch.

I lean over the railing to spot any dark shadows looming under the boat. Nothing but murky water, swirling along the hull.

In the next second, the deck of the trawler steeply lists. Before I have time to react, I'm sinking into the cold water. Without my dry suit, it's like swimming in ice cubes. My jeans cling to my legs, and a shoe is sucked off into a surprisingly strong current. I kick for the surface. My head breaks through, sweet air in my lungs. Noise—hoarse shouts and a groaning roar that's too familiar—hits me at once, loud and disorienting.

I shake the water off my face, try to corral my whirling thoughts.

I'm in the lake. And there's a monster.

"Lemon, swim!" Pappap screams.

I swing my head toward his voice. The boat bobs about ten feet away in the churning water. Pappap's face is chalky. I want to scream back, ask him where the monster is, but my voice sticks in my throat. Is it drawn to kicking legs? If I make a sound, will it find its way right to me? I should stay put. No, that's silly. What am I going to do—float and play dead until it decides it's not hungry for a corpse? My eyes dart back and forth. My teeth chatter.

"Lemon, listen to me now," Pappap yells. "I hain't going to let nothing happen to you." He pauses. "Swim to the island. Reach along the boulder there, pull yourself over. There's a break in the bushes just ten or fifteen feet, you can wiggle through to dry land."

The boat engine chugs hard. The vibration of it jolts up my legs. I fill my lungs with air and do as Pappap instructs.

Something bumps against my foot. I swallow a shriek and a gulp of lake water. Pappap yells again.

A new vibration shakes my legs and squeezes my body. A huge gray bulge breaks the surface of the lake only inches away. Yellow teeth flash in front of my face, and the smell of dead things rushes up my nostrils.

The pulse hits me again. The monster thrashes and groans. Its mouth descends. My brain shocks out, and suddenly it's as though I'm watching from a great distance.

The monster's hard head strikes me in the face. Tears spring to my eyes, and my cheek pulses with pain. I grimace and punch. There's no way I want to die without kissing Troy. The monster squeals and bucks.

I smack and hit at it with all my strength. It jerks and snaps at my arm. A slicing pain rips through me. The monster pulls me under. I sputter icy water and surface again to a churning scream and the roar of the boat engine. Those teeth tug at me again. I suck in another lungful of air. Just before I'm hauled below again, I catch a glimpse of a thin figure standing on the far shore. A thin figure with a shock of bright red hair. Amelia. It has to be. No one else has hair like that. Not missing after all—but what is she doing. Helping or not helping?

I flail as the monster drags me furiously through the water. It's like being propelled by a jetpack. Is Amelia's dad here, too? The rest of the agents? Why don't they *do* something? Or is this part of the plan to kill me and my family? A shaking throb hits me again, and I'm free. I clamp my hand over my arm, if for no other reason than to make sure it's still attached.

I kick, hoping I'm heading in the right direction—toward the surface, toward air. My foot catches. My guts shrivel. No fair. No fair to think I'm getting away only for the monster to come back. My lungs burn. I brace myself to be dragged through the water again, but nothing comes. I open my eyes again to darkness, but there's no hulking shadow, only a sense of urgency in my lungs that makes my brain scream.

I kick again, but something still has my foot. I pat down my leg until my hand touches a gnarled thing. Not alive. I wedge my foot out and lose the other shoe, and a feeling of peace clouds my head. It's warmer now. I'm back to thinking about Amelia, wondering where she's been. Wondering if she was really trying to warn us—if it was all a ruse to get me to this moment.

Grammy's going to be so mad at Pappap—if she's already not dead. Maybe the agents took her out first.

And what about Troy and Darrin? Will the agents leave them alone? I dragged them into this mess and now . . . will Amelia tell them I've died? Will dying hurt? I've read about drowning. It's supposed to be like falling asleep, like accepting what you can't change.

This whole town will die along with us. It probably won't take long for the tourists to completely abandon Devil's Elbow, for the poverty to descend. It's already started, from what Pappap said.

I don't want to accept any of it. I reach along, find something solid to touch. Pull myself along whatever has caught me. A rope? A tree root?

Here it is—death. The light is changing, getting darker. Hell, maybe? I don't know what I believe happens after life ends. Maybe nothing. Maybe it's just *this*. A glow in my head, and then lights out and nothing.

I drag myself along, but the pressure in my chest deepens. *Take a breath. That's what you need to do.* That's a voice in my head, telling me to go with it. End it. Why fight? The voice fogs. I reach again, and my hand breaks through . . . to something. Another heave, and my head follows.

I choke on the air. My lungs expand with a pain that rips me in half. I crawl out of the lake and shake the freezing water from my eyes, but there's nothing but an inky black warmth. The ground beneath me is gritty and sharp, rocky. I cough, and a river of snot and water shoots over my upper lip.

I roll over and clasp my arm, gasping. I can't tell whether it's water or blood. Nothing gushing, at least. Something sharp pokes into my hip bone. I reach down and feel the outline of my phone in my freezing, soggy front pocket. I dig it out and flick the screen. The bright glow burns into my retinas.

I wince and turn the screen away, even as I silently thank Darrin for talking me into a waterproof phone. A look at my arm makes me sigh in relief, too. Whatever caught me—the monster's tooth, maybe—made a cut, but nothing horrible. I'm barely bleeding now. I tear a strip from the bottom of my shirt and wrap it around my arm, thinking of the tourniquet Grammy wrapped around what was left of Will's arm. I gulp against the burn of the scratch, the grief of remembering my cousin is gone.

I pack it way down inside myself. This is not the time to wallow. I take a deep breath and slowly look around.

Rocks. No, a cave. A mostly dry cave—and hot. That makes zero sense. The walls are gray and rough, boulders piled one on top of the other. I shiver violently and climb to my feet while extending my hands—my fingertips don't touch the ceiling. I flash my phone's light along. Water laps along the edge of the cave. Along the far edge, I catch sight of something bright blue. Bright blue marred with dark red. Fabric half wrapped around a torso.

My scream reverberates off the low walls.

There's a pile next the torso. The top is scattered with bones too short and thin to be human bones, jumbled side-by-side with the remains of a hand, flesh green and bloated. A torn orange shirt bearing what I think is the Magic Monster logo. I can't think about what's inside the shirt. I can't think about who's in that pile. The rest of Skeet. Part of Will. Snowflake.

I skitter back and almost drop the phone. I'm trapped, with nothing to do but wait for the monster to come back for a snack . . . or for me. I hope I'm wrong—that this has nothing to do with the agents wanting to kill us all, and that Pappap got away. That he won't assume I'm dead and blow up the island anyway.

I tap my phone again as it dims, and the light comes back stronger. So does the shivering. Not a single bar on the screen—I have plenty of juice but no access to a network. A thousand years from now people will do an excavation of the island, maybe, and then they'll find my skeleton, torn apart and scattered over the cave, too. My breath stutters out, along with my resolve to be calm and positive.

This is it for me. Maybe I can write out my goodbyes on the walls of the cave, but by then who will care? What will it matter that I'm thinking of my grandparents or my friends while waiting to become the next meal? No one will give a crap that I'm half in love with my best friend.

Whoa. I freeze. That's too much. I don't love Troy. Well, I do. I love him like crazy . . . but in the same way I love Darrin. Okay, maybe that's not true. I've never wanted to canoodle with Darrin. Ever. My nervous laugh bounces off the cave walls.

I sigh and scan the cave again. The smell of rot is less obvious here, but still present. There's no clear way out except for the way I came in, and I'm not going back out there. I'm trapped here, just as sure as I've felt trapped in Devil's Elbow, impersonating Old Lucy for the rest of my life. That is probably not a concern anymore on any level. Whatever the case, it seems like I'm doomed to run out of air in this cave eventually, even if the family legacy *isn't* about to be exposed.

I really should text goodbyes, just in case. If the cave collapses, or the monster eats me, or I suffocate, at least a rescue squad—if one ever comes—will find my phone. Even if everyone I know is gone by then, saying goodbye will make me feel better about it. Sort of.

I sit on the ground in my sopping wet jeans and lean against part of the cave wall that's farthest from the nearest entrance. I thumb in my grandparents' names from the directory. I type: *Trapped in a cave under peters island. Send help. Love you both.*

I scrunch my nose and think of Pappap telling me he loves me back at the house this morning. I could add, just out of spite, *I mean that, Pappap, unlike you.* Instead, I type: *I'm okay. See you soon.*

To Darrin, I write: *Went to stop Pappap from getting killed, ended up stuck in a cave on Peter's Island. What a silly way to go. Hope monster/feds will be over now and all will be safe. Take care. You're a good friend.*

My fingers shake so much I can barely type in Troy's name. A million things to say wind around in my head. Stuff I want to say but can't or shouldn't. I thumb in a note to him, wishing I hadn't been such a coward. It probably doesn't matter now.

In a fit of hopefulness, I hit the send button for each message. I crawl to my feet and turn off the light on my phone. Better save it for when I need it, and better not to give the monster a hand in spotting me. Hey, I might never breathe fresh air again, but why help fate along? Nothing is truly over until it's over.

21

T R O Y

S LEEP ISN'T A THING I have anymore. Oh sure, I caught a few hours last night—but my body wants something else. Protect what you love, I guess. The lake is a threat. Those agents are a threat. Mr. Z may or may not be a threat. And Dad told me last night that Vern Jenkins made bail, so now Vern is a threat again, too. Dad had it right when he said everything was cursed.

I flip over, try to force my eyes to shut. Sun's been up for a while. Lemon said she'd text when she wanted us to come over. I should've just stayed parked in her driveway last night, slept in the Buick. Kept watch over the house.

Something taps at the window, like scattered hail.

I slide my phone off the nightstand, flip through. No new texts from Lemon, although there are a few random ones from kids at school. World might be coming to an end, but gossip stops for no one.

The noise against my window comes again. I roll out of bed, squint through the blinds. A handful of gravel bounces off the glass in front of my nose.

I jerk back, pissed. Told Darrin a million times—a text is sufficient. Stones from my mom's garden, they'll break a window. Dad likes Darrin just fine; it doesn't mean he won't try to arrest him.

I lean forward at the window. It's not Darrin. Red hair. Amelia, almost hidden in the bushes below. My agitation goes into blender mode. She gestures at me—*come down*.

I jump back, throw on jeans from the day before. Don't even feel the stairs under my feet. I can barely take a full breath. Mom and Dad are in the kitchen—their muffled voices are audible as I sneak out the back door, hurtle around the corner of the house.

"I don't have time for your questions," Amelia says right away. Her voice is suddenly different—unchirpy. Now she's got a strange accent, flat, broad consonants. She's in black, as usual, feet to throat. Her bright hair is wrapped into two messy horns on either side of her head—and her pale skin stands out like a foghorn. "Get your piece of shit car, and let's go. Your girlfriend's gotten herself into some deep doo-doo."

"What?" I say like an idiot. If there were too many things in my head before, now I'm blank with shock.

"Which word didn't you understand?" Amelia's freckles pulse. "Get your car keys, Romeo. We have to move. I'll fill you in on the way over to Darrin's."

My mouth is dry as chalk. "What happened to you? Who *are* you?"

She shakes her head. "Do I have to do everything around here?" She slips past me into the house.

"Hey." I gawk at her. I should call Lemon, ask her what's going on. I'm fumbling with my phone when Amelia emerges a few seconds later—my car keys dangle from her fingers. "I'm driving."

I seize the keys. "Tell me what's going on."

She snatches back the keys. "I'm here to help. Get on board."

I clamp my mouth shut, follow as she climbs into the Buick. Can't do anything else, really. Least she knows what she's doing. Seems to, anyway. More than I can say. She unlocks the passenger door. I slide in. Can't think of a good reason not to.

I click the seat belt over my chest. "Where are we going?"

"You're hot, admittedly, but sometimes I wonder what the hell Lemon sees in you. I swear, you've got the mental capacity of a snail every now and then. And it smells like sweaty boy in here." She backs up the Buick, fast but quiet. "Look, you already know we've been keeping an eye on Lemon and her family—"

"And everybody else in town," I say.

"It's my role, and I play it," Amelia says. "Same as Lemon plays her role in this whole Old Lucy cock-up. I help my dad with the tech stuff, I collect intel. I stay out of the way."

"So . . . what's this then?" I say.

"It's full-on crazy, that's what. Normally we come in and kill the monster or set whatever it is right, and no one gets in the way because no one knows. I don't want anything to happen to you guys. I mean, sure, you and Darrin are kind of slow on the uptake, but Lemon is really cool—like we'd truly be friends if I weren't watching every move she makes. By the way, Skeet Jenkins's family? Not really a threat. I've been watching them too. They're freaking morons. Couldn't find their butts with both hands."

"Okay, good to know." That's at least one thing less to worry about— if she's right.

"Anyway," she continues. "I was close to convincing my dad's unit to back off and maybe even work *with* you. Oh, and they were never going to tell the world that Old Lucy was a hoax. Lemon's grandfather, though, totally derailed everything. I understand why Lemon didn't want to tell Ike what she overheard. It wouldn't have mattered one way or another—but how did you *not* know he was listening yesterday?"

"Listening?"

She scowls. "The upshot of all this is that Lemon had to go talk Ike out of being a lunatic this morning, and she ended up on his boat and got knocked into the water out at Peter's Island. The Mosasaurus went after her and took her under. I was able to shift it away from her with a high-pitched wave signal, but..."

A ten-ton bomb detonates inside my head. A faint wheeze comes out of me. "But *what*? Is she hurt? Is she dead? That's where we saw the monster."

"Don't lose your shit just yet." Amelia glances over at me, smirks. "None of the equipment we've got on the lake picked up a signal from her dead body. She's probably underground on the island. I mean, that's not great news, but it's not the worst news."

"*Underground*? And what the hell is a Mosasaurus?"

My phone pings.

Lemon: Am stuck in a cave on Peter's Island. Always been a great friend. Maybe prom would have been something more for us. Stay safe. Luv ya. Xo.

My eyes widen. I swallow around the lump that forms. *Something more?*

"For crap's sake," Amelia snarls, "disable your GPS and turn off your phone."

My hands shake when I pass her the phone, try to get my leg to stop bouncing up and down.

"Well, that confirms that," Amelia says a moment later. She tosses the phone at me without looking. "Now would you *please* turn off your freaking phone."

"Shouldn't I let her know we're coming? To hang on?"

She side-eyes me. "I'm surprised she even got a message to you— my dad's unit surveyed the island. Those boulders that surround it? The base of that island is pretty much made up of those. They found a few tunnels and caves, but it would basically be a dead zone down there. Good thing the ultrasonic works in dead zones."

"Ultrasonic?" I'm just repeating what she says now—I'm too shocked for much more than that.

"Yeah, ultrasonic," she says. "Lemon must have found a place pretty close to the surface of the island."

"Right. Surface of the island."

She waves the fingers of her right hand in front of my face. "Hey, snap out of it. I'm on the job. Off to the rescue and all that. You on board or what?"

Her words barely register. Finally, I say, "So are your dad and the rest of agents already there?"

She swings the car onto Darrin's street. "Do I have to talk slower? I said I *almost* had the unit ready to back down—the plan is still a go for tonight. So unless my dad has an epiphany, it's just me to set things back the way they should be before everything goes to hell. No one else. You're lucky I was able to jam the surveillance signal from Lake Lokakoma as soon as I saw what was happening. If my dad's team gets wind of it . . . I don't know what they'll do, but I think I can fix it myself without any bloodshed."

"And this Mosasaurus?" The fuzz in my head is starting to fade— still stuck on the *something more* of Lemon's text, though. My brain's struggling over which to concentrate on more: Lemon in danger, or Lemon having possible feelings. Now that I'm thinking it, disgust wraps over me. The *something more* can wait.

"What the hell are they teaching you in science class here? Ever hear of the Cretaceous period? Dinosaurs?"

My jaw drops. "Gotta be kidding me. Darrin was right about this monster being a dinosaur?"

"Jesus, you ask a lot of questions. By the way, do you have my ultrasonic?" She pauses. "I saw you and Darrin out at the lake yesterday. I couldn't believe Darrin figured out the wormhole—he's not as dumb as he looks. I was rooting for you guys to piece together the earthquake connection."

"Earthquake? What the hell, Amelia? And what the hell is an ultrasonic?"

Amelia shifts uncomfortably. "It's not Amelia, it's Ash. My name is Ash."

"Uh, right. Don't care what your name is. I care about getting to Lemon and you being straight with me. And how do you know about Darrin and the wormhole?"

"Your houses are bugged. Your cars. The school. Do you think the unit went undercover as grief counselors for their health? It wasn't the only reason, but they could get into places I can't as a student. I mean, what do you think my primary function was befriending you three?" She leans over, whips open the glove box with one hand. Plucks something from inside and hands it to me.

It's tiny, the size of a fly.

"Thought for sure you'd figure it out—especially when you started taking stuff apart at your house." She shrugs. "So, the ultrasonic?"

Can't seem to grasp much of what she's saying—it's too much, too fast. I glower at her. "Tell me what it is first—might be able to help you."

She shakes her head. "I told you it was a speaker, remember? That thing? Lemon found it on the lake shore. Ring any bells?"

Irritation crashes over me. "We left it at Lemon's last night."

She pulls an identical pyramid out of her pocket. "It's fine. With luck, Lemon's got it with her. Go get Darrin."

I don't even hesitate. Don't know if I can really trust her or not, but she's got the only plan. Betsy answers the door, pigtails all cockeyed, takes one look at me, and yells, "Darrin!"

Good thing he's dressed when he appears. "Lemon just texted me the weirdest thing." He stops, gets a suspicious expression on his face. "What's with you?"

"We gotta go."

I must look like a madman—Darrin doesn't even hesitate. He snags a pair of sneakers from inside the door and calls, "Be back later,

Dad." Follows after me when I turn, not even a question. He cranks open the back door of the Buick and dives in. "Well, shit, Amelia. Nice to see you."

I twist around. "Lemon was on Mr. Z's bo—"

"I know that part."

"Monster attacked her—she's okay, we think. Maybe."

"Maybe?" Darrin said. "Elaborate, please."

"She got away from it. It's a Mosasaurus—you were right about—"

"Time travel," Ash breaks in. Darrin's brows beetle together. "And the dinosaur."

"But now Lemon's . . . I don't know. She's in Peter's Island or under or something."

"A series of tunnels," Ash adds, scowling. "You guys were on the right track about this thing breathing air and holdings its breath underwater."

"Uh-huh," Darrin says. "Troy, do you not find it questionable at all that Amelia turns up after being disappeared? She's probably been tortured or brainwashed into working with the feds again. It's classic black ops."

"Damn," Ash says, all sarcastic. "You found me out." She huffs. "Deal with him," she says to me. "I have to concentrate."

So I do—deal with Darrin. Takes all of two minutes to tell him what I know—because I don't know much of anything. "So yeah, Ash was about to tell me about the ultrasonic-speaker thing when we got to your house."

"Yeah, great," Ash says, "Now we're all in the know. Coo coo ca-choo."

Darrin bounces on the back seat, pounding on my headrest. "Would now be the time to admit I have now fully freaking embraced a belief in conspiracy theories? So Ash is, what, your spy name?"

"Give me a break," she mutters.

"What's with the ultrasonic?" Darrin says.

"You already figured out that it communicates with the Mosasaurus." Ash's hands clutch the steering wheel—mine are squeezing my knees so I don't go out of my freaking mind. "It . . . works on frequencies, which is the easiest way I can explain it. I can zap the hell out of the Mosasaurus when it's being a very bad boy—like when it tried to eat Lemon. Totally not standard issue. I helped my dad develop it," Ash says with a hint of pride. "And let me head you off at the pass, chief: your earthquake opened a time portal. The Mosasaurus swam through. Yes, my dad's team is basically black ops. Sort of. They track entrances from one time period to another."

"There are more?" I gape at her.

"A lot more."

"Why the secrecy?" I say.

"People are panicky idiots," Ash says. "What do you think would happen if people knew earthquakes weren't *always* shifting tectonic plates or a slip of a fault line? The shifts and slips make it possible for an Einstein-Rosen bridge to open for a hot second."

"You shitting me with this?" Darrin says.

"And what the hell is an Einstein-Rosen bridge?" I say.

"I *knew* it." Darrin jabs a finger from the back seat. "This explains so much."

Ash clicks her tongue. "You know nothing."

"So, this Mosasaurus. How are we gonna get rid of it?" I say.

"The bridge under Peter's Island *can* be reopened. All you have to do is simulate an earthquake," Ash says.

"Simulate an earthquake?" Darrin asks. "How?"

Ash shrugs. "Explosives, usually. Or fracking."

Darrin leans up between the seats. "Tell me fracking companies are in on this. That they're all part of an agenda to cause earthquakes in order to reopen portals."

"Only one that I know of," Ash says. "The rest are just crappy corporations who don't care about the environment. Sorry to disappoint. So, are we done with show and tell yet? When I left to come get you, the Mosasaurus had just eaten Ike Ziegler, so—"

"Mr. Z is dead?" I say. My stomach clenches. "I thought you could control the monster with that thing?"

I gesture to the pyramid.

"Holy fuck," Darrin says softly.

"Hey, it's not like I'm the pied piper of dinosaurs." Ash stares straight ahead, eyes like stone. "I do my best. It didn't work *that* time. If Ike had stayed on his boat, it probably would have been fine, but the second the Mosasaurus dragged Lemon under, he jumped into the water to try to save her. It was—"

"Can't believe Mr. Z is dead," I say. "Lemon's going to . . . don't know what she'll do. Wait—where's Mrs. Z?"

"Still at their house. She was trying to call your dad, so I disabled her phone and the Internet. Lemon took her bike, Ike took the car, so she's probably sitting on that hideous gold couch of hers. Thank god they've only got the one car—I hate fiddling around with car engines."

"You didn't do anything to the Buick, did you?" I reach around to test that my seat belt is buckled.

"Would I be driving it if I had?"

"I doubt Mrs. Z is just sitting around," Darrin says dryly. "Not while she thinks Ike and Lemon are out on the water."

"I can't worry about her right now. Lemon's not going to have a chance unless we can get to her," Ash says.

"Okay, fine." Reality abruptly rushes my consciousness: I'm hurtling down the road in the passenger seat of my own car. James Bond's surly sister is at the wheel. Nothing is okay. "So we have to blow up something—to open this portal, I mean?"

"Uh-huh," Ash says. "Boom. Ike had explosives on his boat when he went out this morning. I'll give him this—he had the right idea, although for the entirely wrong reason. It wouldn't have worked, even if he'd successfully blown the island to smithereens."

Darrin says, "So first, where are we going to get dynamite, and second, how does that help us get to Lemon?"

Ash barks a sharp laugh. "Dynamite? This isn't 1950, like Ike thinks it is. We've got a stash of good explosives in the woods near the fishing dock. We'd have been able to get this done a week ago if you guys weren't practically camped out at the lake. I told my dad we should have just drugged everyone for a few hours and taken care of things quietly while you were out, but no one thinks to listen to a kid. Anyway, we definitely won't blow anything until we get Lemon."

"You didn't really answer my question." Darrin leans forward over the seat a little more.

"Just go with it."

"I might be more inclined if I wasn't worried your dad and his buddies were going to jump out of the trees and kill us dead," Darrin says.

"Oh, stop being so dramatic." Ash sneers at him. "They could—they're authorized—but wet work is a whole big pain in the butt that involves a load of red tape. That's part of why I thought I could convince them to work with you, even if they didn't listen to me before. No one likes paperwork."

"Comforting," I say.

"Won't your dad be pissed when he finds out what you're doing?" Darrin says.

Ash's nose crinkles up. "What's he going to do about it? By the time anyone knows, it'll be done. I left a note."

"But aren't they going to figure out how to undo all the signal jamming and whatever else you did? Aren't they watching *you*?"

"Smartest question you asked all night." Ash nods gravely. "A bunch of the agents—my dad included—won't be back until the morning. They're off checking another site a few towns over that they got a call about. Another reason why I thought I could talk them out of tonight's deadline, by the way. The rest of us, well, two agents are off shift, sleeping to get ready for blasting apart the lake tonight, and then there's me and another guy, who are supposed to be surveilling. I slipped him a sedative. He'll be out for hours."

"And you think this *isn't* going to take hours?" Darrin says.

Ash looks at him and grins.

22

LEMON

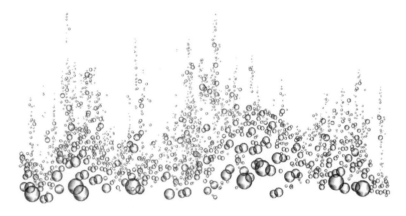

THE CAVE BREATHES. THE AIR should be cold—the lake water is spring chilled, and it's still cool enough outside to need a sweatshirt at night. But when I put my hand on the red-gray stone that forms these walls, it's as if I've lain my hand on feverish human skin. A warm exhale that smells uncomfortably of rot prickles the damp hair at the back of my neck, and the inhale rushes past me but doesn't bring any relief.

Each step through a new cave, a new tunnel, feels like I'm burrowing into the center of the earth. I edge my way forward mostly by touch. My fingertips are raw meat from scrabbling over the rough surfaces in the dark. My feet are soggy and tired.

The monster bellows so close I can feel it, filling the space with its roar. I wedge myself into a crevice and close my eyes. Even *I* can smell myself—mud and sweat and blood and stale lake water—so no doubt that thing can tell exactly where I am by scent alone. It sounds like it's heaving itself across the rocky floor, grunting heavily to propel a bulk that should make it slow on land. I don't want to find out. The sound of it snuffling after me makes me close my eyes. If it's going to start chewing on the part of me it can get its jaws around, I don't want to see it coming, even if all I get is a dim glimpse. There's no way to be sure, of course, but I'm pretty sure Will watched those teeth sink into him—and I can't bear to think of that.

The monster's been shadowing me through the caves since I sent those texts.

Maybe its sense of smell isn't that great—the *slap-thud* of its heft continues but grows fainter. I wriggle out of my hiding place and move as fast as I can in the opposite direction. When the sound of that thing is distant enough, I contort myself around what I hope is something I can hide myself behind.

I light up my phone screen—just long enough to see my surroundings—and the time. It's been almost two hours since I was on the public dock, although it feels like much longer. Still, without a door marked "Exit Here," I'm screwed because this cave is more of the same: craggy caves, mucky puddles, mud, and slicks of white goo that look like bird droppings but emit the stench I've come to associate with the monster. I might still be lost and alone when the USGS agents blast my lake apart, and me with it.

Under my hand, the walls grow more jagged. The hot air tastes gritty on my tongue, with the damp tang of standing water in the back of my throat. Sometimes the water pulsates so loud I'm sure the lake will bust through and drown me—or mask the sound of the monster crawling back in my direction.

My fingers scrape over the walls again, pulling me ahead. Soon it's not just the wind on my face I imagine but someone whispering my name and the sound of small feet skittering nearby. No doubt I'm hallucinating the voices, but the skittering—mice, maybe. Or rats. It's impressive they've survived with the monster prowling through the cave system, but there are little cracks everywhere. Lots of hiding spaces for small things. Still, if I die here they're going to gnaw on me, and it's going to be terrible. Should anyone ever find my body, I hope Grammy has passed on—seeing what's left of me in that state will be enough to kill her.

Of course, if Pappap was able to get away, maybe I just need to hide, like the mice and rats. Amelia *did* see what happened—I'm sure of it. Maybe she'll be able to convince her dad to help me. Or maybe the agents decided not to wait, and everyone's dead.

Ten more steps, and a faint glow of phosphorescence suddenly condenses overhead on the roof of the cave. I reach for it. Stretch up toward it on tiptoe. The hazy outline of my bloody fingertips emerges from the darkness of the cave. Behind me, in the distance, comes a roar.

I jump at the dim light, hand outstretched. My hand hits something softer than the walls around me. Dirt and rock crumble onto my forehead. I sputter and brush it away from my eyes and mouth. A small bit of light—weak and gray—filters through. A hint of the sweet almond perfume of forsythias trickles in. I mean to shriek in surprise, but my mouth is parched. Only a strangled wheeze emerges.

A dull *slap-thud* echoes through the cavern. Not close, but never far enough away.

I jump again toward the light. This time I knock out a small hole. Cool air pushes at my face, but only for a moment. Again and again, I gouge out small bits of dirt until I can make out a snatch of sky.

The sound of the monster seems a little closer. My heart beats loud enough that it screams in my ears. I press myself against the cave wall and into the corner, listening.

I'm trying to work up the courage to dig more dirt from the hole overhead when something clamps down on my shoulder. The screech that tears out of me is grainy terror. My throat burns. My arms and legs flail. If this thing wants to kill me, it'll have to work for its dinner. My fist connects with something hard. I wince and kick out harder. Clench my eyes shut. My toes bash into something firm.

A red glow flares beyond my eyelids. Someone says, "Lemon, stop. It's me." It doesn't register, though. I fight until my lungs burn, too. Until a pair of strong arms wraps around me.

"It's okay," Troy says.

"Hey, Lemon. Snap out of it," Amelia says.

I stop wriggling and peep one eye open. Troy's anxious face is just visible in the gleam of a flashlight, one cheekbone slightly swollen. Without thought, I tilt forward and kiss him. *Really* kiss him. Hard.

He jumps, then tightens his grip on me and leans in. My breath has to be disgusting, but I don't even care—he's safe and strong and *here*, and that's enough.

Darrin whoops. "Damn, get a room."

"Seriously," Amelia says. "Could we break this up for the moment? Less kissing, more blowing stuff up."

I freeze, lips still touching Troy's, and squint. There's enough light to see his dark eyes peering down at me, wide. I shift backward and hate the loss of his comfort immediately.

"I have a million questions," I hiss, "and I'm happier than you could possibly know, but right now we have to get the hell out of here. I don't know where the lake monster is, but it can breathe *air*—it's in here with us. We were right, remember?"

A flashlight beam bumps along the cave floor until it lights a pair of black hiking boots and black-clad legs. It tilts up to Amelia's pale, squinting face and her ginger hair sprouting out in messy cones. She gives me a two-fingered wave. "I don't think the monster will be much of a problem."

"In what universe?"

Darrin laughs. "Funny you should say that."

Amelia sighs. "You're right about one thing: we've got to get a move on."

"Are you not paying attention?" I say. "Hungry monster. Big teeth. Not just water-bound."

"Yeah, I know," Amelia says. "My dad's unit has a decent enough map of the cave system—we need to get to the place the Mosasaurus came through, which isn't too far from where we were able to get underground."

Panic wells in my chest. I can feel the stone shaking—it's coming right for us. "We—"

She nudges Troy out of the way to stand right in front of me. "Lemon, I've got this. If can you trust me, I promise this will all be okay."

Darrin says, "We'll explain everything, Lem. For now, just go with it."

I scrunch up my face. "But—"

"You asked me to trust you, no questions asked." Troy—at least I think it's him—brushes his thumb along my cheek. "Remember? Can you do the same for me right now?"

"Yeah," Darrin says. "What's a guy got to do?"

"All right." Anything short of not leaving immediately to avoid death seems ludicrous, but I trust Darrin and Troy—with my life. They've proven themselves to me over and over again—not just during the last week, but always. I breathe, try to calm myself. Try to ignore the stench of blood and rot in the hot air.

Amelia's hair gleams in the light as she nods. "Great, let's go." She turns and walks through the cave. "Are you coming?"

Darrin scurries after her, and Troy takes my hand and leads me along. His face is shadowed in the light from the flashlight he holds—he doesn't look scared, but I can't read his expression. Determined, maybe. We pass into a cavern that should be far too big to exist below the surface of Peter's Island. There's a huge stand of water covered over by branches and more bones, mostly animal from the look of it. At least I hope they're animal bones.

Troy hustles me along, shining his flashlight at the ground. There's too much light, and we're making too much noise—feet stomping over stone, all these random conversations. I want to say something, but Amelia seems so sure. She gestures at us to walk close to the wall.

Troy glances at me and smiles, tight-lipped. "You're okay?" he says under his breath.

I force my heart to slow, force myself to breathe evenly, to be calm. "I guess."

"I got your text."

My brain explodes with a million thoughts. The text...the one I assumed he'd never get until long after I'd died. Ten minutes ago I would have given anything to get rescued, and now I want nothing more than for the ground to open up and swallow me whole. I might get my wish in one way or another, because I can hear the monster advancing—but I can only seem to focus on my own mortification.

"Don't worry—I know you were scared." His words cram together, fast and slippery. "People say things they don't mean. I'm not holding you to it."

"This is just pathetic," Amelia says from ahead of us.

"Neither one of them has got any game at all," Darrin says.

"You mind?" Troy says.

"Are they really this oblivious?" Amelia pauses, then barks, "Get in front of me. Quick."

Darrin turns and shoves me ahead. Troy has his hand on my arm a second later, bumping me forward. The monster pokes his head into the cavern from behind us and bays so loud I have to clap my hands over my ears.

I've seen this thing too many times for my liking, but still I've never noticed that the shape of its head looks a bit like an alligator. It heaves itself in on the same flippers we saw on the fish cam recording. With the light shining in its direction, it's easy to see they're huge—nearly the size of my body. The thing barely fits into the cave. Its claws click on the stone floor.

"Be ready to run," Amelia says.

Troy tightens his grip on my hand. My chest squeezes, hysteria only a few breaths away. Another *slap-thud*, and the monster snaps its teeth. Hot breath, hotter than the air, hits me with an even viler stink. Amelia pulls a clone of the speaker I found at the side of the lake out of her jacket and smacks a button. The monster staggers sideways and screams. I hold my ears again and wince. It struggles upright and screams again, flops into the puddle. I've never heard anything as angry—not even Pappap. Branches fracture. Amelia steps backward, pushing us along with her. My legs shake so badly, it's hard to keep moving.

The monster hurls itself and breaks through into the water—and disappears down, long tail writhing and splashing until it's gone.

For half a second, the monster's similarities to an otter pop into my head. "What—" I start.

"Nope," Amelia says. "Things to do, explosives to detonate. We can talk about evolution later. There are a few more pools like that in this system, so keep an eye out—but we have to motor."

"Just . . . hang on. I have to do one thing." Darrin's face appears in the murk. Amid Amelia's protests, Darrin positions himself in front of me and Troy. "You guys are being morons, and I think we're past it, don't you? Life-threatening situation. Off to save Devil's Elbow and all that. So. Lemon, Troy's had a thing for you since forever." Troy drops my hand. "Troy, Lemon's text wasn't a trauma-induced accident. There, you're a couple. Discuss while we're evading death on flippers." He abruptly smiles and takes off after a still-muttering Amelia.

If I thought the awkwardness was bad when Troy said he'd received my text, now it's as if the hot air has been stoked by a mocking fire, setting my skin to blaze.

Troy swallows hard and turns to follow Amelia and Darrin. I fall into step next to him, even though diving after the monster and tracking it myself is preferable to hearing Troy say he feels no such way about me. Whatever the case, we're two seconds from possibly being eaten—entirely the wrong time for Darrin's crap.

I trudge along in painful silence until Troy says, "He's right, y'know. Been following you around like a lovestruck puppy for most of our lives."

The fire burning me lessens just enough for a spark of hope to light instead. The sound of Amelia and Darrin grumbling quietly to each other ahead is louder than the thoughts banging around in my head, but not by much.

Finally, Troy says, "No idea what to say right now."

The spark grows, and words pop out of my mouth. "I guess . . . we like each other, right?" When he doesn't respond, I say—much calmer than I feel, "Maybe we should try, I don't know, being together. Giving that a shot. If we make it out of here."

His hand finds mine again in the dark. He stops, and I turn toward him. My skin is still on fire, but it's different now. He says, "Wait. So . . . what does this mean?"

The screeching in my brain quiets to a dull bleat—and I lean in. His lips on mine are a shock, I think, to both of us.

A roar somewhere ahead sends us shooting apart.

"Okay, lovebirds," Amelia calls. "Time to get to work."

"What is she talking about?" I can feel my forehead crinkling in the dark.

"Ash—she's planning to set off explosives, punch a hole to another world," Troy says. "The Mosasaurus goes through, we shut the wormhole, and everything goes back to normal."

Just like that, my brain is back on overdrive. "Who's Ash? And another world? A Mosasaurus? What—"

"*She's* Ash—but never mind that now. Come on." He tugs me to catch up with Darrin and Amelia, but I'm turning the word over and over again in my brain—*Mosasaurus*. I'm ticking through animals in my brain, trying to pinpoint where I know the word. And did . . . whatever her name is . . . say something about *evolution*? As I cross over into the next chamber, where Darrin and Amelia stand, heads close together, I gasp. This cavern is bigger than the last. It's damper here, and the sound of water echoes all around. It's possible that I might have stumbled through it before in the dark, but the sound is amplified, different from anything I've encountered.

"Hold up," Amelia, Ash, whatever, says. "I'm going to need a lot of light for this. I've got some halogen lanterns."

"We couldn't have used those when we were looking for Lemon?" Darrin says.

"No," she says tersely. A few moments later the cave erupts with a blinding whiteness.

I squint, trying to see around the glare of her lantern, but it's nothing but a hazy yellow-red starburst. Amelia-Ash sets her backpack on the ground. It's so big that Darrin could fit in there, which I haven't noticed until just this moment.

She unzips the bag. "Okay, look. Here's how this is going to go: I need to position these"—she waves the beige block in her hand— "around the wall over there. See where the rocks have all piled up?"

"And on the other side of those rocks is what?" Darrin says. "Jurassic Park?"

"Not quite." She unpacks her bag, a mass of blocks and wires. "If our calculations are correct, I can reopen a wormhole into the Cretaceous period for another twelve hours or so. Boom, lure the Mosasaurus through, set off a secondary blast to reseal the rift, and done."

This is making zero sense.

"Any chance the entire island collapses?" Troy says.

"No," she says. "I do know a little something about explosives."

I can't waste any more energy trying to piece everything together. My brain immediately shifts into problem-solving mode, shoving my anxiety down with the other fears I can't deal with right now. "So . . . you need to get the monster here, right? How do we do that?"

"Hey, nice to have you back in fighting shape," Amelia-Ash says and grins at me. "There's a scent marker I'll put in the water—there's another pool in the next cave over—that will draw the Mosasaurus close, and if it doesn't respond, we'll need bait to reel it in, draw it here." She eyes me. "Which means either Conspiracy Boy over here," she jerks a thumb at Darrin, "goes in the water and flails around, or one of you lovebirds do."

"What about you?" Darrin says. "If this is such a great plan, why don't you act as bait?"

"Because I'm the one with the detonator," she says. "Plus I've got the ultrasonic," she brandishes the speaker, "so if our Mosasaurus gets too close I can use it to keep it from snacking on you."

"No other option?" Troy says.

Ash gazes at Troy for a moment. "No. So you decide who plays the helpless victim." She picks up a handful of blocks and wire and hurries away.

"I'm it," I say with a bravado I absolutely do not feel. "I'm a better swimmer than either of you—and I can run faster."

"You could have gills and scales, still wouldn't be playing bait," Troy says. "I'll do it."

"I'm not excited about the idea of being eaten," Darrin says, "but my short and sexy bod puts me at an advantage to either of you giants in this regard, don't you think? Less of me to eat."

"Oh, would you quit it," I say. "Darrin, you're not a strong swimmer. And you." I jab my finger at Troy. "This is not the time to get all testos-terone-y and stupid. You're not any less of a manly man if you stand by and watch a girl take a risk."

"Noted. But you're not just any girl." Troy touches my cheek with the tip of his finger, and I shiver. He pulls himself up straight. "But nah, not about that. Anything happens to me, you're the backup plan, Lem-on. If I screw this up, I know you won't."

Ash rolls her eyes, palms the speaker, the ultrasonic, whatever, and pushes a button. A terrible thrashing pounds against the wall of the cav-ern. She says, "This scene you've got going here is all very sweet, but we've got business."

23

TROY

L EMON'S GOT HER ARMS WRAPPED around herself. Darrin's pacing. The thrashing against the stone has stopped, but the noise of water is relentless. Watching Ash flit around, place the explosives—that's what's keeping me from losing my mind. Every nerve ending in me is on fire.

Ash is solid, calm. Like she's done this a million times. Maybe she has—she did say this is what her dad's unit does: chasing down monsters. She rummages through her big-ass bag and looks up.

"Lemon, can I get your help?"

Lemon touches my arm, crosses the cave to Ash's side. Ash hands her a lantern. "Could you hold this while I place the last couple of packs?"

"I think you better stop giving Ash the stink eye," Darrin says when Ash and Lemon move to the far side of the cave. "Your face is going to freeze that way, and she's likely to tranq you." He pauses. "You didn't tell Lem, did you? About Ike?"

"Nah, man. But maybe Ash is wrong—maybe we *should* tell Lemon now."

Darrin's brows shoot up. "Give Ash the benefit of the doubt. She's saving our asses. *All* our asses."

"You hope."

He nods at me. "Even if we all die, it's fine. I asked her about what happens if everything goes to hell. She set up a chain reaction that gets triggered if we're not safely out of here by the time her dad's unit would start their, uh, wet work. It's partly a threat of taking the unit's entire mission public, but it's solid. She said Lemon came up with something similar that would have worked—something her dad overheard on surveillance, I guess. She thinks Lemon's a fucking genius."

Ash calls from across the cave, "Heading over to put the scent markers out. It'll take a few minutes for them to work. Get ready."

My body tenses. Maybe it's the heat or the stink of the monster, or even the threat of that thing busting in here before we're ready, but I'm not confident we're getting out of here. Lemon's picking her way back to where Darrin and I stand. I hold out a hand to her when she's close. Her fingers are hot. Much as I want to push her up against the wall of the cave, make out with her for my final few minutes on earth—freaking her out seems counterproductive.

Darrin ducks away, turns his back, and starts muttering. For once, I'm grateful he's been rooting for me and Lemon for so long that he wants us to have a private moment.

"Guess maybe this is our goodbye scene, huh?" Lemon says like she can read my mind. Pulls me closer. Our noses almost touch. "You're supposed to say things like, 'I know you'll rescue me if something goes wrong' or 'when we get out of here, let's go out.'"

The sound of something big trouncing on stone reverberates through the space. "Here it comes," Ash yells from the cave next door.

I don't move. "What comes next?"

"You're supposed to kiss me." She moves her hand to my hip. "Oh, screw it. I have to do everything."

There's just enough time to think that Ash said the same thing to me. Lemon's mouth is warm, sudden. Everything in my brain except Lemon—it's silent. Least for thirty seconds. Then reality butts back in. The monster. What my parents will say if anything goes wrong. What Mrs. Z must be going through, what Lemon will say about Mr. Z. If Ash is setting us all up.

Still, a joy hits me, too—like a plucked piano wire. It vibrates through my chest. Lemon bites my lip gently, lets me go.

Ash comes sprinting back in and yells, "No need for bait—it's coming! Stand your ground. Wait for it."

"Wait for *what*?" Darrin says. "Until it chomps us in half? Shouldn't you be blowing a hole in the wall?"

The smack of the monster's body on stone is deafening. Adrenaline hits me hard. Darrin, Lemon, and Ash yell at each other—sounds weird in my ears. Darrin crashes into me, knocks me flat onto sharp stones. Pain blossoms in my ribs. Hands grasp my arm, tug. I flip over with a groan. Lemon's terrified face looms above me.

"Move," she screams.

"Go," Ash yells. "I'm coming."

I manage to get my feet underneath me, scramble out of the way of a large gray-orange head with snapping jaws. Its skull plows into the rock—right where I'd been standing.

Lemon runs nearly toward the Mosasaurus and lets out a high-pitched screech—the same as she did in the boathouse when we skipped school. It's the Old Lucy call, and it's deafening. Everything stops for a moment. The monster seems to sniff the air, makes a beeline for Lemon.

Ash pushes her out of the way. "Here, right here."

It turns, lunges at her. Lemon makes a run toward me.

Darrin snags my shirt. I don't realize I'm straining toward Ash until Lemon's hip slams me. I jerk upright. Darrin shoves me into another cave. I break free. Ash is still out there.

"Here, monster," Ash's voice calls. "Get your ass back where you belong."

Darrin spits, "What the hell is she doing?"

"Ash!" Lemon lurches as if to sprint to Ash—I catch her around the waist. Darrin ducks up next to me at the corner of the cave. Ash flattens herself against the rocky wall. Even in the now-dimming light, that red hair blazes. She's got a detonator in her hand.

The Mosasaurus swings its head toward me, Darrin, and Lemon. Roars guttural and loud. It seems bigger than I remember. Ash grimaces, stoops to pick up a rock. Hurls it at the giant head. It bays again. The sound of it rings 'til my ears pop.

"Come on now, come and get me." Ash waves her arms, hops. It swings back toward her, hurls itself, swiping at her with a flipper. "That's right. Just a little more."

The expression on her face, man. Tears me out of my trance. She looks ticked off, sure. Triumphant, too. And determined. Like she knows she's going to win.

The Mosasaurus heaves itself forward again, snaps its teeth at her. It's so close.

She hollers, "I know three people who are going to get blown to smithereens if they don't get the hell out of here in three seconds. Three . . . two . . ."

I throw myself backward, taking Lemon and Darrin with me. I land hard, breath whooshing out of me. Five thousand thunder bolts hit at once. High-pitched ringing pitchforks my head.

I open my eyes. Didn't feel Darrin and Lemon crawl off me, but there they are. Lemon's face—it's dim in the glow of a flashlight. Her lips move—no sound but the ringing. She seizes my wrist, pulls me upright. Her face is drawn, tired, terrified, all at once.

"You okay?"

She nods. I tug at her hand. "See Ash?"

Darrin gestures wildly with his flashlight. He winces, holds his arm close to his chest. The mouth of the cave behind us is gone—blocked by rock. Darrin nudges us both toward the other side of the cave with the tip of the flashlight.

Bells keep pealing in my head. There's rumbling under my feet again, then a wave of something thick, hot pushes me against the rough wall, squeezes the air out of me.

Right, second blast. Ash said that second one would be set automatically to seal the portal after the first blast. Trying to remember what else she said about it when Darrin's light flickers, goes out. Can't see a damn thing. I close my eyes, like that'll help. I reach out, feel my way. Nothing but rock, then soft hair pulled back into a ponytail under my hands. The curving bones of a forehead, a nose, a chin. What I assume is Lemon jerks, gropes at my arms.

I pull her to me—it's her all right. Finding her whole, not leaking blood—relief shoots through me. There's enough time to take a deep breath, pull her closer. A flutter of lashes—I kiss her eyelid. Hell, I don't care. A few inches south, I have it. She kisses me back like we're the only two people left in the world. Maybe we are.

Yellow lights pulse beneath my eyelids. I squint directly into a flashlight. It lowers—there's Darrin. The ringing dims. Darrin's yelling replaces it. "Let's go. This whole place could collapse."

Ash. She made us repeat back to her every turn we made in the caves. Showed us a map of the complex. She knew. The whole time, she knew how it would go. There's no way she survived. She's either dead from the blast or sucked through the wormhole—or trapped in the cave with the monster, getting eaten.

Darrin darts away. I follow, keeping Lemon within reach. She's quiet. Least I think so—my ears may be playing tricks. I'm quiet, too, though. What am I supposed to say? Suppose we'll know soon enough if Ash's plan worked—if we go topside, get eaten by a super pissed off dinosaur: that'll be a sure sign. I put my hand on stone, feeling for a vibration—any sign that the Mosasaurus is alive, following us through the caves. There's nothing.

I take Lemon's hand. She squeezes. It feels like a dream, but this—her hand in mine—is real. We stay connected at the fingers even as we approach the boulder that hides the crevice up to the surface of the island. Light filters through. The red-gray rock is lit by the sun.

Lemon sniffs beside me. Her voice is tinny, but I can hear it when she says, "God, I can smell the forsythias. I never thought . . ." Her voice wavers. "What are we going to do about Ash?"

"Don't worry," Darrin says. He leans against the wall. "Ash can take care of herself. She hasn't spent the last however many years with her dad and his unit without learning a couple of things."

"What do you mean?" Lemon says.

"She planned for failure, but she probably has a plan C and a plan D and at least another six lives to spare."

"You really don't think she's dead?" I say. "Those explosions—knocked us on our asses in the next cave. She was standing right there."

"No way," Darrin says. "The girl's got skills we couldn't dream of. I mean, come on—she comes with her own bag of explosives. She's like CIA Barbie. Well, USGS Barbie. That doesn't have quite the same ring, though." He turns and crawls into the crevice, gasping and holding his arm. "Think I broke my fucking elbow."

We wait until he's through—the sound of him swearing drifts back to us.

"So maybe everything goes back to normal now," Lemon says.

"Not everything, I hope." I lean forward, kiss her like I've fantasized about doing a million times.

Lemon grins. "Yeah, maybe not everything. At least not for a few months anyway." Her smile dims.

"What happens in a few months?"

"College. You'll leave here, go to school, and I'll be here"—her face pinches—"pretending to be a fish."

"But—"

She flaps her hand at me. "No, I know. You'll come back for Thanksgiving and Christmas, and we'll see each other then."

But I'm not going anywhere. Not this year. Maybe not next year, either. A smile cracks my face 'til it hurts my jaw. "Lemon, think I have an idea."

24

L E M O N

IT'S BEEN JUST OVER A WEEK—and every morning I jolt awake, only to wonder if I imagined everything: the Mosasaurus, the USGS agents, Ash . . . the insanity that an earthquake opened a wormhole to the past and let something horrible into our world, and that it was reversible. But then the sound of Grammy crying leaks through my closed bedroom door, and I remember that Pappap is dead. It makes it all very real. Plus, every bone in my body still hurts. Every muscle. Every hair. My arm aches like crazy. That's as real as it gets.

This morning is no different. I roll out of bed, avoiding Bob's feet—he's sprawled over most of my bed, and his head pops up when the mattress dips, but only for a moment. He goes right back to sleep. I go to my bedroom window, though—the one that overlooks the lake. It's my ritual now. I suppose I'm just making sure nothing has changed. Or maybe I'm hoping to see a flash of Ash's red hair out there.

Today it's just the water of the lake, a blue sky, and the equipment that the construction guys brought in to repair the stairs and rebuild the dock and boathouse. Right on cue, Grammy sniffles from somewhere in the house. She blows her nose a moment later.

As far as Grammy is concerned, it's Pappap who killed the Mosasaurus. The monster and Pappap went down together in the lake—the two of them. It was the last thing I could give her—the idea that Pappap died sacrificing for the lake. For Old Lucy. For Will and for Snowflake.

Sheriff Ramirez and the USGS agents ran underwater cams and sonared the lake. They found Pappap's body and pieces of the trawler, the pile of bones the monster left behind . . . but not the monster itself. The sheriff chalked that up to the explosion he thinks Pappap set off. I stayed away from all that, but Troy said the agents acted like they *hadn't* been planning to kill us all when they stopped at his house one last time.

Ash's dad must have known she told us all about his unit—and he had to have known we'd been with her when everything went down. He didn't ask any questions, though, or hint that he was planning to leak anything about Old Lucy being a hoax—Darrin said it's probably a case of mutually assured destruction, whatever that means. Ash's dad only said the unit would be keeping an eye on the town, in case there was another earthquake.

No, Grammy knows more than almost anyone else, but we didn't tell her everything—not about the Mosasaurus or the wormhole, about me nearly drowning and getting eaten. She thinks I was standing on the public dock watching Pappap battle the lake monster.

She has zero idea that Troy, Darrin, and Ash stole a motorboat from a neighbor's house, or that the boat is how we got back to shore after it was over.

Grammy's sitting at the kitchen table when I emerge from the shower. She grips a mug of tea, a faraway expression on her wrinkled face. Butterbeans sits on the chair next to her, tongue hanging out.

"Merciful heavens, honey. You startled me." Grammy smiles sadly. "You feeling okay today? Do you want some breakfast?"

"I'm okay, I guess. No breakfast, though. It feels weird to be here without Pappap." Even saying his name in the house isn't right, like it's coming out in the wrong tone of voice.

"Yes, it sure does." Grammy reaches over and scratches Butterbeans' brown ears. Bob catches up with me and curls into a tight ball in the doorway to the living room.

I sit on the chair opposite Butterbeans and think about Ash and the wormhole. "Hey, I talked to the latex guy yesterday after school about a new Old Lucy costume. He said it should be a month or two to manufacture it. Not ideal, but I think there are some things I can do to simulate a sighting or two without it. It might even be a good idea to make something like that a regular part of the impersonations."

"That's a good idea. Flo Benscoter did say she saw you on the news the other day, swearing up and down the monster was just an overgrown alligator and not Old Lucy. Your grandfather would have been so proud of you for thinking of that."

I gnaw on my bottom lip for a moment. "Speaking of Old Lucy, I want to talk to you about something."

Grammy pats my hand. "Of course, honey."

I take a deep breath. "I'm going to college."

"That's great, Lemon." Grammy nods. "The community college has a lot of great online programs."

"No, not to the community college. I'm going to Penn State. I have a full scholarship for their animal science undergrad program, and I've decided to accept." Before Grammy can get another word out, I rush ahead. "Troy has decided to stay here and go to community college because he doesn't know what he wants to do with his life anyway. We worked it all out. When he's ready to transfer to a four-year, or when I have to do my doctorate, we'll figure out a new plan. Darrin's going to help, too. We'll be a team. But for now while I'm away, Troy will take over Old Lucy sightings and help you run the ferry business until you decide to retire."

Grammy's mouth works, but no words come out. Her eyes go glossy.

"If that's okay," I add. "About the ferry business, I mean. I'm not trying to edge you out. And I'll be home in the summers to do the heaviest lifting on the Old Lucy sightings and help with the ferry tours during high season. Darrin, too. He'll pitch in."

Grammy brings her hands to her mouth.

"And Darrin can help with Old Lucy gossip," I blurt. "His sister Betsy is like a one-girl gossip factory. One word to her about a new sighting, and everyone will be talking about it. Not that she'll know she's part of the secret. You'll see, Grammy, this will be gr—"

"Oh, Lemon, that's wonderful!" Grammy smiles tremulously. "I know Ike said . . . well, now really is the perfect time to make a change of this magnitude. I said before that this is all yours to run your own way—and I meant it."

Something heavy lifts from my body, and I weigh nothing at all. I'd expected Grammy's support—eventually, after a lot of discussion— but hearing it makes everything solid. I lean over and gently hug her. "Thank you. I'm so happy you think it's a good idea. You'll see—this is going to work. Troy really wants to do this. And Devil's Elbow needs a veterinarian since our old one retired last year—and who better than a vet to offer public opinions about Old Lucy?"

"I daresay you might run into resistance from Bobby and Nan, but we both know it doesn't matter." Grammy sips her coffee. "I mean it— Ike would be proud. He was always proud of you, and loved you so, even though he wasn't one to show his feelings much." A tear slips down her cheek.

"I know, Grammy."

And I do. He told me right here in this kitchen. Maybe he was manipulating me, but he could have done that a hundred different ways. I'm choosing to believe he meant every word he said. Family is never easy. Sometimes you have to give people grace. Sometimes you have to make up your own narrative about their intentions and hope with all your heart that what you believe is true.

"There's one more thing," I say. "Troy is giving up a lot to take things over for me. I mean, he says he's not, and this is a good solution for him, too, but what he's offering... I want to give him a piece of ownership in the ferry business. Like half. He tried to say no, but I insisted."

Grammy swipes at her face with the tips of her fingers. "That's up to you, Lemon. I know you'll do the right thing—for the town, for Old Lucy. And for yourself. That's not a small thing."

"You really think so? You don't think I'm being selfish?"

"So what if you are? There's nothing wrong with thinking of your own future and what you really want. Heavens, Lemon—if you were being truly selfish you would tell me to deal with all of this myself and wash your hands of it. You've figured out a way to keep everything going, make sure I can retire, and help Troy and this town. I'd say that's the opposite of selfish. Now why don't you go get into that prom dress, and I'll pin up the hem to take it in to the tailor?"

I kiss the top of Grammy's head when I pass behind her on the way to my bedroom. Everything is different now. *Everything*. Even I feel different.

Prom is only two weeks away, graduation is a week or two after that. I have three months with Troy before I move to Penn State. It's not enough time, especially now that there's an *us*. It's only a ninety-minute drive between here and campus. It'll be fine, I think, but I want to fit in as much time with him as possible now, while I can. And with Darrin, too, but in a very different way.

I grin and change into my dress. The dress that Ash helped me pick out. The shoes are next. The heels click on the old hardwood on my way back to the kitchen.

Grammy has her box of sewing pins out, waiting for me. She shoos Bob when he prances around me, and he leans his chin on the chair where Butterbeans still sits. Grammy turns back to me. "Now stand up straight. Shoulders back."

She fusses with the bottom of my dress, pinning it into place. Meanwhile, I'm thinking about Troy's arm around my waist. The smell of him. That first time I kissed him down in the cave, the stench of death all around us.

Grammy says, "I forgot to ask—how's the rumor mill going at school?"

"People are mostly talking about the giant alligator being dead and telling me they're sorry about Pappap dying. It's been relatively tame. You know the folks that own Monster Pepperoni downtown?"

She mmm-hmmms.

"I overheard their daughter say that they had a few early tourists come through for lunch. Not nearly what it should be right now, but maybe the summer's going to be okay."

Grammy smiles. "It'll be fine."

"Darrin has this idea that maybe Ziegler's Ferry Tours should start advertising on conspiracy theory websites. There are apparently a few devoted entirely to Old Lucy—he thinks we can drum up some interest in dark tourism that way."

"Dark tourism?"

"Yeah, people who like to plan vacations around places that have ghosts or serial murders or—in our case—a mysterious lake monster that survived the invasion of an overgrown murderous alligator." I don't mention that the real lake monster and the deaths of Will, Skeet, Pappap, and Snowflake have only made Old Lucy more popular. She doesn't need to know.

"I'll leave that to you kids." She laughs and climbs to her feet. "There. All done. By the way, the mail just came—you got a postcard." She points to the kitchen counter.

"A postcard? I never get mail." I swish across the kitchen, mindful of the pins, and take the postcard off the stack of mail.

The front bears a glossy photo of a lizard-like dinosaur crawling down a dock. The postcard edges are crisp and new. Large looping letters spell out the words, *Ding dong, the dinosaur is dead.* The word *dead* is crossed out and replaced by *gone.*

I turn it over.

Lemon,
Tell Darrin I said he screams like a horny baboon.
—A

I gasp. No. No, it *can't* be. An excited frizzle stirs in my stomach.

"Something good?" Grammy says.

I can't help it: a slow smile breaks across my face. "Yeah, something good." I slip the postcard into the pocket of my dress. "Hey, so . . . I'm going to go meet Darrin and Troy in a bit, but they're going to come here tomorrow afternoon, okay?"

"I'm sure there's a lot to talk about," Grammy says.

"And maybe in another week or so we'll have Troy over to talk about the ferry business? Do you think you'll be up for it by then? I know you must be feeling—"

"Yes, of course. And invite Troy to Sunday dinner tomorrow. He's your young man now, isn't he?"

The tips of my ears warm. "How did you know that?"

"I'm not completely oblivious. I noticed you holding his hand at Ike's funeral. Plus, I know you wouldn't go to your senior prom with just anyone." She winks and heads out to the living room. Butterbeans hops off the chair and waddles after her.

Bob leads the way back to my bedroom. When my door is safely closed, I fish the postcard out of my pocket and read it again, smiling as big as my face will hold.

"I'm glad you made it, Ash," I say aloud . . . just in case anyone is listening.

~~~

THE EDGE OF the lake is alive with sound. A light wind jostles the trees, rustling branches and leaves, and the crickets are extra loud, like they've been holding it in. An army of birds chatter overhead. There's even a heron flying low over the water. Troy, Darrin, and I ducked behind a stand of bulrush to watch before hiking the trail around toward what used to be our boathouse and past it, skirting around the weeping willows.

Troy's fingers are twined with mine, and our hands swing between us. "Can't believe she sent a postcard," he says. "Low-tech for Ash."

Darrin laughs and plucks at the cast on his arm. "The girl defies expectation, that's for sure. *Horny baboon . . .*" He cackles.

I pull Troy to the shallow pebbled beach. It's littered with broken wood from the dock and small bits of leftovers from Pappap's boat that have floated over this way. When I close my eyes, I can still see the Mosasaurus attacking Will . . . going after Snowflake . . . even coming for me over at Peter's Island. The only lake monster now is Old Lucy—that's what I have to keep reminding myself. "I wonder where she is. The postmark was Philadelphia, but do you think she was just passing through?"

"I guess we could maybe make a guess by searching for the most recent earthquakes in the state," Darrin says. "But she probably doesn't want us looking for her."

"Probably not." Troy smiles and kisses my knuckles.

Darrin makes a gagging noise. "Do you have to do that stuff in front of me?" he teases. "I'm happy for you and all, but it's like watching my brother and sister make out. The prom is going to be torturous. I can't believe I felt the need to get you two together for that. What was I thinking?"

"Too late now," I say.

"We should really get started on what we came here for anyway," Darrin says. "I'm taking Cara to the movies tonight. I don't want to be late."

"Are you taking her to see something sappy?" I laugh.

"So she can witness your sensitive side?" Troy says.

Darrin cracks up. "Hey, I'm secure in my manhood, and I'm not afraid to cry."

"Things never change."

Troy laughs, too. "Oh, hey, forgot to tell you—speaking of things changing. Dad took the detail off the Jenkins house. Says it looks like Skeet's mom is getting life insurance money from what happened at the lake—sounds like you're off the hook."

I tighten my grip on Troy's hand for a moment before releasing him to dig through my back pocket. "That's good. I mean, Ash said they were never much of a threat anyway, but it's nice to not have to worry about it . . . although it makes me feel kind of bad for Skeet. What kind of mom gives up her vendetta for cold hard cash?" I pull the map out and unfold it carefully.

"Only you would feel sorry for someone who threatened to have you executed," Darrin says. He and Troy gather around me.

"Are you positive you guys want to get in on this?" I ask. "It's a lot. I kind of feel like I'm taking advantage of you."

"Done deal, Lemon," Troy says. "We're in."

"No arguments," Darrin says.

The smile hurts my face. "Thanks. I mean it." I turn back to the map and point, giddiness coursing through me. "Okay, so here's the route you swim for Old Lucy sightings. And remember: you do it how we train when the time comes. We've got a month, maybe a little longer, before the new Old Lucy suit is ready."

"Ike's not going to haunt us from beyond the grave, is he?" Darrin says. "Like he might choose to haunt the sighting route?"

"Could be," I say. "But Grammy is on board. She says he would be, too."

"Doubt that." Troy chuckles. "Can't believe I get to be Old Lucy. The new suit will fit me?"

"Yeah, of course," I say. "And it's new and improved to make the tail flip easier. The tail flip is the key to being a particularly great fake lake monster." I look out over the lake—*our* lake now—and go back to the map. I trace Pappap's hand-drawn line on the paper with my finger, following the trail back home.

ACKNOWLEDGMENTS

BLAME THE LOCH NESS MONSTER for *A Misfortune of Lake Monsters*. I certainly do. To be more specific I blame Nessie, having to wash dishes as a chore when I was a kid, and Briar Creek Lake, the lake within view of the sink at my childhood home. Briar Creek Lake is too shallow and small for Nessie or any other kind of monster, but that didn't stop me from fantasizing about a monster lurking out there.

A (ferry) boat load of people deserve thanks for bringing this novel to the, uh, surface.

I promise: I'll stop with the puns now.

So . . . thank you to all the folks at CamCat Books for their work on *A Misfortune of Lake Monsters*—and for taking a chance on me and Old Lucy and the world of Devil's Elbow, publishing the book, and putting it front of readers. (And, speaking of readers—it should go without saying that I have sincere gratitude to everyone who decides to give *Lake Monsters* a read and falls in love with the sheer weirdness of Devil's Elbow).

Randi Flanagan and Jessica Olin, thanks for your good humor and opinions on everything from cryptids to explosives to small-town living, not to mention for letting me vent when needed and for acting as tour guide when I visit each of you.

Thanks to my local SCBWI writing group—Amy Beth Sisson, Laura Parnum, Hilda Burgos, and Susan North. They have spent a lot of time looking at pages and chapters, to the point where Lemon must feel like their little sister. Nicole Valentine has spent time in Devil's Elbow (and with our writing group) as well. Thanks to all of you for everything!

Carla G. Garcia, Nicole Green, and Suja Sukumar have been excellent critique partners in the world of Devil's Elbow—thank you! I have the distinct pleasure of sharing a debut year with Suja, and I'm so excited about that!

Thank you to my husband Craig. I have holed up with my laptop, left him to fend for himself, and otherwise ignored him in favor of hanging out with Lemon and Troy on many a night. I don't think he minded it too much when I dragged him to Scotland for a Nessie hunt, though. Who would?

Finally, thanks to my mom, and the librarians and my English teachers in my rural hometown of Berwick, Pennsylvania. My mom never cared what I read when I was a kid—she was just happy I was reading and getting good grades and not getting myself into too much trouble. The librarians who manned the circulation desk never batted an eye when a ten-year-old me checked out stacks of books written by Stephen King, Toni Morrison, Judy Blume, and J.D. Salinger, among others. No one tried to usurp my mother's parental right to raise me reading as she (and I) saw fit. No one called in bomb threats to my small-town public library for stocking books a few very loud people found scandalous. No one pitched a fit about my senior year English class reading list including Ralph Ellison's *Invisible Man*—or about my junior year English teacher encouraging me to read everything James Baldwin ever wrote. I never really thought of my mom or my librarians or my teachers as heroes of free speech and access to education—not back when I lived in my hometown. Today, though, I do. They are the people who helped me become who I am, along with every book I've read and every new idea to which I've been exposed, and I am grateful. Because of them, I will always know how to fight the monstrous, aquatic and otherwise.

ABOUT THE AUTHOR

NICOLE M. WOLVERTON GREW UP in the rural hinterlands of northeast Pennsylvania, wondering what lurked in the dark cornfields outside her bedroom window—which certainly fed her interest in writing horror and speculative fiction.

Today, Nicole lives in the Philadelphia area in a creaky hundred-year-old house (which also serves as nightmare fuel for her work). She is Pushcart-nominated for her short fiction, and is the author of *The Trajectory of Dreams*, an adult psychological thriller (Bitingduck Press, 2013). She also served as the editor of *Bodies Full of Burning* (Sliced Up Press, 2021), a first-of-its-kind short horror fiction anthology that centers menopause.

Her short fiction, creative nonfiction, and essays have appeared in dozens of anthologies, magazines, and podcasts. *A Misfortune of Lake Monsters* is her first young adult novel.

Nicole earned a B.A. in English from Temple University and a Master's of Liberal Arts in storytelling, horror, and society (with a creative writing certificate) from the University of Pennsylvania. She is an election official and communications professional, as well as a travel enthusiast (25 countries to date) and a dragon boat steersperson, paddler, and assistant coach.

She still wonders what lurks in the dark.

Join Nicole at
nicolewolverton.com;
or on Instagram, Threads, or Bluesky
@nicolemwolverton

If you liked
Nicole M. Wolverton's
A Misfortune of Lake Monsters,
please consider leaving a review
to help our authors.

And check out
Taylor Munsell's *Touch of Death*.

BLOOD DOESN'T SCARE ME. That's not the reason for the tremor in my hands. There are things far worse than a little blood.

"I can't believe you're making me do this," I grumble, kicking the toe of my boot against the gym floor.

"I'm not making you do anything." Felix bumps me with his broad shoulder. "I simply suggested you should go through the blood drive. It's expected."

My snort earns a narrowing of his brown eyes. Expected. I don't know how a blood drive honors the memory of a student, but he's right: every person in the school is "doing their part."

"But that doesn't mean I have to like it." I reach up to fiddle with the peridot crystal pendant at my neck. If nothing else, maybe it'll actually shield my emotions today. "I should have asked Gran to make me a draft to calm my nerves."

Though, I'm not sure even Gran, the most powerful witch in the coven, could make a draft strong enough for that.

Felix lowers his voice. "We can leave."

I shake my head. "We've already been seen. Time to be a big girl." And, we're next. The line of students waiting to donate blood still stretches behind us, but any second now Felix and I will be whisked away to one of the portable beds now lining the school gymnasium.

"Your call." Felix shrugs. "Anyway, no harm can really come from it."

Not true.

I glance around the gym. Every light is on, but they aren't really bright enough. The stench of stale sweat hangs in the air, mingling with the too-strong smell of antiseptic.

A shudder courses through me as I try, and fail, not to think about what that antiseptic smell is covering up. Blood might not scare me, but it's still not my favorite.

At least there are no unwelcome guests so far. I tug on the hem of my glove, more out of habit than anything. They're one of my favorite pairs: the black lace is almost as smooth as the silk that lines them. If I have to wear gloves, might as well make a statement.

"They'll be wearing gloves, too," Felix says gently. "They won't touch you."

Nodding, I hope I seem more confident than I feel. The last thing I need is for an unknowing nurse to touch my skin and send me slipping into her death in a gymnasium full of my classmates.

"Felix Davies," another junior girl calls. Her sleek black ponytail falls to her midback. She's dressed in scrubs, so she must be in the school's nursing program. Her dark eyes move to find Felix grinning at her. Color floods her beige skin.

Felix has that effect on most girls, and boys, to be honest. Between his warm brown skin, easy smile, and dark, inviting eyes, he can charm anyone.

Except me. Even just thinking about it gives me the creeps. He's basically the big brother I never had.

"Come with me," she stammers. Poor girl.

"Georgiana Colburn?" an unfamiliar voice calls.

"George," I say reflexively. Felix glances back and gives me a thumbs up.

The nurse and owner of the unfamiliar voice smiles at me, her eyes only momentarily snagging on my blue hair.

"Right this way, young lady," the nurse says as she escorts me down the row of beds. I glance back, trying to catch Felix's eyes, but he's busy charming his nurse while she gets him settled.

I follow her to an empty bed, palms slick with sweat inside my gloves as I sit down. The crinkling of the paper lining the bed as I adjust makes me cringe.

As the nurse works, my mind races, trying to think of any spell or incantation, anything that would make this situation less daunting, but I come up with nothing. For being a witch in a coven so connected to death, an event with so much blood should send power coursing through me, especially considering my particular gifts. But I got nothing. Maybe I should actually pay attention in my magic lessons.

There's the snap of gloves, a tear, and then the smell of alcohol burns my nose. In a few swift movements, she is tapping on my wrapped arm, looking for a vein. The nurse notices the way my whole body tenses as she touches me.

"Take a deep breath," she says, probably thinking I'm nervous of the needle, not that her skin might touch mine and I'll wind up experiencing her death. Even with her gloves on, I don't feel safe.

A hiss escapes my lips as the needle slides in.

"Good girl." She adjusts the bag before pulling off her gloves and tossing them in one of the bins along the center of the room. The blood drains from my face at the sight of her bare skin. "You're all set. I'll be back to check on you in a little while."

She heads to another student down the row, leaving me alone. It's been a long time since I've experienced someone's death on accident. After almost a lifetime of dealing with it, I've gotten quite good at avoiding touching. Gloves, covered skin, even the attitude are all ways to keep me safe.

The bed to my left is empty, but the poor kid in the bed to my right looks like he's trying to scoot as far away from me as possible. My attitude might work a little too well in keeping people away.

It still hurts my feelings, even after all these years. I wish I could tell my classmates that I don't want to get near them either. The encounter is always worse for me than it is for them.

My eyes find Felix, and he flashes me a grin, just as cool as ever. His poor student nurse is still standing by him, black ponytail bouncing as she talks.

I scan the rest of the gym. My gaze catches on a girl with dark skin and tight curls. She smiles and gives a little wave. I stare back at her as my brain tries to process if she meant the wave for me.

It's possible. She's a witch, too, and with Gran as the coven's Supreme, she'd know who I am. She's at lessons every Friday with me, so her birthday must be soon since we're in the same ascension class, but I don't know that I've ever actually spoken to her.

She's new, only moving here at the beginning of the school year. I rack my brain trying to remember why she moved here. Something about a divorce, I think.

Intercoven marriages can be tricky, especially when the spouses have two different magics. Almost every witch ends up in the coven that's not ours. Death witches make other witches kind of jumpy. Ridiculous, but true.

I realize I've let my mind wander too long, but the boy on her left catches her attention before I can decide to wave back.

Closing my eyes, I lean against the headrest, trying not to think of ways to kill Felix for talking me into this. I know he meant well, but still. It's not like he has to worry about the risks. Not only the touching, but ghosts don't appear to him if he lets his guard down.

My breathing and the squeaking of shoes on the gym floor fill my ears. A heavy feeling settles on me, raising the hairs on my arms. Someone's watching me.

Popping my eyes open, I immediately look to Felix. He's chatting with the student nurse as she wraps his arm and definitely not looking at me. While I didn't notice the feeling at first, it's impossible to ignore now. I try to find the source, but everyone's attention is elsewhere.

Maybe it's just my anxiety playing tricks on me. I close my eyes again, trying to relax. Not a minute goes by before there's a touch on my arm and I yelp.

"I'm sorry dear," the nurse says. Her hand is on her chest like I startled her. That's better than the alternative though. I really don't want to know how this poor woman dies. "I just wanted to check your bag. Looks like you're about done."

As soon as the nurse pulls the needle from my arm, I'm off the bed and leaving the blood drive, completely ignoring her as she scolds me about needing to take it easy.

Felix is hot on my heels as I try to put distance between myself and the gym. He had been ushered out of the gym as soon as he stood up from the bed, despite his very loud protests. No students in the gym unless you're actively donating, Principal Hawkins had told him as she shooed him from the gym.

He was waiting at the doors when I came out, and despite my trying to brush past him, he still follows me.

"What happened? Are you okay?" he asks.

"You're such a worrywart."

He jogs in front of me and stops, almost making me run into him.

"What happened?" Felix asks. I sway a bit on my feet. He reaches out like he'll catch me but stops himself before he makes contact. I give my head a small shake to clear it.

"Nothing. Something in there just gave me the ick. Plus, the nurse just startled me. I thought someone was touching me."

"But she didn't touch you, right?"

"No skin-to-skin contact was made."

Felix's shoulders sag in relief. "Good. I shouldn't have made you do that."

"You didn't make me, just strongly suggested."

"Still." The look of guilt on Felix's face would be enough to melt the iciest of hearts.

"It's okay. I promise. No harm, no foul."

"Buy you an ice cream after practice?" he asks.

"Trying to assuage your guilt with bribes?"

"Maybe." His shoulder lifts in a lopsided shrug.

"I accept."

"Hoped you would. Can I walk you to class?" Felix offers me his arm like we're in some ill-fated historical romance even though he knows I won't take it.

"Okay, now you're doing too much. Bathroom first though."

Felix looks around the empty halls and catches my drift.

"I could pee," he says before walking down the hall.

"So gross," I mutter under my breath and follow him.

2

T HE HALLWAYS ARE EMPTY SINCE everyone is still in class as I exit the bathroom. I usually only go to the bathroom during class. No nosey glances or gossip that way.

My black lace gloves are tucked into my back pocket. I've never much liked wearing gloves; it's more of a necessary evil than a comfort. Still, I feel naked without them, too exposed. But I refuse to put them on before my hands are fully dry.

Unfortunately, the bathroom was out of paper towels again, so I'm stuck wiping my damp hands on my pants as I leave. I'm in a hurry, intent on beating Felix out of the bathroom so I can harass him about having to wait.

As the bathroom door swings shut behind me, I take a step forward and my foot slips out from under me. My arms fling out, intent on stopping my tumble.

A hand reaches out, catching mine on the descent. And I fall in a new way . . .

☙☙☙

SHE LOOKS OUT of place in this too bright room, the blue of her hair like a shining halo. Her teeth are bared, those emerald eyes shining with a feral rage.

"Big mistake," she growls.

I can't help but smile. I love a girl with spunk.

A scream erupts from her small throat as she launches at me in a tear of blue. She slams into me, the full weight of her slight frame toppling us to the floor. I barely have time to draw breath before her knife sinks into my shoulder.

I didn't even see her grab one. She moved so fast.

Pain erupts as the blade slices deeper, black dots flooding my vision. Now, I'm the one screaming.

Is this it? Is this how I go? At the hand of a sixteen-year-old girl?

I try to shove her off, but she's like a woman possessed. She rips the knife from my shoulder.

She straddles me as she raises the knife again, this time with both hands gripping the handle, and sinks it in.

Again.

And again.

The pain is unbearable, muddying my thoughts. There are so many explanations I have, but now, all I can think about is getting her off, making her stop.

I try to push again, but my arm fails me. I'm just so tired.

My struggles don't phase her.

She's coated in my blood. A vision in crimson. It spatters her face, coats her stomach, slicks her hands, but still she keeps stabbing.

She's screaming words, my blood flinging into her mouth with reckless abandon.

Is this what it feels like? Is this death?

Is it finally my time?

I try to cough but a wheezing sound escapes as something warm drips down my chin.

She sinks the knife in again.

I feel it as it pierces my lungs, my heart. Pain pounds through my chest.

Tears are tracking down her beautiful, bloodstained face. Clean streaks between the gore.

"Go. To. Hell," she says through clenched teeth.

Darkness seeps around my vision, so I can only see her face as I—

MY EYES FLY open, my breath coming in heaving gasps. I can't get enough air into my lungs.

My throat squeezes tighter.

His face is above me, concern furrowing his brow.

Blood thrums through my body, thundering in my ears.

"Miss, are you all right?" the boy asks. He looks so familiar, but I can't place where I know him from. I barely hear him through the buzzing. He reaches for my elbow.

It all comes back to me: my fall, his hand reaching out to catch me. He must have lowered me to the ground when I slipped into his death, because that's where I find myself. I scurry back, shoving my hands behind me to scoot away.

Sweat coats my palms, and they slip out from under me. My elbow slams into the tile. I keep pushing.

I can't touch him again. I won't go through that again.

Whatever that was, I never want it to happen again.

Not real. Not real. Not real.

I close my eyes, but the image of my blood-slicked form is seared into the back of my eyelids. My eyes fly open.

"Are you okay? You passed out." His tone is concerned, but there's something in his eyes, almost like he's accessing me.

Tears flood my lashes. My head is shaking. He moves forward again.

"Fine," I choke out, pushing away from him again. My whole body trembles, adrenaline, fear, and confusion sparking too many connections in my brain.

I need to leave. Now. I can't stay here.

Felix emerges from the bathroom, his eyes going wide when he sees me on the ground.

"You don't look fine. Here, let me help you up. We should get you to the nurse." He reaches for me again.

The sound that comes out of me sounds more animal than human. He pauses. Felix shoves him out of the way and bends down to grab my elbow and yank me up, the sleeve of my shirt a barrier between our skin.

"I'm fine. Really. Happens all the time." I've repeated this so many times it actually feels natural. I want to sink into Felix, pretend like whatever just happened was a dream.

The boy is still eyeing me. There's no fear like I'm used to, but something more than curiosity in his gaze.

I need to get out of here.

"She's anemic," Felix says, tugging me away. "She gets light headed from time to time."

Desperately, I try to remember how to walk. I can't think of anything but his blood slicking my hands.

I choke on a sob.

Anything. I need to think of anything other than the knife sinking deeper. Anything other than the feel of the blade as it split my, his, chest.

"I don't think you are." His gaze is piercing as he watches Felix drag me away. "You really should be more careful. Water can be a beautiful thing, but it's been known to kill." He glances at the puddle I must have slipped in.

"I'm fine." I start to stumble, but Felix's grip is firm. "Fine." I say, backing away from him. I should turn away, at least watch where I'm going. I can't do anything but watch him as Felix finally gets to the end of the hall and drags me out into the cold.

3

T HE CHILL OF THE DAY rips through my lungs in heaving gasps. Felix has me propped against his Jeep, another item in a long string of "forgive me for not being around" gifts from his parents, his face inches from mine.

"George, look at me. Take a breath," Felix says, gripping my shoulders.

My hair spills from my ponytail, sticking to the wet streaks on my face as I continue to shake my head.

"No, no, no, no, no, no," I hear myself muttering, but it's like someone very far away is speaking.

Since Felix got me out here, I haven't been able to say the words, to tell him what I saw.

What I'll do.

"George!" I can hear the panic in his voice now.

"No, no, no, no, no," I keep muttering, mascara tears tracking down my cheeks.

Warmth spreads through my skin as Felix's hands touch either side of my face . . .

❧❧❧

"GOODNIGHT MY DEAR," I hear as I close my eyes, sleep calling to me. My breath evens, slowing to a steady rhythm. I wonder . . .

❧❧❧

EASE FLOODS THROUGH my body as I open my eyes, but pure rage quickly follows it. My hands collide with Felix's chest, and I shove him with all of my strength. Despite our considerable height difference, my anger must bolster me because he lets out an oomph as he stumbles backward.

"What. The. Hell. Felix!" I yell.

He's never touched me without permission before. Never. It is a violation of everything that makes us, us.

"I'm sorry!" He's rubbing his chest.

Good. I hope it hurts.

"I didn't know what to do. I've never seen you like that." When I say nothing, he continues. "I panicked. George, I'm sorry."

My eyes search his face, rage draining as quickly as it flooded me. "Don't do it again," I mutter, a sudden exhaustion weighing on me. I slide down the side of the Jeep to sit leaning against the tire.

He crouches in front of me. "I won't. What happened?"

I'm not even sure how to answer that. The sun's shifted behind the clouds, and I shiver, not just from the cold.

My jacket's still inside. And my backpack. I don't think I can bring myself to go in so I just rub my arms for warmth.

Stop.

I suck in one shaky breath. Exhale. Another less shaky breath. "I touched that boy."

"Snotty Silas?"

"Who?"

"Snotty Silas. Remember? He went to elementary school with us but moved away in fifth grade. I didn't know he was back but apparently he is." So that's where I know him from. I nod. "I know you hate when that happens, but there has to be more. You don't break."

I lift my glasses on top of my head and swipe the tears from my cheeks. My fingers come away black and my mind registers that my hands are still bare.

My gloves are still tucked into my back pocket. I pull them out and tug them on. My carelessness with them today has already cost me too much.

There's no sensible way to say what I'm about to say that doesn't make me sound like a monster.

Maybe I am the monster.

"It was me," I whisper.

"What was you? Wait, it was your death?" Felix's brown skin turns ashen.

I shake my head. "It's worse than that." Inhale. Exhale. Another tear slips free. "It was me," I say again. "I—" Another breath. "I killed him." My eyes fall to the asphalt. I watch Felix's shoes, unable to look him in the eyes.

When the silence stretches on, I finally look up. Felix's lips are pulled into a thin line, the charm that usually oozes from him replaced with something that feels like pain.

"Felix?" I say cautiously.

"It must be a mistake."

"You know it isn't." Felix knows, better than most, what these visions mean. Once a death is written, it cannot be changed.

"When?"

"I don't know. Soon? I was a little overwhelmed by what was actually happening, but I looked the same, I think."

"Why?" He's not asking how I knew what I looked like.

"You know I don't see that much."

He pushes up, pacing in front of me. I watch him for a bit, grateful for the distraction of his movement, before I clamber to my feet.

"What are you thinking?" I'm suddenly flooded with the fear that he'll want nothing to do with me. I am a murderer, after all.

Murderess? Soon to be murderess? Murderess in training?

Shut up, brain.

"We have to tell your Gran," he says, still pacing.

It was my first thought too, but as I try to put distance between myself and what I saw, it's clear I don't want anyone else to know. Even Gran. "Absolutely not."

"Who else will know what to do?"

"There's nothing to do, Felix. It can't be changed."

"That's bullshit and you know it."

His words startle me. Felix almost never curses.

"Felix, you know I can't change—"

He cuts me off. "You've done nothing yet. No one can be convicted before a crime has even been committed." His fists are clenched, knuckles shining white, as he keeps pacing.

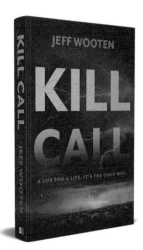
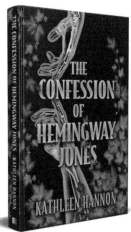